The Rise of the House of McNally

or

About Time Too

Bestselling author Philip Ardagh is probably most well-known for his Eddie Dickens Trilogy, which started life as a series of letters to his nephew, Ben, but has since been published in 25 languages around the world, receiving both critical and popular acclaim. *The Rise of the House of McNally* is the third of his *Unlikely Exploits*, which began with *The Fall of Fergal* and *Heir of Mystery,* and concludes the exploits of the extraordinary McNally family.

The Rise of the House of McNally

or

About Time Too

PHILIP ARDAGH

illustrated by David Roberts

ff

faber and faber

First published in 2004
by Faber and Faber Limited
3 Queen Square, London WC1N 3AU

Typeset by Faber and Faber Limited
Printed in England by Mackays of Chatham plc, Chatham, Kent

© Philip Ardagh, 2004
Illustrations © David Roberts, 2004

Philip Ardagh is hereby identified as author of this work in accordance
with Section 77 of the Copyright, Designs and Patents Act 1988

Coke and Coca-Cola are registered trade marks
of the Coca-Cola Corporation

A CIP record for this book
is available from the British Library

ISBN 978–0–571–21099–2

2 4 6 8 10 9 7 5 3

In loving memory of Beanie,
put to sleep on 27th March 2003
in her eighteenth year.
You were the bestest Bean there's ever been.

A Word to the Wise

There are those of you who were saddened by Fergal's death in *The Fall of Fergal*.

Now Fergal is back.

There are those of you who recoiled at yet more death in *Heir of Mystery*.

This should cheer you up.

There are those of you frustrated by not knowing what was causing the terrible outbreak of holes across the land.

Your frustration will soon be at an end.

There are those of you eager to find out the secret of Mr Maggs's teddy bear.

The wait is over.

And as for Le Fay, Albie and Josh's particular powers?

Just give me time.

PHILIP ARDAGH

'A fine wind is blowing the new direction of Time.'
From *Song of a Man Who Has Come Through*
by D. H. Lawrence

Prologue

Tick tock tick tock . . . *Brrrrrrrrrrrrrrrrrrrrrrrrrrr!*

Chapter One

There's a hastily assembled barricade in front of the door, made from a large filing cabinet pushed onto its side, a heavy table, a pile of chairs and anything else they could lay their hands on: angle-poise lamps, a water cooler, and even an empty fish tank. There are four of them making up the 'they' in question. Carbonet is the smallest and apart from his height – or lack of it – his most distinguishing feature (as it says on WANTED posters) is his hairy ears. I don't know if you've ever seen those little battery-operated gadgets designed for trimming nostril and ear hairs (they're often advertised in mail-order catalogues) but I suspect a whole drawer full of them wouldn't be enough to tackle his growth.

Next to Carbonet at this precise moment is Doyle. He looks a-bit-of-a-smoothy by nature but, deprived of a recent haircut and any hair oil, he looks less than at his best. He's looking forward to new clothes and a pampering . . . if they manage to escape.

Crouched down next to Doyle – and the only one who seems to be *doing* anything apart from worrying about being caught – is Smeek. Smeek is the tallest of them all and is most certainly the strangest looking. I'm not talking about his face. It's almost impossible to *see* his face. He has long straight jet-black hair (rather like an outsized hippie wig) growing down to his knees, and he has very spindly limbs.

Finally, there's Byron. What makes her stand out from the others is that she's a she. She's incredibly thin and has a permanent frightened rabbit-caught-in-the-headlights-of-an-oncoming-car expression on her face.

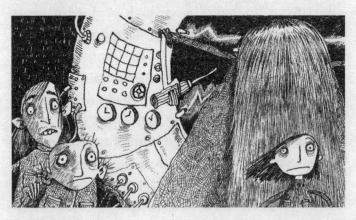

Until recently, one of the most frequently-heard expressions in Byron's life has been: 'Cheer up, it may never happen.' Now, unfortunately, it *has* happened and Byron has every right to be looking scared half-witted.

All four of them are wearing similar-looking slate-grey jump-suits (which presumably got their name from those suits parachutists wear when jumping out of aeroplanes). Each has their name stencilled in large black letters over their breast pocket: **CARBONET**, **DOYLE**, **BYRON** and **SMEEK**. For some reason, Smeek has an additional 'X' in square brackets after his name: **[X]**.

They're all bare-foot and, by the state of their feet, have been for some time. Their soles have become hard-skinned; toughened from walking without footwear and, yes, they're more than a little grubby. Smeek appears to have five toes on one foot and seven on the other. In a way, it wouldn't look quite so strange if his twelve toes had been shared out evenly between the two.

The banging against the door is getting louder as someone on the other side, egged on by those around him, swings the metal cylinder of a fire extinguisher against the wood, causing the uppermost chairs on the barricade to teeter.

'Hurry, Smeek!' says Carbonet.

Smeek, who is using a red-handled screwdriver

3

to tinker with a large piece of machinery in the middle of the room, simply grunts. He is holding a double-ended spanner in his mouth like a dog holding a bone. 'I'm doing my best, old friend,' he manages to mumble.

'Do you think this will work?' asks Byron, her voice all nervous and jumpy.

'It better,' says Doyle, gently running his fingers through his collar-length hair. It's a nervous trait rather than a wish to look particularly handsome at this particular moment in time. 'It's our only way out of –'

He's interrupted by a loud splintering noise as one of the door's panels splits apart.

'Time's running out,' says Carbonet.

'This is hopeless!' wails Byron. (I'm sorry it's the only woman doing the wailing, but there it is.)

'I think we're ready,' says Smeek. He stands back to admire his handiwork.

Imagine a giant car tyre, or rubber ring, or ring doughnut, but made from numerous pieces of metal held together with rivets and screws. Then imagine a tangle of wires trailing off to one side, and a key pad – rather like one used for setting a burglar alarm or opening a door when you punch in a code – set at chest height on the right-hand edge of the ring. This is what's in the centre of this room. This is what Smeek has been fine-tuning.

The machine is humming now, like the over-heated valves of an old radio, back in the days before transistors and microchips. (You'll have to take my word for it.)

'What if it doesn't work?' asks Byron.

'Then we're no worse off than if we didn't try it in the first place,' Carbonet points out.

'We hope,' mutters Doyle.

'WHAT?' demands Byron.

'No reflection on you, Smeek. I'm simply pointing out that this could be suicide,' says Doyle.

'What are you saying?' asks Carbonet.

'He means that there's no guarantee that using the Doughnut will be safe,' Byron jitters. She reaches into her breast pocket and pulls out a small mouse. 'Which is why I must let you go,

Kevin.' She gently strokes the tiny rodent's head, with trembling fingers. 'I'll miss you.' She gives the mouse a quick kiss, puts him on the floor and he instinctively scurries for cover. With hindsight, this kindness will be a terrible mistake.

'It's a risk we're going to have to take,' says Smeek. 'We can only fit through one at a time. Who goes first?'

Someone has found a fire axe and is now using that on the door. It won't be long before their pursuers have made light work of their makeshift barricade and are on top of them.

'Let's stop talking and ACT!' says Doyle. He pushes in front of the others and, before they can stop him should they want to, he jumps through the hole in the middle of the Doughnut . . . and disappears.

'You next, Byron,' says Carbonet.

'No, you.'

Smeek takes Carbonet's hand. 'Come on, old friend,' he says. 'We go together.' He jumps through the Doughnut pulling Carbonet after him. At that very moment, a number of things happen at once: the barricade gives way, a group of uniformed men spill into the room and Kevin the mouse finishes chewing through one of the wires attached to the Doughnut, giving himself a nasty shock.

Seconds later, Byron jumps through the humming metal ring.

There is a loud 'FIZZ!' followed by a bang, followed by silence. The humming has stopped. The machine is dead. Sadly, so is Kevin the mouse.

'They got away!' shouts one of the uniformed men.

'That's the least of our worries,' says another, striding over to the Doughnut. 'With the machine down we've lost their co-ordinates.'

'What do we do?'

'Do? We tell no one, or . . .' He doesn't bother finishing the sentence. They all know how serious the situation has become. 'Now let's get this mess cleared up.' The room starts to rumble and shake.

The year is 1993. It is 28th May and the clock on the wall is edging towards three minutes past eleven, local time. In the seismology lab of the Zanger Institute Earthquake Monitoring Station the needles of the earth-tremor recording equipment suddenly come to life, scribbling peaks and troughs across the graph paper like the lie-detector read-out of a babbling suspect, or a medium frantically scrawling out 'automatic writing'; apparent messages from the spirit world.

Dougie – with an 'ie' not a 'y' – is the scientist who's supposed to be monitoring the equipment, which usually means drinking plenty of coffee and doing crosswords and word-search puzzles. (Angie – also with an 'ie' – who does the other shift, prefers logic puzzles and occasionally leaves her puzzle books lying around the lab. Dougie had a go at some of her logic puzzles once, but just couldn't get his head around them.)

Now puzzles of any kind are banished from Dougie's thoughts. He sits bolt upright in his swivel chair, mutters 'Strewth', turns to the keyboard of his computer and frantically taps various keys. A zigzag line appears on a graph on his screen.

'Strewth,' he says again, this time with even more feeling.

This is incredible. Somewhere in the Great Victoria Desert an earthquake or some kind of explosion or something has caused readings like nothing he's ever dreamed possible. Whatever's making the earth shake is well over *a hundred times* more violent than anything he's ever seen recorded for the region.

Dougie grabs the red-coloured phone, the one without buttons or a dial – like the ones you see very important people use in films when they need a direct line to the President of the United States. 'Hello?' he says. 'Hello?'

'Hello,' says a bleary voice at the other end.

'We have a Code Blue in the Great Victoria Desert,' says Dougie, barely believing his own words.

'Code Blue?' says the voice.

'Code Blue,' confirms Dougie.

'Strewth!' says the voice.

Over the next few days and weeks, scientists at the Zanger Institute will begin to try to piece together a picture of what occurred, combining results from scientific monitoring with eye-witness reports from people having seen what most of them describe as a 'blinding flash of light in the sky', and ear-witness reports from people having heard what most of them describe as 'the loud boom of a distant explosion'.

Zanger's experts, along with other experts from around the globe, will eventually rule out the possibility of an earthquake, a crashed meteorite, 'something to do with UFOs' or even, as some will later claim, a secret and highly illegal underground test of a nuclear weapon developed by a Japanese terrorist group. The truth is that it's highly unlikely that they'll ever come up with the truth. Perhaps it's too incredible to believe . . .

But happen it did, and you don't just have to take my word for it. It's history: 28th May 1993, near Banjawarn Sheep Station in the Great Victoria Desert, Western Australia.

*

'Is everyone okay?' asks Smeek, stumbling to his feet. He has a pounding headache and his hair has somehow become all tangled and full of sand. Sand? He looks around. It's a clear, dark night. Where on Earth have they ended up? On a beach somewhere, perhaps? That'd be nice.

'Aoawpth!' says Doyle, spitting sand from his mouth. He's found himself face-down in the desert. He too has a headache like his worst ever hangover (and, for those of you who've never drunk as much alcohol as Doyle, let me tell you that his worst ever hangover was b-a-d).

'Carbonet!' cries Smeek, running over to his small friend who's lying, bleeding into the ground, the thirsty sand eagerly soaking up his blood. 'He's badly hurt!' With the care of a father, Smeek gently lifts Carbonet's head.

'We made it?' asks Carbonet. 'We got away?'

'We got away,' nods Smeek.

'Where . . . when are we?'

Smeek forces a smile. 'I've absolutely no idea whatsoever!' he confesses, surrounded by darkness.

10

'I hurt,' says Carbonet.

'Where, old friend?'

'All over.'

'Smeek!' Doyle groans from a short way off.

'What is it?' asks Smeek, carefully laying Carbonet's head back down on the ground, pushing some of the sand into a pile to make a pillow. Doyle calls out to him again. Smeek looks down at Carbonet. 'I'll be back in a moment,' he reassures him.

'Fine,' says Carbonet forcing the words. 'I'm not . . . not planning on going anywhere.'

Smeek gets up and strides across the sand to Doyle. 'What is it?' he whispers. 'Carbonet is in a bad way and –' He stops and peers down at what Doyle is looking at through the blackness.

It's Byron . . .

. . . what's left of her. He can make out little

more than a pile of blood-soaked clothes.

'Oh no . . . wh-wh-what have I done?' cries Smeek falling to his knees. He buries his hair-hidden face in his hands. 'What have I done?'

'She knew the risks,' says Doyle, who's had time to prepare a response, but still doesn't sound half as tough and heartless as when you read his words on the printed page.

'I don't understand . . . I don't understand . . .' sobs Smeek, unaware, of course, that it was Byron's own pet mouse Kevin chewing through the electrics that has caused the harm to her and Carbonet, and was nothing he himself had done.

'Get up!' Doyle urges. 'We've got to get moving. Who knows how long before someone works out exactly where to find us and follows us through the Doughnut.' His head is pounding, pounding, pounding and he's finding it hard to focus his eyes, but the horrible death of Byron has helped him to focus his *mind* on the matter in hand.

'Carbonet is too badly hurt to move,' Smeek says in a harsh whisper.

'But move him we must, Smeek,' says Doyle, 'or we could all end up dead.'

*

Another time. Another place. Le Fay McNally is standing in a room. Much of it is in shadow.

12

Something about the perspective seems a little strange: a little *off*. The walls don't quite meet the floor at right angles. The ceiling and the floor aren't quite parallel. Everything is in shades of grey. The window – yes, there's a window, though she hadn't noticed it before – is not quite square. It's as though she's on some arty set in a black and white movie; a cross between a Salvador Dali painting and a 1950s cartoon which exaggerates and distorts everyday objects.

In a corner stands the being Le Fay knows as Mr Maggs; the being she saw fall to his inevitable death. His head is large, bald and pumpkinlike. His teeth like shark's teeth. He looks up from whatever it is that he's doing.

'Who are you?' he asks in the familiar voice Le Fay thought that she'd never hear again.

'It's me, Le Fay McNally, Mr Maggs,' she says.

'What did you call me?' the being Le Fay knows as Mr Maggs demands.

'Mr Maggs,' she repeats.

'And why do you call me that?'

'Because that's the name you insisted I call you,' says Le Fay, stepping closer to him across the bare grey floorboards. 'With the Mister and everything.'

'When –?' begins Mr Maggs. 'Oh,' his expression changes. 'I think I understand.'

Since those unlikely events in Fishbone Forest,

13

Le Fay has often wondered about his insistence on being called 'Mister'. Had he demanded the title so as to sound more human? Sure, he has two eyes, two arms, two legs and just one head and nose, just as it should be – not too many, not too few – but, put them all together, and you are left with something not quite so human after all.

'Mr Maggs,' says Mr Maggs, slowly rolling the words around his mouth, as though trying out the name for size. He grins in the shadows. 'I like that . . . You say we've met?'

'Yes,' Le Fay nods. 'In Fishbone Forest. I was the girl looking – er – for her dog. Don't you remember?

You had a fall . . . We all thought you were dead.'

'And what was I doing in this Fishbone Forest?'

'You were planning to implement your *Manifesto of Change* . . .' Le Fay is really close to him now. There isn't a scratch on him. Not a bruise. Even if Mr Maggs has somehow survived the fall – and she finds that very hard to believe – surely there'd be some sign of injury?

Mr Maggs – and Le Fay has absolutely no doubt now that this is him – gives her an enormous grin. 'A manifesto of change? What an excellent idea. Our meeting like this is most fortuitous, Le Fay McNally. Really most fortuitous . . .'

They're so close now that Le Fay can smell the familiar strange sweetness of his breath. Frightening though she finds Mr Maggs, a part of her is glad that he survived. All he did was frighten them, he never did them any actual harm . . . though, it's fair to say that if that big hole hadn't opened up beneath him, there's no way of knowing what he *might* have done.

'How did you get out?' she asks.

'Out?'

'Of the hole?'

'Mr Maggs . . . Fishbone Forest . . . *Manifesto of Change* . . . The hole,' says Mr Maggs, as though all these names and concepts are somehow new to him, like unfamiliar items on someone else's shopping list. It's almost as if he's making no real connection with them.

Of course, thinks Le Fay. The fall. He must have hit his head in the fall down the hole. There must have been amnesia . . . loss of memory . . . cognitive deficits. (How can she, a young and poorly educated girl, know a phrase like that?) Then she notices how small Mr Maggs now is. No, that's wrong. Compared to the other items in this strange and sparsely furnished room, Mr Maggs is the same size he ever was; it's his size in comparison to *her* that has changed. She has become larger which is why he looks smaller.

'I wish I understood what's happening,' she says. 'Everything is so strange.'

Mr Maggs – surely it really is Mr Maggs, whatever he's calling himself now, and whatever he does or doesn't remember? – is staring intently into her eyes.

'You work it out,' he says.

Le Fay looks down to see what he was working on when she came into the room. Her eyes widen. She screams. If this were a dream she'd wake up now.

But this isn't a dream.

Chapter Two

It's hot hot *hot* and the McNally children – though, of course, Jackie the eldest is actually an adult – are in Garland Park (which is rather a grand name for a not-so-grand area of mud and grass, with a single tree roughly at its centre). Like many places around town, it's named after the Garlands, a rich local family who used to own much of the land on which it's built. By far the richest local family, however, used to be the Lyonses. It was a Lyons who'd had Fishbone Forest planted and had Fishbone Hall built at its heart. The McNallys sometimes sit in the tree in Garland Park but it's currently occupied by a whole gaggle of other kids, legs swinging from the branches under the shade of a 'roof' made from a sheet of very rusty corrugated iron, the edges of which have given many a child a nasty deep cut over the years.

There's no room for the McNallys, but they don't seem too bothered by the heat anyway, except for Fergal and his shaggy dog's fur. His brothers and sisters like to throw sticks for him and he likes bringing them back; which you may think is weird what with him apparently having an ordinary boy's brain with an ordinary boy's thoughts. But the reasons are straightforward enough. First off, since occupying Bumbo the dog's body, Fergal has found that he has inherited a few doggy habits, and Bumbo must have been a big fan of fetching sticks. Secondly, it really is fun. He can't play most human games but here's one he can get involved in with the others, and the twins in particular love the idea of getting their brother – yes, brother – to chase after sticks! Of course, with a 'dog' who really does understand absolutely everything you say to him – rather than simply seeming to – they can develop some quite complicated rules too. Their antics often attract the attention of other dog owners who make comments such as 'smart mutt' and 'boy, isn't he well trained!'.

They're not playing stick games now, though. Too hot for Fergal. They're all sitting on the dry straw-like grass, patchy in the baked-mud earth, their backs up against part of the brick wall which has been built around a large hole that opened up in the ground one day last year – just one of the ever-increasing number of holes that have been appearing across the country. Though nowhere as big as some of the other holes, it's still far too deep for anyone to attempt to fill it in, hence the wall. Since it was built to replace the temporary barriers, a few foolish kids have walked around the top of the wall for a dare, but only a few. One slip or stumble and it really is a long way dow-ow-ow-ow-nnnnnnnn.

Life is good for the McNally family. With their father no longer drinking and his friendship with ex-naval and retired detective Charlie 'Twinkle-Toes' Tweedy firmly cemented, wooden-legged Captain Rufus McNally is a happy man for the first time in years, and *his* happiness adds to that of Jackie, Le Fay, Albie, Josh and Fergal. And then there's the computer Le Fay won in the Tap 'n' Type competition. With Fergal falling from their hotel window on the night of her victory, all thoughts of ever claiming the prize were forgotten . . . until Fergal came back to them, even if in four-legged form, that is. Since then, she and Jackie have gone and chosen the equipment, paid for it with the winning voucher and then set up in their apartment. It's by far the most valuable item in their home and, on more than one occasion, Le Fay's suggested they sell it, but Jackie – and later their dad, Cap'n Rufus – insisted that she'd earned it and she should keep it. It hasn't taken long for Le Fay to get to understand most of the programs, and to show Albie and Josh how to play games on it, but she can't really use the computer quite as often as she'd like because they can't afford spending much on electricity. And she can't go on-line because the phone's been disconnected. But these are only minor niggles in the grand scheme of things, and not something she'd dream of ever telling the others.

Sometimes, the McNallys still find themselves talking to each other about the events triggered by Le Fay getting to the finals of the competition. They discuss the hole that caused them to abandon the coach, meeting Mr Peach the ventriloquist, Fergal's fall, and all those strange goings-on in Fishbone Forest. They wonder whatever happened to Mulch and the teenager Toby but, more often than not, the conversation returns to Mr Maggs. What might have happened if that second hole hadn't swallowed him up? Would he really have tried to put his crazy *Manifesto of Change* into operation? Was he mad and bad? Both? Neither? He still seems to haunt their thoughts. Perhaps this is because he fell to his death, as Fergal had fallen, and they'd been helpless to help him.

'I wish we had money for an ice-cream,' says Josh.

'Me too,' says Albie. 'Just one between the four of us –'

Fergal barks.

'– the five of us,' Albie corrects himself, 'would be nice.' (He doesn't really like sharing food and drink with Fergal. It usually comes back all slobbery.)

'Sorry, guys,' says Jackie. 'You know we can't afford it, but when I start my job we should be able to splash out on a few luxuries.' For years she's been responsible for looking after the others, it's not been something she's been able to trust her father to do. But now things are different. In the past she's been able to earn a little extra money doing a few odd jobs for other people from home – sewing, stuffing envelopes, making shuttlecocks (yes, making shuttlecocks), that kind of thing – but now she's got a job working at the SNAP-E-DREZZA clothing factory, less than an hour's walk from home. She's due to start in a couple of weeks.

'I wish we'd got that paper round,' says Albie.

'Yeah,' says Josh. 'It's not fair that we have to have a bike.' They'd tried arguing that they were used to walking and, anyhow, there were two of them prepared to work together doing the one round for just one person's pay, but Mr Ratsby who organises newspaper deliveries, was having none of it. 'No bike, no job,' he'd told them.

21

'I was wondering if we could get a job in a circus or on the stage or something,' says Josh.

'What as? A pair of clowns?' grins Le Fay. Josh gives her a friendly punch on the shoulder. 'Argh!' she says, deliberately over-acting and rubbing her arm. 'Bully! Picking on a poor defenceless girl!' This isn't a description any of them would use to describe their sister. Le Fay seems to have an ever-increasing sureness about everything she does nowadays. It's something that's hard to put into words.

'We were thinking that it might be useful for a magician –' begins Josh.

'– to have almost-identical twins –' continues Albie.

'– in his act,' Josh finishes. 'The audience would think that we're the same person, which would make it a lot easier for the magician –'

'– to do some amazingly magical tricks.'

'You've obviously given this a lot of thought,' says Jackie, 'but we live in a world where people like watching magicians with beautiful female assistants, wearing sparkly clothes with feathers in their hair.'

'One look at your ugly mugs and they'd know there was something fishy going on!' says Le Fay. She's mocking herself as much as the twins because these three all have the McNally red hair and gappy teeth. Jackie shares the red hair but, in both jackal and human form, her teeth lack the McNally gap. Fergal used to have both gappy teeth *and* red hair . . . but now, of course, he's inherited Bumbo's and not the McNallys' genes.

Albie is about to say something, then stops. He leans forward, away from the wall, a puzzled expression on his face. He clutches his right arm with his left, holding it close to his chest. Suddenly, before their very eyes, his right arm – including his hand – swells up to an impossibly enormous size then goes back to normal. In that brief moment, it's like Popeye's in the cartoons, after he's swallowed a can of spinach and his arms bulge with incredibly exaggerated muscles. Imagine it: your arm ballooning out and growing in length, your hand becoming bigger than a strongman's. Then, seconds later, it's back to how it was before.

23

If this happened to one of our relatives, we'd either think we'd been imagining things, or we'd take him straight to hospital. If it happened to us in person, we'd probably be thrown in a terrible state of panic. All five McNallys are shocked all right, perhaps even a little frightened, but they know one thing for sure. Whatever just happened to Albie, it's to do with his secret power. Jackie, they know, can turn into a jackal. Whatever Fergal's power was going to turn out to be, it stopped his brain being splatted to nothing when his body had hit the pavement outside The Dell hotel. But Albie, Josh and Le Fay's powers have yet to reveal themselves. Here is the very beginning, the first inkling, of what Albie's is going to be.

'What the –?' gasps Albie.

'Are you okay?' Josh asks his twin.

'Sure. Fine . . . My arm's a little numb, that's all.' He flexes his back-to-normal fingers on his back-to-normal hand at the end of his back-to-normal arm.

Jackie's already up on her feet. Le Fay's halfway there. 'We're going to have to go home, NOW,' says Jackie. 'Who knows what might happen to you next.'

'Do you think anyone saw?' asks Josh.

'If they did, they'll think they've caught heat stroke and are hallucinating,' says Le Fay.

A short way off, by a litter bin stuffed full of discarded drinks bottles, cans, and ice-cream wrappers, a pair of eyes is watching them and has been for the past half-hour or so; eyes belonging to someone who saw Albion McNally's fleeting transformation and doesn't doubt it for a single second.

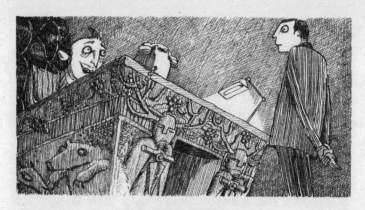

Chapter Three

Malcolm Kent knocks on the huge mahogany door to the office of the chairman of Tap 'n' Type.

'Come!' says a voice.

Malcolm swings the door open and begins his walk across the acres of deep-pile gold-coloured carpet towards Count Medoc Silverman's desk.

The desk is an extraordinary affair. Carved from one enormous piece of dark wood, it is covered in the most unusual carvings of vines and bears and wolves and hunters wearing antlered head-dresses. You'd expect a Viking warrior to be seated behind such a threatening-looking piece of furniture. Instead, that position is occupied by Silverman, with his slicked-back hair, thin moustache and perfect teeth. He is wearing one of his trademark pinstriped suits.

26

'Ah, Kent,' he says with a welcoming smile. 'Come in! Come in!' He glances at his chunky gold watch. 'Thank you for being so prompt.'

Malcolm has only ever been in the chairman's office on a couple of occasions and the same thought strikes him this time as before. It seems strange that the man who has founded Tap 'n' Type 'Providers of Keyboards to the Crowned Heads of Europe & Beyond' doesn't have a single typewriter, word processor or computer in his office. Count Medoc Silverman even writes company memos by hand, with one of his selection of gold fountain pens, in that distinctive red ink of his.

Count Silverman leans forward, placing his elbows on the large green blotter that takes up much of the top of his desk. 'Forgive the cliché, but I expect you're wondering why I asked you here today, Malcolm.'

'Indeed, Count,' says Kent, who hasn't been thinking about much else all morning.

Count Silverman picks up the gold paperknife which he uses to slit open the tops of envelopes containing his private correspondence. The handle is as ornately carved as his desk. He runs the tip of the blade under his perfectly manicured fingernails. 'It was a terrible thing when that brother of the Tap 'n' Type competition winner fell out of that window last year.'

'Fergal McNally,' says Malcolm, feeling a little put out that his boss appears not to remember the name. 'It was awful, sir. Quite awful.'

'And not the kind of publicity I intended the competition to generate.'

'No,' says Malcolm, taken aback.

'But accidents happen, and this was through no fault of your own. I felt the competition itself generated just the right buzz. You put the whole thing together very well.'

'Thank you, Count. I've become a friend of the McNallys since then. They really are lovely peop–'

The Count's eyes seem to open that little bit wider. 'Of course we missed out on the damage limitation exercise of paying for a grand funeral. The hotel beat us to it on that one, I seem to recall. And didn't it rain? I imagine it was a wash-out.'

Malcolm Kent looks down at his shoes, sinking into the plush pile of the gold carpet. 'The Dell paid for the coffin, if that's what you mean . . .' He remembers the funeral clearly. Surprisingly, there'd been laughter as well as tears thanks to the twins' rubber ball. (You had to be there.)

Medoc Silverman stands up, looking every bit the slightly flash used-car-salesman that he isn't. He walks around his monstrosity of a desk to stand by Malcolm Kent. He puts his hand on his shoulder.

'But the past is the past, and I've asked you here to talk about your future. I'm promoting you to Publicity Director, effective from now.' He grasps Malcolm Kent by the hand and shakes it. 'Congratulations,' says the Count.

'Th-Thank you, sir,' says a somewhat surprised Malcolm.

'We must toast your success.' Silverman walks over to a wall unit and pulls down a flap to reveal a row of bottles of red wine. He selects one, handing it to Malcolm along with a gold corkscrew. 'Perhaps you would do the honours?'

'Er, thank you,' says Malcolm.

As Malcolm uncorks the bottle and Count Medoc Silverman places two large wine glasses on his blotter, Malcolm reflects that, despite the name *Silver*man, the Count seems to much prefer gold. His cufflinks, his watch, his ring, his fountain pens, his corkscrew, even the colour of his carpet? All gold! On the walls of his office are mounted various musical instruments – a saxophone, a trumpet, a flute, a trombone and a tuba – and they too are made of gold.

The bottle open, Count Medoc Silverman half-fills the two glasses, handing one to Malcolm Kent and raising the other himself. 'To your promotion,' he says. The two men drink. Malcolm thinks the wine tastes delicious. 'Do sit,' says Silverman, going back to his side of the desk.

Malcolm looks around. There appears to be nowhere *to* sit. 'Thank you, I prefer to stand,' he says, which is probably the best answer to give when there are no other chairs in a room.

'I insist,' says Medoc. 'Use that ugly elephant-thingy as a stool.' He points in the direction of a small elephant carving beneath the large window which lets the brilliant sunlight into his office, showing the thousands of usually unseen dust particles floating in the air.

Malcolm strides over to the elephant, carrying it back to the front of the chairman's desk, then squats on it. His position reminds him of a picture he once saw of Puddleglum the Marshwiggle in a book called *The Silver Chair*. He feels that he's all knees and feet.

They drink.

'There are exciting times ahead,' says Silverman.

Later that same afternoon, Count Medoc Silverman stares up at the ceiling deep in thought, listening to jazz on the office sound system, when there is a tap-tap-tapping. It isn't coming from the door to his outer office, but from the door leading to his private staircase down to his private garage beneath the Tap 'n' Type building. The door with the lucky gold horseshoe on it.

He frowns. 'Who is it?' he hisses.

'Duffel,' says a muffled voice.

The Count jumps up out of his chair and over to the door, yanking it open. There in front of him stands an out-sized teddy bear, his thread unravelling in places and looking very grubby indeed. You wouldn't look too great either if you'd had to crawl your way out of a huge hole and had been sleeping rough ever since. For here is Mr Maggs's one-time constant companion.

The Count is silent for what seems like an age. 'How on Earth did you find me?' he gasps at last.

'It was only a matter of time,' says the teddy bear, fixing him with a glassy stare. 'You may have changed your name, but you've not lost your flare for publicity.' He pads across the plush carpet, leaving a slightly sooty trail.

'Where's . . .' Medoc pauses whilst he remembers the name. 'Mr Maggs? I thought you two are supposed to be inseparable.'

Duffel puts his paws on the seat of the Count's chair and then clambers up into it. 'Dead,' he says.

The Count switches off the jazz. Silence. 'When? How?' he asks eventually.

'Last winter. I can't remember exactly,' says Duffel. 'I've lost track of time.' At the mention of the word 'time' he lets out a strange laugh. Come to think of it, any kind of laugh from a teddy bear would be strange. Generally they don't laugh . . . or walk . . . or talk. Then again, Duffel isn't like other bears. 'We fell. He didn't stand a chance. Luckily for me I have all this padding . . . and,' he adds quietly, 'I landed on top of him. He cushioned my fall. That's what I'm here about. The rips –'

There is a knock at the main door to the office and, before the Count has time to say anything, his secretary Miss Willis strides into the room. She immediately sees the grubby teddy bear on Count Silverman's chair.

'H-How sweet, Count,' she says politely.

Count Silverman picks up Duffel and hugs him to his pinstripe jacket. 'An old family heirloom,' he smiles. 'It's been a much-loved member of the family for many a year.'

He opens a bottom drawer of his huge desk, places Duffel inside it and slides it shut.

'Just a few letters requiring your signature, Count,' says Miss Willis placing them on the Count's blotter and unscrewing the lid of one of his many gold fountain pens for him. 'And you asked me to remind you that you plan to tour the factory at three-thirty.' She hands him the pen.

'Thank you, Miss Willis,' says Medoc, signing each letter with a flourish of red ink, turning it over to dry on the blotter.

Miss Willis leaves the room.

There is a banging coming from the bottom of Count Medoc Silverman's desk.

'Let me out of here!' comes a muffled cry.

For the time being, Silverman leaves him where he is.

Chapter Four

As the chairman of Tap 'n' Type makes his way down his private staircase to his private garage beneath his office building, he has Duffel tucked under his arm. It is unlikely he'll run into anyone as he makes his way to his gold-plated Bentley – that's a car, and a rather nice one at that – but he isn't going to take any chances. It would look strange enough him carrying a battered out-sized teddy bear, but a teddy bear running alongside him would have been pretty much impossible for him to explain away!

'And don't say a word,' Silverman insists before scooping Duffel up out of the drawer and wedging him under his armpit.

Duffel does as he is told. He is used to keeping his mouth shut after years with Mr Maggs. He'd never spoken when anyone else was around, and had had to be careful even when there wasn't. With so many holes in the walls and missing doors at Fishbone Hall where they'd lived, they could never be sure who might overhear them.

Duffel is also used to seeing the world from a teddy bear's angle. Picked up and plonked down here, there and everywhere.

Once Duffel is in the front passenger seat and Medoc Silverman in the driver's, he feels that it's okay to break his silence.

'I should have known that you'd do the best out of all of us,' he says as the Bentley drives up the ramp and out of the underground garage, into the brilliant sunshine. 'You always were the smart one.'

Medoc Silverman keeps his eyes on the road in front. 'And, in this time and this place, my name is Count Medoc Silverman and I'll thank you to remember that.'

'If you say so,' says Duffel. He looks at Silverman with his neatly slicked-down hair, his perfectly pampered moustache and expensive (but rather flash-looking) clothes. 'Is Medoc Silverman a real person whose identity you borrowed . . . or did you make him up?'

Medoc Silverman eases the gold-plated Bentley to a halt at a junction. The traffic lights are red. He turns to face the teddy bear. 'You spent too much time with Maggs,' he says, his voice even, yet somehow menacing. 'He was the evil genius –'

'There was nothing evil about him. He was just misunderstood –' Duffel protests, but the Count ignores him.

'Well, whatever he was, he was the one with the big schemes. I, on the other hand, went down the simpler hard-work route and am now a highly successful businessman. Tap 'n' Type is a well-respected company providing an excellent service across the globe. I didn't need to steal anyone's identity. I created Count Medoc Silverman out of nothing.'

'Don't you think that blending into the background might have been safer?' asks Duffel.

The traffic lights change to green and Medoc Silverman drives the car across the junction. 'I can't believe I'm hearing that from a talking teddy bear!' he laughs.

Duffel puts a paw on Silverman's arm and stares at him with his glassy teddy-bear eyes. The chairman of Tap 'n' Type looks down at him in his plush leather seat.

'I have no choice,' he says quietly. 'This is what I have become.'

'I know,' says Silverman, his tone gentler now. 'I'm sorry. I shouldn't have said that . . . but why shouldn't I have a new name and a new lifestyle and all the very public trappings of success that go with it? I created Count Medoc Silverman, founded Tap 'n' Type and built it up into the success it is today. And I want to enjoy that success. We all got a second chance and I've grabbed it with both hands.'

Duffel looks down at his own threadbare paws. 'Some guys have all the luck,' he mutters.

The Bentley reaches a stretch of open road. 'I'm happy to help you, Duffel,' says Silverman. 'Happy to feed you and . . . er . . .' He is about to add 'and clothe you' but it occurs to him that he isn't sure whether teddy bears generally wear clothes or not. '. . . er . . . give you some money, but I can't afford risking you being around. The past is the past. We have to look to the future.'

Duffel makes a strange noise. It is the teddy-bear equivalent of an indignant snort. 'We all know what the future has to offer,' he says. 'That's what got me into this mess.'

Silverman says nothing, he simply pulls the car into the fast lane and puts his foot right down on the accelerator.

★

Tick tock. Time to move. Forwards. Sideways. Backwards. Time ticks on. Time for a thought or two. Or three. Ready? *At the time it happens, every moment in history takes place in the present.* Hmmmm. *The very latest craze is only the very latest craze until the next very latest craze comes along.* Mmmmm. *Today's baby is tomorrow's grandparent.* Have a banana.

★

It's a beautifully clear silvery moonlit evening. There are few people about and Jackie and Fergal are chasing each other back and forth across a local playing field. Jackie is in jackal form and, so, can communicate with her doggy brother without spoken words. They're 'talking' as they run, chase and play.

38

JACKIE: *Are you happy?*

FERGAL: *Happier than I've ever been, Jacks. If only we could explain to the others what it's like to run on four legs and to feel the wind in your fur.*

JACKIE: *Ouch!*

FERGAL: *And to be able to nip your big sister's tail!*

JACKIE: *And the smells. What about the smells?*

Fergal stops and cocks his leg against a tree. He can't help it. There'll always be a little bit of Bumbo in his behaviour.

FERGAL: *I'm still having to get used to them. I never knew that everything smelt so strong through a dog's nose!*

They chase each other round and round and in and out of a small clump of trees at the edge of the field.

Suddenly, an elderly man crosses their path. His skin looks blue in the moonlight.

FERGAL: *!?!*

JACKIE: *What's wrong?*

FERGAL: *It's him . . .*

JACKIE: *Who?*

FERGAL: *The man from Fishbone Forest . . .*

JACKIE: *WHO?*

FERGAL: *Lionel Lyons!*

JACKIE: *Who?*

FERGAL: *Lionel Lyons! Well . . . it's his body.*

JACKIE: *You mean . . .?*

39

Jackie and Fergal stand stock still. The old man bends down and pats Fergal on the head.

'It *is* you!' he says, with obvious pleasure, studying the scar in Bumbo's head where Mulch had cut it open. 'So you survived the scalpel too, did you, boy?'

Jackie is intrigued. Here is a man who can not only tell them more of what went on last winter in Fishbone Hall before she and the others arrived on the scene – Fergal's recollection is patchy and he spent much of the time locked up in an outbuilding anyway – but he's also probably the only person Fergal will ever get to meet who shares the almost unique experience of being a brain in someone else's body. Dashing behind a tree, Jackie turns back into human form and slips into her clothes, which she's left neatly folded on the grass. She emerges in the moonlight.

'Hello,' she says to the man in Lionel Lyons's body.

'Oh, hello,' he says. Fergal bounds over to Jackie. 'Is he your dog?'

Jackie nods.

'Just the one?' he asks. 'He was playing with another very handsome beast a moment ago.' His voice sounds old but not frail. In the same way that Fergal speaks with Bumbo's bark, this man must sound a lot like Lionel Lyons used to.

Jackie glows with inner pride. She's never been called a handsome beast before. 'Just Fergal,' she says, bending down and giving her brother a good solid pat. 'You're Lionel Lyons, aren't you?' she adds.

The man is visibly surprised. 'You . . . You must be mistaken,' he says.

'Technically, I suppose,' says Jackie. 'I mean, all your thoughts and feelings aren't Mr Lyons's, but you are in his body, aren't you?'

'I – er –' The man who had his brain placed in Mr Lyons's body – he was a French teacher, wasn't he? – actually splutters.

'There's so much I want to ask you,' says Jackie. Fergal is jumping up barking at his big sister but, because she's now in human form, she can't understand him. But *he* can understand her. 'Shall I tell him?' she asks. Fergal nods. Jackie looks up at the man. 'I was at Fishbone Forest. I met Mr Maggs, Mulch and Toby. I know about the Lyons fortune and your brain being put in that body.' She pauses. 'You're not alone. This,' she says, looking back down at Fergal, 'is my brother.'

For the first time in this brief encounter, the man looks really *really* surprised. He may even have turned a funny colour, but it's hard to tell in the moonlight.

Let's fast-forward. Just a little. Not too far. Stop! Back a bit. Great! Here's fine. We're back at the McNallys' apartment with Smoky the cat in the 'nest' she's made for herself on top of the wardrobe in the bedroom.

In the front room, all the McNallys are assembled, including their father Captain Rufus who is the only McNally sitting in an actual chair. Perched on one of its arms is Albie and on the other is Josh. The two remaining chairs are

42

occupied by the French teacher inside Lionel Lyons's body and Mr Charlie 'Twinkle-Toes' Tweedy the retired police detective who was paying one of his regular visits to the apartment when Jackie and Fergal turned up with their surprise guest.

Le Fay was using her computer when they arrived. The twins were in bed. Now they're all very wide awake indeed, and giving the newcomer their undivided attention. Le Fay is sitting on a windowsill, the moonlight filtering through the grubby glass, with Fergal curled up at her feet, whilst Jackie – who is very much in charge of these proceedings – is sitting on a very large (and very lumpy) home-made cushion opposite their guest.

'Please tell the others what you started telling me on the way over,' says Jackie.

The ancient gentleman – well, that's what he is on the *outside* at least – looks around the assembled company. 'My name is Tom Dwyer,' he says, sounding a little nervous, 'and I used to teach French in a truly terrible school in Hartingly called Gravel Hall . . . where the only thing worse than the students was their parents. It was a horrible, horrible job.' He takes a sip of tea.

Despite Twinkle-Toes Tweedy helping Cap'n Rufus get all the benefits he's entitled to, money is still tight in the McNally household and, except on very special occasions, teabags get used time and time again, until the last trace of tea-colour has gone. (Flavour has very little to do with it.)

What none of them knows is just *how* special their meeting with Tom Dwyer (in Lionel Lyons's body) will turn out to be.

'I hated teaching. I hated my home life,' Dwyer explains. 'My parents died when I was little and I was brought up by an aunt who fed me and cared for me and always tried to do what was right for me, but she never knew how to show her *love* for me, if she actually felt any.'

Albie and Josh watch him speak with fascination. They remember Mr Maggs talking about his hare-brain scheme in which he'd needed the dead Lionel Lyons to make 'one final appearance' so that Mr Maggs could be made heir to the Lyons fortune and now here he is. Here is Mr Lyons's body with another man's brain inside his head, of course . . . living and breathing (and drinking tea-coloured water) in front of them. It's weird enough having a brother who's now a dog, but imagine if he'd come back looking and sounding like a completely different *person*. In a way that might have been even harder to cope with.

'When I left home I went to France for a few years. I didn't like it . . .' Dwyer continues.

Le Fay begins to wonder whether the French teacher has ever liked *anything* much!

' . . . so I came home and taught the language. I wasn't much qualified for anything else.' He finishes his tea and places the mug on the arm of his chair, next to a hole where the stuffing is poking through the cover. 'I never married. I never even had a girlfriend.'

Fergal is studying the newcomer more intently than anyone else in that room. Of all those present, only Fergal really knows what it's like for Tom Dwyer's thoughts, ideas, reactions – his very *being* – to be occupying a different body; a body that was once occupied by someone else . . . by someone else who has died and vacated it. Both he and the French teacher are new tenants in old properties left empty when their previous occupants moved on.

'My last memory as Tom Dwyer in my original body was down by the docks. I fell in the water. Perhaps I jumped . . . I'm not altogether sure. I remember fighting for breath . . . drowning . . . then I was hit by a boat . . . and then the next thing I remember clearly is waking up in what seemed like a hospital room with a teenage boy and a – er – man clutching a teddy bear . . . I was confused . . . Then I saw my hands . . . They didn't seem to belong to me . . . It was like a nightmare.'

Charlie 'Twinkle-Toes' Tweedy produces a small metal flask from the hip pocket of his checked jacket and pours a splash of something into Dwyer's empty tea mug.

'Have a sip of this,' he says. 'It'll do you a power of good.'

Captain Rufus McNally raises a quizzical eyebrow. He's never seen Twinkle-Toes produce his hip flask before, and has never touched a drop of alcohol himself since he first learnt of Fergal's fall.

Dwyer swallows the drink gratefully, then resumes his incredible tale. 'It took time to adjust to my new body and my new surroundings, but, as it transpired, I was Mr Maggs's pet project and he went out of his way to make sure that I adapted and was comfortable –'

'So long as you did exactly what he said.'

The man inside Mr Lyons's old body nods. 'He told me that he and Lionel Lyons had been old

46

friends and that, having no family left, Lionel had intended to write a will leaving everything to him but that, sadly, Lionel had died before he'd had the chance to do it.'

Which was almost the truth, Le Fay thinks. In fact, by his own admission, Mr Maggs had deliberately befriended the old man with the sole purpose of trying to persuade him to leave him the Lyons family fortune.

'He explained that he needed me to play the part of Lionel – and argued that the flesh and bone part of me really *was* Lionel anyway – and that I must visit Mr Fudge of the lawyers Garland & Fudge and write a will making Mr Maggs sole beneficiary . . . which I did.'

'Did he threaten you? Say what would happen if you didn't go along with this extraordinary state of affairs?' asks Twinkle-Toes Tweedy, his detective instincts coming to the fore.

Dwyer shakes the head he's come to think of as his own. 'No. He pointed out that he'd given me back my life . . . and, in return, all he wanted was this one small favour. Little did he know how little I valued his gift at first . . .'

Albie and Josh look at each other from the separate arms of their father's chair. Tom Dwyer certainly isn't a bundle of laughs.

The 'cheer up it might never happen' line would

be rather wasted on him too, I suspect. And phrases such as 'Let's do it for the fun of it', 'just for a laugh', and 'hey, let's party' are unlikely to roll off his tongue which, given what he's been through, is understandable, I suppose.

'Of course, it took me a while to realise the other implication in Mr Maggs's plan as he presented it to me. Writing a will wasn't *all* he needed from me. There was more. Much more.' Dwyer pauses, looking at his old, gnarled hand clutching the mug on the arm of the chair. 'As Lionel Lyons, I went with Mr Maggs to the offices of Garland & Fudge, met with old Mr Fudge and said all the things that Mr Maggs had coached me to say. I had them draw up a will leaving everything to Mr Maggs, just as he wanted. But . . .' He trails off into silence.

'But, of course!' cries Le Fay, with a look of horror. 'For Mr Maggs to inherit the Lyons fortune, *you had to die first!*'

Chapter Five

There is a loud gasp in the McNallys' sparsely furnished front room, made up from all the barely audible sharp intakes of breath coming from each and every one of them, except for Charles 'Twinkle-Toes' Tweedy, whose years as a detective have trained him to hide his emotions, and for Fergal, who lets out a puppy-like yelp instead.

'When did it occur to you that you were going to be required to – er – die?' asks Tweedy, leaning right forward in his chair, reminding Le Fay of a bird-of-prey on the lookout for a passing mouse.

'It didn't,' confesses Dwyer. 'I was still trying to adjust to the fact that I was alive again and, in one sense, was someone else. Then there was the fact that I was more or less a prisoner in a semi-derelict house in the heart of some godforsaken forest in one of the wettest winters on record. It was his

49

assistant Mulch – Jackie says you children met him – who warned me.'

Fergal's ears are twitching at the mention of Mulch, the nickname of one Stefan Multachan, petty crook, assistant to the late Mr Maggs and a skilled surgeon in his own right. He was the one who'd put Fergal's brain in Bumbo's body.

Le Fay's legs are going numb from being perched half-on and half-off the window sill. She stands up and steps over Fergal, who is having a good old scratch behind his left ear with a hind leg (something which not all brothers can do).

'But I don't get it, Mr Dwyer. When we had the misfortune to meet Mr Maggs his plan was complete. The way he told it, he'd *already* inherited the millions. He claimed that he was the owner of Fishbone Hall and was ready to spend some of the fortune to make his *Manifesto of Change* come true! But you're still alive.'

'Yes,' says Albie.

'How come?' asks Josh.

'Thanks to Mulch,' says Dwyer. 'He not only pointed out the less pleasant aspect of Mr Maggs's plan but also helped me to escape.'

RRRRRRRRRRRRRRRRRRRewind.

'We've got to get you out of here,' says Mulch, the

rain dripping from his plastic raincoat onto the already sodden and warped floorboards.

'I thought I'd done everything your Mr Maggs had asked of me,' says Dwyer, looking up from his chair.

'There's no time to argue,' Mulch insists. 'The master could be back at any moment. Here. Put this on.' He throws a shabby mac into Dwyer's lap.

Dwyer gets to his feet; feet that once belonged to Lionel Lyons, mind and body. 'You mean Mr Maggs doesn't know you're moving me?'

'No,' says Mulch with added urgency. '*Pleeease!* We must hurry.'

Pulling on the mac as he walks, he follows Mulch through various holes in the crumbling walls of Fishbone Hall and down a flight of back stairs. Outside in the terrible rain now, they pass an outbuilding, triggering off a spate of excited barking from within.

'Sssh!' hisses Mulch. 'That stupid dog is going to give us away!' He and Dwyer clamber into Mulch's English-mustard-coloured van.

'You love that dog,' says Dwyer, pulling the seatbelt across the late Lionel Lyons's body which he's already beginning to think of as his own. 'I've seen you nurse him and play with him. Since Mr Maggs – er – brought me back, that's the only love I've seen in this horrible place. You and that boy Toby seem to obey your so-called "master" out of fear and there's no love lost between the pair of you.'

The little van is speeding down the driveway, heading between spiny trees, windscreen wipers frantically sweeping back and forth, back and forth, trying to cope with the ceaseless rain.

'You're forgetting Mr Maggs and Duffel,' says Mulch, craning forward over the steering wheel to try to see his way through the downpour.

'You mean that there's more than the four of us in that crumbling excuse for a house?'

'Five, if you count the dog,' says Mulch.

Dwyer counts off the occupants on the fingers of one of his new (second-hand) hands: 'You, me, Mr Maggs, Toby and the dog makes five. Then who's Duffel?'

'The master's teddy bear.'

Dwyer snorts. 'Yes, I'll grant you that. He certainly seems to love his bear.'

Mulch swerves the van around a bend a little too sharply and almost loses control of the vehicle.

'Careful!' says Dwyer. 'I don't want to end up dead again so soon –'

'Which is why I must get you away from here,' says Mulch, sweat breaking out on his brow which is already splattered with rain.

'W-Why?'

'For Mr Maggs to inherit the Lyons billions he needs a death certificate, and for him to get a death certificate he needs –'

'A body.'

Mulch nods.

Tom Dwyer, ex-teacher of French, sits in silence as the little van the colour of English mustard speeds towards one of the exits of Fishbone Forest.

Back at the hall, there is a knock on Mr Maggs's study door. 'Come!' he says.

Toby the teenager ambles in, the headphones to his Discman around his neck. His T-shirt reads 'DON'T SHOOT ME, I JUST WORK HERE'.

Mr Maggs is standing by a window; one which isn't simply a hole in an outer wall but has a frame and glass and everything. The effect of normality is slightly spoilt by ivy growing across it *from the inside*.

Duffel is leant against the wall beneath it.

'Well?' demands Mr Maggs.

'Mulch has just smuggled the patient out of the house,' Toby reports.

A satisfied smile spreads across Mr Maggs's extraordinarily wide face. 'O, goodie!' he says. 'I want you to buy me a bunch of plastic tulips.'

'What's that got to do with –?'

'All you need to know is that I want a bunch of plastic tulips. What it has or hasn't to do with is my affair!'

Mr Maggs is struggling not to fly into a terrible rage. He doesn't want to. He doesn't need to. He must simply impart his orders to the boy as coolly and calmly as possible. But there's that tell-tale tremble in his voice.

'Sorry . . . Yes. Of course . . .' Toby mumbles.

'Yes?' Mr Maggs pauses.

'Yes, *master*,' Toby adds hurriedly.

Mr Maggs bends down, picks up his teddy bear and holds him tight. 'If this all goes to plan, Toby – and it *will* go to plan – I will soon inherit this

54

house, this forest and all that lovely money and I shall be able to implement my *Manifesto of Change* . . . and you, Toby, shall be richly rewarded for your loyalty. Remember that. Richly rewarded.'

'I'll remember,' Toby assures him. To him, cash and lots of it is what this is all about.

'In the meantime, first thing tomorrow morning you will take what money you need from the kitty in the egg-bowl in the kitchen, go into town and *buy me some plastic tulips*.' These last few words are spoken through two rows of pointy little teeth, clenched together.

'Thy will be done,' Toby intones, without a trace of irony. He leaves Mr Maggs to his thoughts, closing the door quietly behind him.

★

'There's nothing like discovering that someone else is planning to take your life away to make you want to keep it!' Dwyer tells the assembled McNallys. 'Mulch took a big risk helping me. A big risk.'

Fergal stops scratching and barks his approval. He's a big Mulch fan.

'Have you any idea how Mr Maggs ended up inheriting Lionel Lyons's wealth without a body?' asks Twinkle-Toes Tweedy.

'Oh, yes,' says Dwyer. 'According to Mulch,

he managed to aquire a death certificate by unscrupulous means.'

'He forged one?'

'I think it involved a genuine doctor signing a genuine certificate,' Dwyer explains, 'but how Mr Maggs got him to sign it is another matter. Mulch was very hazy on the subject.'

'Which means you've seen him since he helped you escape?'

'In fact, you still see him, don't you?' says Le Fay. It sounds like a challenge to deny it. 'In fact, it was he who told you that you might find Fergal and – er – another dog chasing each other up on the playing field. What you didn't expect was for us to recognise *you*. You didn't run into Jackie by coincidence, did you?'

'Y-Yes,' confesses Tom Dwyer. 'I mean no. No I didn't. I do still see him . . . How did you know?'

'She has brains –' says Albie, which is an unfortunate choice of words, given who he's talking to.

'Not in jars,' Josh adds, helpfully.

Le Fay frowns. How did she know? How does she know so many of the things that suddenly seem to be competing for space in her mind nowadays? She shrugs. 'I just worked it out,' she says.

Chapter Six

The following morning, Tom Dwyer returns to the McNallys' apartment and takes Jackie, Le Fay, Fergal and the twins to see Mulch. Their father wants Twinkle-Toes Tweedy to go too but, as an adult herself, Jackie assures him that the children have nothing to fear.

They walk. It's not far and, anyway, the McNallys certainly can't afford to take the bus. Fergal keeps bounding excitedly ahead, his long pink tongue lolling in the morning heat. He's very much looking forward to seeing Mulch again, but the others aren't quite so sure.

It turns out that, all this time, Tom Dwyer has been living in an apartment less than three-quarter of an hour's walk from the McNallys' home! (Three-quarters of an hour if they were striking out on their own, that is. This particular trip takes well over an hour because Tom Dwyer is in the body of a very old man, remember.)

'This was where Mulch brought me the night he drove me away from Fishbone Hall,' Dwyer explains as they walk across the lobby towards the lift.

'No dogs,' says a security guard seated behind a small counter.

The twins are impressed. All they can see of him is the dome of his head poking up above the top of the large newspaper he's reading, and his feet, which he has up on the counter . . . and, if that's all they can see of him, how did he manage to spot Fergal (who didn't make a single yap, bark or whimper)?

'We haven't got a dog,' says Le Fay, frantically signalling Fergal to hide before the man lowers his paper.

Fergal darts behind a large square plant pot made of the same pinkish simulated marble as the foyer floor. This probably makes the entrance to the apartments sound far grander than it really is. Of course, this is far grander than the building the McNallys' apartment's in, but that's not saying much. The Garland Apartment Building, which is where they are now, was probably once far grander. The old phrase 'it's seen better days' seems very apt. The floor has lost its lustre and the plant pot, behind which Fergal is now hidden, is badly cracked and contains a plastic pretend-plant which hasn't been dusted since the day it was placed there.

The security guard pulls his feet off the counter and folds his paper as he stands up.

'Don't mess with me, lady,' he says. 'These ears ain't ever been wrong.' His accent sounds strange.

'Are you an American?' asks Le Fay because, don't forget, which ever country you think this story is taking place in, you're W-R-O-N-G.

'I surely am,' says the guard who, incidentally, is called Arthur P. Peabody III. The Roman numerals 'III' after his name mean that he is the third Peabody to have been given the name Arthur P. Peabody, so the correct way to address him – and I don't mean you to confuse him with an envelope or a package – would be as Arthur P. Peabody the Third . . . which is probably more in keeping with the name of a senior vice-president of a multi-global sock-making company or a software giant, whatever a software giant may be, than with a security guard in what he himself once described as 'a two-bit flea-pit of a building'.

'I've always wanted to go to America –' says Le Fay. Fergal's tail is sticking out behind the pot plant and she's trying to push it out of sight with her foot whilst keeping her eyes firmly fixed on Mr Peabody.

'I strongly suspect that you're trying to change the subject,' declares Peabody. 'I believe we was discussing the fact that I distinctly heard the pitter-patter of doggy paws on my marble floor.'

'Well –' begins Le Fay, relieved to see out of the corner of her eye that Fergal has pulled his tail in.

'The clackety-click of claws on marble floors –'

'You're a poet!' grins Albie.

'Like little knitting needles,' continues the security guard, ignoring the boy.

'Well –' says Le Fay.

'Good morning, Arthur!' Tom Dwyer interrupts. 'I've got a little something for you.' He shuffles across the foyer, digging his hand into the pocket of his lightweight summer jacket, already a little damp with sweat from having caught a cab to the McNallys' and then walking back with them.

 'Oh really, Mr Smith –' says Peabody, because that's the name the kindly old gentleman gave him when he moved in. (It would have been extremely unwise to refer to himself as either Dwyer or Lyons now, wouldn't it?) Dwyer produces a small lozenge-shaped tin of pilchards in tomato sauce and places it on the counter by the folded-up newspaper. '– You shouldn't have.' Peabody slips the tin out of sight. 'I'm sure I must have imagined those doggy sounds. My hearing ain't quite what it used to be. My ears must have been hallucinatin' again.'

The others aren't quite sure whether ears really *can* hallucinate, but they get his meaning. Arthur P. Peabody III sits back down, unfolds his paper and puts it up as a screen between himself and the lift. He's already looking forward to his lunchtime pilchard sandwich. He has a loaf and a sharp knife in his cubby hole. In this weather, there's no point in bringing any butter, margarine or even that low-fat spread his wife (Alice Peabody) would far rather he ate. It would melt in minutes, and the management of the Garland Apartment Building are too mean to provide him with a fridge. Not even a small one. Which is why Mr Peabody's bottles of beer are annoyingly warm in their hidey-hole under the counter. Peabody sighs a silent sigh to himself – an inner sigh – and ruminates on the fact that life is, in his opinion, not always very fair. (It may have occurred to you that this is not a particularly original thought, but at least it's true.)

Tom Dwyer and the McNallys meanwhile are taking advantage of the window of opportunity the bribe has afforded them. In other words, they all nip into the lift, Fergal included, before the security guard changes his mind; Fergal's paws clackety-clacking those last few steps across the foyer.

'My ears never lie,' Peabody can be heard to mutter.

Up in Mulch and Dwyer's apartment, the McNallys recognise some of the items dotted about the place. Mulch must have brought them from Fishbone Hall after Mr Maggs fell to his death. Of course, his book – his *Manifesto of Change* – has been lost. Jackie had thrown it into the hole after him.

Dwyer makes them all sit down before Mulch makes his entrance. Jackie can clearly recall the time she last saw him.

It is raining. Still raining. It's hard to remember when it *hasn't* been raining. Jackie's heart feels like bursting with joy. Looking into the eyes of the dog sitting on Le Fay's lap, and being petted by the twins, she knows that Fergal is well and truly back.

She looks up and – through a large hole in the ceiling above, and a large gap in the roof of the room above *that* – can clearly see the sky, splashes of falling rain mixing with the tears on her face.

'We did it, Mum,' she whispers. 'Thank you.'

She looks down to see Mulch kneeling by the hole in the floor of Fishbone Hall into which his master has fallen. The earth smells rich and damp. He is sobbing gently.

A pang of guilt stabs Jackie, but it's quickly replaced with one of confusion and anger. But what harm has Mulch done them? Not a lot. Mulch has brought Fergal back to them. She puts her hand on his shoulder. He looks up at her with such sadness.

'He wasn't a bad man,' he says, for the umpteenth time.

'Maybe not *all* bad,' Jackie concedes.

Mulch gets to his feet. 'Are you going to call the police?' he asks, wiping his eyes with the back of a sleeve, mixing dust from the fallen masonry with his tears and the rainwater, giving his face an impressively smudged look.

'The police?' asks Le Fay, still in the towel dressing gown Toby gave her to wear. *Where is Toby?* she wonders. *He must have run off into the night.* 'Of course we're going to tell the police! A man –' she stopped. Mr Maggs was certainly no man. 'Someone *died* here tonight. We can't just ignore it and pretend it didn't happen!'

'And he was crazy and wouldn't let us go!' Albie points out.

'And . . . And . . .'

'And, *no*,' says Jackie. 'We aren't going to tell the police. Who's going to believe a bunch of scruffy kids with a story about reanimation and not-quite-human beings . . . about brains in jars and fortune tellers . . . No, the matter ends here, Mulch, with the death of your master.'

In amongst the smudges, a look of relief appears on Mulch's face. He even manages a smile. It's not a pretty sight.

'You've been mixed up in some bad things,' says Jackie. Mulch is about to say something, but Jackie puts up her hand. She's cold and tired and wet and it's been a traumatic day . . . and they've all got to go home and face the wrath of their father who's probably worried sick about where they are and what's happened to them. 'But we have a lot to thank you for too,' she says.

'Woof!' agrees Fergal loudly, and trots across to Mulch and licks his fingers; those same fingers which nimbly connected his brain up to this new body. 'Woof! Woof!'

'No police?' say the twins.

'No police,' Jackie repeats.

'No police,' Le Fay agrees, with a change of heart. 'Can we take Fergal home now?'

'You'll show us a way out of here, Mulch?' Jackie asks.

'I'll do better than that. I'll drive you home,' says Mulch. 'You should all fit into my van.'

'And then what will you do?' Le Fay asks the little man.

Mulch shrugs. He thinks of the ex-teacher of French in Lionel Lyons's old body in the apartment in town. 'I'll survive,' he says.

They follow him out into the rain, avoiding as many puddles as possible in the short dash to his van the colour of English mustard. Le Fay sits in the front next to Mulch, with Fergal on her lap. Jackie and the twins pile into the back.

At the East Gates of Fishbone Forest, Mulch jumps out of the driving seat, unlocks them and drives his van out into the road. He's about to jump back out and lock the gates behind him, when Le Fay puts a hand on his arm. 'You don't need to do that any more,' she says, with wisdom beyond her years. 'It's over, Mr Mulch –'

'Multachan. My real name's Stefan Multachan,' he corrects her. 'You're right.' He drives on, leaving the East Gates wide open behind them. 'You're right!' It's not just common sense, somehow it's a symbolic gesture.

Mulch and the McNallys part company just around the corner from the McNallys' apartment. He stays in the van. Perhaps he's worried that they'll change their mind and inform some authority or other.

'Thank you,' says Jackie from the pavement. He's not sure whether she's thanking him for the ride home or for Fergal or for what.

She's not sure either.

Le Fay steps forward, with Fergal still in her arms. They've only just been reunited and neither is in a hurry to let go.

She leans forward and speaks to Mulch in a lowered tone through the open side window of the van. Back on the kerb, neither Jackie nor the twins catch what she says.

'There are no such things as bad people, Mr Multachan,' she says. 'Some of us do bad things sometimes, that's all. But what you've done for us is amazing.'

Fergal's approach is much more direct. He leans forward in his sister's arms and gives Mulch a great big lick across his face.

'Goodbye,' mutters Mulch at last. He releases the handbreak and drives his English-mustard-coloured van into the night.

The McNallys turn and head for home. It's only when they reach the doorway to their building – the single remaining door swinging on its single remaining hinge – that Jackie realises something quite remarkable. It's stopped raining.

Whooooooooooooosh! Forward to Tom Dwyer stepping aside to let Mulch enter the room. He looks smaller. Older. He's obviously nervous.

Fergal leaps forward and greets him, tail wagging.

Hello, Mulch! he says. *It's good to see you again. Really good! You smell fantastic!* What it comes out as is a series of 'woofs!'.

Fergal's obvious pleasure at seeing him again breaks the ice. The small man visibly relaxes a little.

'Hello, everyone,' he says. 'I'm glad you all came. Thank you.'

Le Fay is looking past him to a bookcase. On the middle shelf is a very familiar object. It's the paperweight from Fishbone Hall; the one she slipped in the pocket of the blue towelling dressing-gown to use as a weapon if needs be. Fortunately, it hadn't been necessary.

Soon everyone is seated and, unlike the McNallys' own apartment, there are plenty of chairs for everyone . . . *and* they've all got drinks that actually taste of something. The adults are drinking orange juice (with bits in), the twins lemonade, and Le Fay Coke from a bottle with a straw. Le Fay has never tasted Coca-Cola before and she's never drunk anything out of a bottle with a straw. The McNallys don't have money to throw around on 'non-essentials' like this and Le Fay would be the first to admit that the whole experience is very novel. (And, whilst I remember, Tom Dwyer has given Fergal a nice big bowl of water, which he's lapping away at noisily.)

Le Fay takes the straw out of her mouth. 'Why did you get Mr Dwyer to track us down now, after all these months, Mulch?' she asks.

'Someone asked me to, Miss McNally,' says Mulch. 'Someone who needs your help and says that time is running out.'

Chapter Seven

Oooooops! We're heading ɘɯiɟ ni ʞɔɒd again. Lionel Lyons, who will turn out to be the last of the Lyonses of Fishbone Hall, is sitting on his father's knee. He's never sat there before. His father isn't generally a fan of using his body parts in the seating arrangements. Fortunately, Lionel is only eight years old and is good and light, and there's no danger of him wearing a patch in his father's fine trousers. His father smells of shaving soap, hair tonic and mothballs.

'Lionel,' says his father. 'Today I want to talk to you about duty. There is a newfangled notion that life is about enjoyment . . . about "having a good time". Well, not in the Lyons family it isn't. It never has been and it never will be. Are you with me so far?'

Knowing that it's expected of him, Lionel nods his eight-year-old head wisely.

'Good chap,' says his father. 'You see, my boy, it is the duty of each Lyons to pass on an even bigger fortune than the one he himself has inherited on the death of his predecessor. His duty, I say. Since I inherited the Lyons millions, I have managed to make that money work for me and have turned it into more millions. It is your duty – yes, duty, little Lionel – to make sure that, by the time you pass away, you'll be able to leave an even bigger fortune to your son. Is that clear?'

'Yes, Father,' says Lionel. Sitting on his father's knee he has a good view out of the broken window and is watching a bird on the rotting handle of an abandoned garden roller. He doesn't like their rare visits to the ruinous family seat of Fishbone Hall. There are very rarely any animals about – few birds, squirrels, mice or badgers. He's pleased to see the little brown bird.

'Some families waste their money on the upkeep of huge family estates,' says his father. 'One of our ancestors even wasted many thousands on building this house, but later Lyons generations learned better! Yes, slave labour was used to build this house – hence the railings around the forest to discourage escape – but those slaves could have been put to work on something far more practical! Our town house is much cheaper to heat and light which is why we live

71

there and not here. These are things you should consider, Lionel. It all adds up.' He pauses and stares into space, remembering when his own father – Lionel's grandfather Leonard Lyons – had a similar conversation with him, and how it had fired his imagination and made him determined to make more and more money when his time came.

'As well as a sense of duty, Lionel,' he continues, 'it is vital that you as a Lyons have one other attribute. And do you know what that is?' He studies his eight-year-old son.

'Yes, Father,' says Lionel.

'You do?' asks his father, somewhat surprised.

'I mean no, Father,' Lionel adds hurriedly. He was rather pleased with his wise nod and his previous 'Yes, Father'. He doesn't want to go and mess things up by saying the wrong thing at the wrong time now. He really *must* try to pay more attention.

The bird has hopped off the handle of the roller and is now rooting around in the soil.

'The other attribute a Lyons needs is a thick skin,' says his father. 'Like a rhinoceros.'

'A rhinoceros,' says Lionel, who has learnt from experience that repeating the last few words a grown-up has just said often makes him or her think that you have some idea what they're on about.

72

'And the reason why you need such a thick skin? Because there are people out there in the big wide world who are jealous of us, Lionel. They're jealous of the way we Lyonses amassed our fortune so they turn on us at every opportunity.'

'A rhinoceros,' repeats Lionel. The bird is pecking at a wriggling beetle or some such thing. Poor beetle, thinks little Lionel.

'What?' asks his father.

'Every opportunity,' says the boy.

'Yes,' agrees his father. 'Absolutely. There's no shame in earning a fortune from selling weapons to both sides in foreign wars, for example, my boy. They're going to kill each other somehow anyway, and someone's got to sell them guns and ammunition. It might just as well be a Lyons. It *should* be a Lyons. It's good business sense, that's all. Who are we to judge? And piracy. Take piracy. Today piracy isn't an acceptable way to behave, of course it isn't. It's not the done thing. But back in the days when we Lyonses were pirates some of the best families were at it . . . well, some of the more adventurous ones, at least, and a Lyons pirate never killed women or children. Unless they were foreign. Or it was absolutely necessary . . .'

Lionel's father is really getting into his stride now. 'And take grave-robbing. There are those who see it as some barbaric act, but it wasn't as if the bodies were going to be used in some awful rituals. They were used for the advancement of science. For doctors and surgeons to get a better understanding of how the human body worked. Without graves being robbed for the dissection table, many of the surgical advances we take for granted today wouldn't exist, Lionel. It's true that we Lyonses charged good money for each body provided, but our ancestors were, yet again, providing a vital service.'

The little brown bird now has a beak full of grubs and creepy-crawlies. *It must have a nest nearby,* thinks Lionel. *It must have young to feed.*

'Do you understand what I've been telling you?' asks his father.

'Yes, Papa,' says Lionel. 'When you die I get all the family money and I must make even more money so that I can pass it on to my son. And it doesn't matter if other people are jealous so long as I make pots of money any way I can.'

Lancaster Lyons beams with pride. He glows with pride. Every fibre of his being seems to be *humming* with pride. He gives Lionel, his only son and heir, the only hug he will ever give the boy in his entire life.

'You're a true Lyons!' he trumpets.

When I grow up, I'm not going to marry and I'm not going to have any children and I'm going to leave all of my money to lots of different charities to help people and animals and things, thinks Lionel. But he's wise enough not to speak these thoughts out loud.

'There's one thing I don't get, master,' says Toby. He's wearing a T-shirt with the slogan 'I'M JUST THE MONKEY, ADDRESS ALL COMPLAINTS TO THE ORGAN-GRINDER'.

'Just the one thing?' sneers Mr Maggs. Toby doesn't seem to get the subtle put-down. Either that or he's not bothered by it. 'Well?' demands Mr Maggs. 'What is it?'

'It's just that for you to inherit all this money –'

'I assume you're referring to the Lyons family fortune.'

'Yeah, that's the stuff, Mr Maggs.'

'Continue.'

'Well, for you to inherit it – and for me to get my cut – Lionel Lyons Esquire needs to be dead.'

Mr Maggs stares at the boy as though he's an idiot. 'He *is* dead, Toby. He died while enjoying an orange-flavoured ice-cream, remember? His dead body was in my fridge for I don't know how long. H–'

'Sorry, master. What I meant to say . . . What I meant was . . .' Toby is all flustered now. He doesn't like to make Mr Maggs angry. Who in their right mind would beat a wasps' nest with a big stick? (That's a cross between a metaphor, a rhetorical question and a very *stupid* question. In equal parts.) 'What I mean is, you put that French teacher brain your Cousin Ralphie sent you into Lionel Lyons's body so that he could *appear* to be alive –'

'Yes,' agrees Mr Maggs. 'Guilty as charged! The shame! The shame!' He suppresses a giggle. 'And we toddled off together to the poky little offices of the over-stuffed Mr Fudge of Garland & Fudge and my pretend-Lionel Lyons wrote a nice big official will leaving everything to *me* when he dies!'

Mr Maggs puts his hands above his head and does a triumphant little pirouette like a ballerina . . . at least it would be like a ballerina if ballerinas had pumpkin-shaped heads and rows of pointy little teeth. He comes to a halt. 'Oh, I see what you mean, my spiky-haired boy! You're thinking that I'm going to have to take away the patient's life in order to claim my fortune!'

'Yes, master. That's it.'

'And Toby-Woby isn't happy with the idea?' He
sticks out his lower lip and pouts.

'Well, the truth be told, Mr Maggs. Not really.'

'But you knew what this project would involve
when I hired you. You knew that the ultimate goal
was implementing my *Manifesto of Change* and
that for this I'll need the Lyons fortune, and for
that –'

'Yes, but I hadn't thought that far ahead,' Toby
protests. 'I hadn't thought of all the little details.'

'What's that saying, Toby? Ah, yes. The *devil* is in
the detail . . . and if you think killing a man is a
small detail . . .'

'I didn't say that,' Toby protests. 'Well, that's not what I meant anyway.'

Mr Maggs comes in close. 'Want to know a secret? Promise not to tell? *We aren't going to harm a hair on the patient's head.*'

Toby visibly relaxes. It's like there's a great weight off his mind. 'We're not?'

'No, we're just going to make him *think* that we are.'

'But I don't understand, master. What good will that do?'

'Simple. Now that he's tricked ancient old Fudge of Garland & Fudge, he's fulfilled his purpose. His work is done and dusted. I don't need his dead body to get a death certificate. I've got death certificates coming out of my ears.'

Toby finds himself looking at Mr Maggs's ears to see if he means it literally. The master doesn't usually use such colourful language. What he doesn't know is that Mr Maggs spent much of last night reading a book of colloquialisms – everyday phrases – to improve his language skills; to help him to blend in when he finally implements his *Manifesto of Change* and ventures out into the big wild world again.

'So what happens to the French teacher?' says Toby.

'Well, we can't have him walking around as

78

Lionel Lyons once I've told old Fudge that he's dead.'

'Yeah, that could really mess things up,' agrees Toby.

'And we can't have him telling everyone that he's really Mr Thomas Dwyer, either, now can we?'

'No.'

'So what we need to do is make sure that he goes into hiding. Lies low. Keeps his trap shut.'

'Uha.' Toby nods. 'But what if he doesn't agree to?'

'This is where my enormous brain comes in!' grins Mr Maggs.

Which is why you have such an enormous head! Toby thinks but, like young Lionel Lyons on his father's knee all those years before, very wisely, doesn't say what he's thinking out loud. 'What have you come up with?' he says instead.

'We let Monsieur Dwyer *think* that we're going to have to kill him, and make him go into hiding.'

'In other words, making him think that going-into-hiding is his own choice. That's BRILLIANT, Mr Maggs!'

'Some of us are born great, Toby,' beams his master. 'I'll get Mulch to sneak him out one evening. Little does Dwyer know that it's with my seal of approval!' With that, Mr Maggs throws

79

himself into his chair behind his desk. It's sodden with rainwater from a leak in the ceiling – well, a hole open to the sky, actually – directly above it. He leans back and picks up Duffel from the floor. 'Why didn't the mummy horse hear her tiny foal's cry?'

For a fleeting moment, Toby is thrown by the sudden switch of subject. Then he realises that it's one of Mr Maggs's riddles.

'I don't know, Mr Maggs. Why didn't the mummy horse hear her tiny foal's cry?'

'Because it was a little horse. A little horse. A little hoarse: h-o-a-r-s-e. Do you understand?'

'Yes . . . Yes, of course. Very good, master. I must go and get lunch ready.'

'Very well,' says Mr Maggs. 'Soup would be nice. A pink soup. Yes, let's have pink soup.' He gives Duffel an extra hug. Of course, the teddy bear remains absolutely silent as teddy bears do.

'Until this week, the only people I've seen from the master's house' – he means Fishbone Hall, of course – 'is Tom,' says Mulch. He looks across at Dwyer, who is sipping his orange juice. 'We've been sharing this apartment since the day Mr Maggs died. Since that day, I haven't seen Toby and I hadn't –'

'Seen us –'

'– until now,' the twins interrupt.

'It wasn't you I was – er – referring to,' says Mulch.

'Who then?' asks Jackie.

'A few days ago I made contact with Duffel,' says Mulch, as though it would mean something to the assembled company.

The McNallys look at each other blankly, as if to say: *Are we supposed to know who Duffel is?*

'Who?' asks Le Fay.

'Sorry,' says Mulch. 'Of course you don't know him by name. Mr Maggs's teddy bear, Duffel.'

Albie laughs. 'You found his teddy?'

'That's nice,' says Josh.

'But he was clutching it when he fell into that hole,' says Jackie. He was even singing about the pair of them on the way down, she remembers with a shudder. 'You didn't climb down into the hole did you?' she asks. Had he crawled all the way down into the darkness to try to rescue Mr Maggs, or to bring up what was left of him?

'No,' says Mulch with a shake of the head. 'You see, the thing is . . .' He pauses for a moment and runs a finger around the rim of his glass. It makes a whining sound – and no jokes about 'whine glasses' please. 'You see . . . it was Duffel who crawled *out*.'

Jackie gives him the benefit of one of her funny looks. Not funny ha-ha but funny peculiar. It's the kind of look which says *Pull the other one, matey, it's got bells on.*

'The teddy bear crawled out?' says Le Fay.

'And tracked me down,' says Mulch. 'All the way up here to this apartment.'

'And this teddy bear –'

'Duffel.'

'And Duffel walked into the foyer downstairs, past a security guard who can detect a dog scuttling across the floor without even having to look out from behind his newspaper, and came up the stairs or in the lift –'

'The stairs, I suspect,' says Mulch. 'I don't think he's tall enough to press the lift button to this floor.'

'– or in the lift,' Le Fay continues, 'and knocked on your front door.'

'Because he couldn't reach the bell.' Mulch nods.

'And nobody thought it was strange that there was a teddy bear taking a stroll around the place?'

'Le Fay!' snaps Jackie. She's brought the others up to be polite and, crazy though Mulch's claims are, there's no need for her sister to sound so . . . so sarcastic.

'Sorry,' says Le Fay, sucking another slurp of Coke through her bendy straw. 'But you must admit that it sounds a little odd.'

'And, unless you're in the know, so does the idea of walking around in someone else's body,' Dwyer points out.

'Woof!' Fergal agrees.

'Or turning into a jackal,' says a voice from the doorway.

Five pairs of McNally eyes turn to the doorway. In it stands a rather battered, threadbare-looking teddy . . .

. . . which would be quite a dramatic entrance I suppose, if he didn't look quite so *saggy*.

Chapter Eight

'We've already met,' says Duffel, his arms flopping teddy-bear-like to his side, which is hardly surprising. He walks rather awkwardly into the centre of the room. 'Don't look so shocked by a walking talking teddy bear,' he says. 'You of all people have no reason to! Tom Dwyer and you –' he lifts a paw and points to Fergal, '– are out and about thanks to borrowed bodies and you –' he looks Jackie straight in the eye '– have some remarkable transmogrifying abilities of your own.'

'Is that a word?' asks Josh.

'If it isn't it should be,' says Albie.

'Ssh!' says Le Fay.

'How did you know?' demands Jackie, assuming that 'transmogrifying' must be another term for shape-shifting or turning-into-a-jackal-and-then-back-again.

'I've been watching you,' admits Duffel. 'All of you.'

'*Why?*' ask Jackie, Le Fay and the twins.

'Woof?' asks Fergal.

Duffel heaves himself up onto the sofa between Mulch and Tom Dwyer. Le Fay notices Mulch edge away from him; perhaps to give the new arrival more room, or perhaps because he feels uneasy in his company.

'I need help,' says Duffel. 'It's a unique and delicate matter and I think that anyone who's faced up to Mr Maggs and has a brother who's now, on the outside at least, a – er– *dog* would have a better understanding of things than most . . .'

'So you decided to check us out?' asks Le Fay, the half-drunk bottle of Coke now completely ignored on a side table.

'Yes,' says Duffel.

I'm having a conversation with a teddy bear, thinks Le Fay.

'How did you find us?' asks Josh.

'I think we'd have noticed a bear following us,' adds Albie. 'Even if he was wearing a hat and a raincoat with a turned-up collar.'

'I found Mulch. That was easy. I knew about this apartment here in town –'

'And he already knew where *we* live because he drove us home the night . . .' Jackie falters.

'The night that me and Mr Maggs were swallowed up in that rip. Yes.'

'That what?' ask the twins.

'That hole,' says Duffel.

'If you don't mind me asking, how come you weren't killed?' asks Jackie. 'That was a very deep hole and it opened up very suddenly.'

'Isn't the question how come you were alive in the first place?' asks Le Fay. 'I thought most teddies were filled with stuffing. Don't tell me Mr Maggs somehow managed to put a brain in you too?'

Duffel shakes his badly-stitched head. 'No. Mine is a very different story. As to how I didn't die . . . I not only have plenty of padding –'

'But you also landed on Mr Maggs,' says Le Fay.

'Yes,' says Duffel, his voice barely above a whisper.

Jackie is still far from happy that someone – more than some*one* – outside her family and very close circle of friends knows her secret. Now it seems that this extraordinary ragbag of a trio, comprised of a petty crook who stole brains to order, a French teacher in an old man's body and a teddy bear all know about it too! How safe a secret is that?!?

'What's this delicate matter you think we can help you with, Duffel?' asks Le Fay.

'I need to put a stop to the rips – the outbreak of holes.'

'And, because of what we've seen and what we've been through, you think me and a bunch of scrawny kids –'

Fergal barks.

'– and Fergal can help you?' says Jackie.

'Teddy bears can't be too picky when it comes to seeking assistance,' says Duffel. 'And don't undersell yourselves.'

'We certainly have looks,' says Albie.

'And charm,' says Josh.

'And intelligence,' says Duffel, his eyes once again on Le Fay.

'Do you know something about me I don't?' she demands.

'I'm simply wondering whether a family with a sister who can turn into a jackal might also have siblings with other talents,' says Duffel. This time he stares at the twins remembering the strange incident he'd witnessed at Garland Park when one of them – he can't tell which – had that amazing ballooning arm!

'My abilities have been a secret up until now . . . At least I thought they were,' says Jackie. 'I'd very much like to keep it that way.'

'Who are we going to tell?' says Tom Dwyer. 'We three are the biggest bunch of misfits I've ever been a part of.' It's the first time the McNallys have seen him smile.

'It's difficult for a talking teddy bear to get taken seriously. Lionel Lyons is supposed to be dead, and Mulch here is . . . Mulch,' Duffel shrugs. A shrugging teddy bear is a strange sight to behold.

'In all the time I worked for the master,' says Mulch, 'I never knew Duffel was alive. I simply assumed that he was a well-loved stuffed toy. I still find it hard to believe . . .' He looks hurt, upset that Mr Maggs had kept such an important truth from him. 'I was at a loss for words when he first arrived at our door.'

'So our secret's safe with you?' asks Jackie. 'If we don't have your word on that – from all three of you – we're not even going to stay here and listen to a thing you say, let alone even think of helping you.'

'Though we *are* going to finish our drinks first,' says Albie.

'Absolutely,' says Josh, gulping at his glass of lemonade.

'No one's going to tell anyone anything,' says Duffel. 'We promise you that.'

'I promise,' says Tom.

'Me too,' says Mulch.

'We all have plenty to hide,' says Duffel.

'Which brings us back to you wanting our help,' says Le Fay. 'What is it that you'd like us to do?'

'Three things. I'd like you to trust me. I'd like you to come with me now, and I'd like you to help me to try to stop this outbreak of holes. In return, I offer you a glimmer of hope. A possibility – and only that – a possibility that we might be able to bring Fergal back to how he was.'

Fergal's ears prick up. He raises his doggy head, his doggy tongue still lolling from the side of his doggy mouth.

'But that's impossible!' gasps Mulch. 'You never said anything about –'

'There's plenty I haven't told you, Mulch,' Duffel confesses, putting a paw on the little man's hand. Mulch jerks it away as though he's received an electric shock. 'I'm sorry.' He looks directly at Le Fay. 'But I won't lie to you. Will you come with me now?' For some reason four pairs of McNally eyes turn to Le Fay to see what she wants to do.

There's something which anthropologists or psychologists (or some such ologists) call 'the group dynamic'. The group dynamic is the way a bunch of people or animals behave *as* a group as a result of the way roles are formed and individuals behave *within* that group. In groups of animals, it's often the Alpha Male – the biggest, strongest, wisest male animal – who is in charge. As he gets older, he's challenged by younger males and, in the end, one of these becomes the new Alpha Male and the new boss of the group. Then the group dynamic changes, because he has different favourites amongst the other members of the group, and different ideas as to where they should go next to feed, or what they should do.

The group dynamic in the McNally household used to mean that poor old oldest sister Jackie did just about everything whilst their dad, Captain Rufus McNally (retired) sat in the back room emptying bottles. If any decisions needed to be made for the welfare of her siblings, Le Fay, Albie and Josh, and Fergal, it was Jackie who made them. They relied on her and looked up to her.

Sometimes they grumbled that she 'wasn't fair' but, in their heart of hearts, they knew that she was trying to do what was best for them. Add to this the fact that she could turn into a jackal, and she made a very good leader!

Now, following Le Fay winning a place in the Tap 'n' Type finals and Fergal's dreadful fall, the group dynamic has subtly begun to change; so subtly to begin with that none of them has really noticed, including Le Fay herself. More and more, she is now the one with the knowledge, the ideas and the gut feelings. The McNallys are acting more and more on her suggestions and advice.

It's obvious to everyone in the room that, rightly or wrongly, everything now rests on her decision whether to go with Duffel or not.

'We'll come,' says Le Fay.

★

The hands on the clock go backwards. The dates on the calendar run in reverse. Here we go again:

Smeek and Doyle bury what's left of Byron – mainly her bloodstained jump-suit with **BYRON** on the breast pocket – in the sand, which is much cooler the further down they dig with their hands. This is partly out of respect for their fellow escapee, and partly to try to cover their tracks should anyone discover their co-ordinates and come through the Doughnut in search of them. Smeek has torn off strips of his clothing to bandage Carbonet. Add to that the fact that great clumps of his hair are falling out – a side effect of coming through the Doughnut that doesn't seem to have affected the others (the hair in Carbonet's ears, for example, being one of the few things about him that doesn't appear to have been horribly mutilated by his recent experience) and the (very) strange numbers of toes on Smeek's feet, and you'll appreciate what a strange sight he is . . . not that anyone is likely to *see* any of them out here in the desert in the dark.

'Time to move, old friend,' Smeek tells Carbonet, another hank of hair falling from his head.

'You're going to have to pull it all out before we go anywhere,' says Doyle.

'What?'

'Your hair, Smeek.'

'Why?'

'Because if we're going to be carrying Carbonet we can't keep stopping every few metres to put him down and pick it up!'

'But I don't need to keep it!'

'You're missing the point, genius,' says Doyle. 'Your clumps of hair will leave a trail . . . a trail which anyone can follow in daylight.'

'But we'll be leaving footprints anyway!' Smeek protests.

But Doyle isn't going to argue. He grabs the end of as much of Smeek's remaining long black locks as possible . . . and the hair comes away from Smeek's head surprisingly easily and painlessly. 'There,' says Doyle. He hands it to a very bald-looking Smeek, whose head now resembles nothing more than a pumpkin with a shark's-teeth smile. 'Now shall we get going?'

'A br-broom,' rasps Carbonet. 'I can use . . . your h-h-air . . . as a broom.' Every word is a terrible effort. Blood trickles from the corner of his mouth.

Smeek manages to force a smile. 'Good idea, friend,' he says. 'But do lie still.'

Doyle wonders if Carbonet is delirious, but soon sees what the wounded man means. As he and Smeek carry Carbonet between them, Carbonet just manages to keep a hold on the long tress of Smeek's hair between his remaining bloodied fingers, letting it trail on the ground behind them, brushing the sand so as to obscure, if not completely erase, their footprints. Using this method, just a light breeze blowing the surface of the desert could virtually obliterate their trail altogether.

They have been walking for a few hours when the trio have their first piece of luck: Doyle spots a shack: Well, he almost walks slap-bang into it. This is soon followed by their second: inside the shack, they find a hurricane lamp for light, and a few basics, including bottled water.

Carefully lying Carbonet on a table, Smeek opens a bottle and holds it to his injured friend's lips. 'Drink,' he says.

*

Not far from Tom Dwyer and Mulch's apartment is an old bakery. It's disused now since the owner, Donald Lumpit of 'Lumpit's Loaves', died without a will and a dispute arose between ten of his eleven children. (The eleventh child – the third oldest girl, Iris – is a marine biologist shipwrecked on an island paradise somewhere and doesn't even know that her dad has passed away.) As the legal wrangle continues as to who owns what and who should be in charge of which department, the bakery's production has ground to a halt, without a single Lumpit's loaf bouncing off the end of the conveyor belt in over two years, and the building and the machinery it houses are falling into disrepair. It is here that Duffel has asked the McNallys to bring him.

'It's easier if you carry me,' he tells Le Fay, 'and I'll whisper directions.'

On the way, Albie and Josh do plenty of burping and belching. (I use both words in case there's a difference. The word 'belch' somehow suggests something deeper and wetter to me.) The twins aren't used to drinking fizzy drinks, and the lemonade they had at the Garland Apartment Building is taking its toll. Up front, Le Fay carries Duffel (who's heavy but not *that* heavy), with Jackie and Fergal following up at the rear. This weather really is far too hot for dogs, and Fergal is panting badly.

When they finally reach the boarded-up building, Duffel has Le Fay put him down in an alleyway running up the side of the bakery, and whilst the twins stand at the end of the alley to check there's no one coming – Fergal seated between them on the hot pavement, thinking back to the days before thick fur – Duffel shows them his secret way in through a basement window.

Fergal leaps in last of all and is delighted by the coolness of the shade.

Duffel has made a small area of living space for himself in the middle of a vast room, having gathered together pieces of furniture from various parts of the old bakery.

Once the McNallys are settled, he begins to talk. 'What I'm about to tell you will sound

96

completely crazy,' says Duffel, 'but, as I've said before, if anyone's going to believe me, you will.'

'Go on,' says Jackie.

'Let me start with the easy part,' says the teddy bear. 'Do you know what a timeshare is?'

No prizes for guessing that it's Le Fay who answers. 'It's a place – like a holiday home, for example – owned by a whole bunch of people who get to live in it at different times of year,' she says.

'How does that work, then?' asks Josh, absent-mindedly scratching Fergal between his doggy ears, just the way he likes it, and just the way Mr Maggs had sometimes scratched Duffel.

Le Fay switches into brainy sister mode. 'Well, say six people buy equal shares in a timeshare, that would mean they each get to stay in the house for two months of every year,' she explains.

'Huh?' asks Albie, if 'huh?' counts as a question.

'Twelve months divided by six people equals two months each,' Jackie points out.

'Simple!' laughs Albie.

'It's a way of sort-of owning a place you could never afford on your own, and having it to yourself, but only for set times of the year,' says Le Fay. 'When you're there, it's all yours and yours alone. That's right isn't it, Duffel?'

Duffel nods his badly-stitched head.

'You sure know a lot of stuff, sis,' Albie says to

Le Fay, clearly impressed. 'But what do timeshares have to do –'

'– with stopping the outbreak of holes?' asks Jackie. 'You didn't bring us here to go into the holiday homes business.'

Josh looks a little put out. It's *his* job to finish his twin's sentences for him, and *vice versa*.

'There are lots of different ways of timesharing,' Duffel explains, pacing up and down in front of a giant dough-mixing machine, which looks like it mixed its last dough a long, long time ago. 'You can timeshare a bed, for example.'

'A bed?' say Albie and Josh.

'He's right, you know,' says Jackie, remembering something their father, Captain Rufus, once told her. 'Dad's brother, Uncle Erik, used to share a bed. He washed up in a restaurant kitchen during the day and slept in the bed at night and someone else, who washed up in the restaurant kitchen during the night, slept in the same bed during the day. They hardly ever even saw each other!'

'Okay,' says Duffel, still pacing. 'That's the easy part. Think of timesharing . . . Now it gets – er – more complicated. As you probably know, the world's population is getting bigger and bigger all the time. People call it the population explosion. There's only a finite – only a certain amount – of land on this planet that people can live on, and there are more and more people needing to share it.' He stops.

'Woof!' says Fergal. What he's trying to say is *Go on!*

'In the future, the problem will get so serious that people will try to come up with all sorts of different solutions: space stations, colonising the moon, floating cities . . . the kind of things you see in science fiction films and television programmes.' Duffel doesn't realise that the McNallys have never owned a TV set.

'I still don't see –'

Duffel stops walking and turns to face them all. 'Someone once said – or will one day say, I can't remember which – that the past is just another country, or some such thing. If you think of it in that way, then the past could be used as another country *for people to colonise*. A way of helping to solve the population explosion would be to send people back in time to live in the past, where there are fewer people and there's more room.'

'But that's crazy!' says Jackie.

'It's ingenious,' Duffel argues. 'You can have a huge number of people all born in the present, living on the same small plot of land but in different times in the past when it was previously unoccupied!'

Chapter Nine

Albie giggles. He can't help it. 'Are you trying to tell us that people have been trying to travel back in time to timeshare this planet in the past?'

'Not exactly,' says Duffel. 'What I'm trying to tell you is that people from the future have tried to travel back into their past and have succeeded.'

Le Fay stares into Duffel's glassy eyes. 'And the future's past is our present, *here and now,*' she adds, her head buzzing with all the implications.

Duffel nods again. 'Yes.'

'But surely we'd notice if people suddenly started appearing out of nowhere –?' begins Albie.

'And what if people start running into their grown-up great-grandchildren who haven't even been born yet?' says Josh.

'And tried sleeping in our beds and stuff?' asks Albie.

'I think we might notice them if they did!' says Josh.

'Who's been sleeping in my bed?' says Albie, putting on a deep gruff voice.

'Said Daddy Bear,' says Josh. Then, remembering who he's talking to, becomes suitably embarrassed and falls silent.

Duffel seizes this embarrassment as an opportunity to continue. 'Scientists from the future spent years trying to develop time travel but got nowhere,' he explains. 'The best minds in the world were working on it but they just couldn't find a way. Then one day, out of the blue, the authorities stumbled on someone who had built his own time-machine using completely alien technology –'

'And was that someone an alien himself, by any chance?' Le Fay blurts out, barely able to contain her growing excitement as the pieces of the jigsaw fall into place.

'Kind of,' says Duffel.

'And was . . . is . . . will his name be Mr Maggs?' cries Le Fay.

'Yes,' says Duffel, 'though, in the future, his name is Smeek. It's only in your time that he took the name Maggs.'

'Mr Maggs was an alien –' gasps Albie.

'– from the future!' gasps Josh.

'And you're from the future too,' states Jackie, who's been listening silently from the sidelines.

'Yes,' says Duffel.

'WOW!' say the twins.

There is a brief silence. 'Tell us what happened . . . I mean what *will* happen,' says Le Fay.

Duffel wipes his threadbare forehead with a paw. He has their undivided attention. 'In the future, space – not the twinkling stars in the sky kind but the room-to-move variety – is at a premium. Most people live in small high-rise apartments – skyscrapers – because they take up the least room. In one particular skyscraper the local police were getting more and more complaints from residents that the new tenant, a long-haired guy called Smeek, was –'

'Long-haired!' Albie cries out in amazement.

'Sssh!' says Jackie.

'– that Smeek was making a lot of noise in his apartment day and night and, whatever it was that he was up to, he was causing the walls to shake. After a number of warnings, the police gained entry to the flat and found an extraordinary home-made machine in his bathroom. Smeek was taken away for questioning, because he didn't have the papers required to be a resident there . . . and, even more importantly, because he didn't look quite *normal*!'

'Woof!' Fergal urges. *Go on!*

102

'During the course of his questioning, Smeek claimed not to be human, and there were those who were quick to brand him a liar or a madman. Only his machine – which was like a metal ring, big enough for a single man to crawl through – led to him being taken seriously. A few simple tests with animals, proved that he had built a machine that could send living creatures through time. A rabbit was sent into the following Tuesday and, I seem to remember something about a gerbil and a previous Saturday.'

'W–!' says Albie.

'–ow!' says Josh.

'The potential for using Mr Maggs's – Smeek's – equipment to help solve the population problem was spotted immediately. The problem was Smeek himself. The authorities didn't want an alien to have anything to do with the project. They knew that they'd have to choose the time and place to send people to with incredible care. Mess about with Time without rules and who knew what might happen? So they locked him up. Don't go thinking that society will be any more tolerant in the future.'

'I'm finding this very hard to believe, Duffel,' says Jackie.

'Here we are listening to a teddy bear, and you're telling me what he says sounds unbelievable?' says Josh. 'Our life is unbelievable!'

'It's just one unlikely exploit after another,' adds Le Fay in agreement. (It's this comment that gave me the idea for the title of this series.) 'And the holes?'

'I'm coming to them,' says Duffel. 'Smeek was locked away with some other prisoners considered high-security risks while top-secret experiments were carried out on his Doughnut.'

'His *what*?' asks an incredulous Albie.

'His machine,' Duffel explains. 'The scientists named it *Doughnut I* because of its appearance. They built a bigger version – *Doughnut II* – based

on the original specifications, and kept it in a wing
of the prison where Smeek was being kept, so that
they could haul him out of his cell and get him to
explain things if they needed to.'

Le Fay thinks back to the Smeek she knew: the
Mr Maggs who loved riddles and his teddy bear
and whose *Manifesto of Change* contained simple
and childish ideals. She felt bad that humans had
treated him – sorry, that should be *would one day*
treat him – this way.

'So did the experiments work?' asks Jackie. 'Are
we now timesharing our present with people from
the future?'

Duffel sits down on an upturned plastic crate
labelled LUMPIT'S LOAVES . 'Not when I left. You
see, Smeek and a few other prisoners managed to
escape from the cell they were sharing, and to get
to the Doughnut and jump through it, into this
time frame, but something went wrong . . .'

Inside the shack.

'I'm going to have to operate,' says Smeek.

'What, are you crazy?' says Doyle, looking
around the shack. 'This place is filthy, we don't
have any anaesthetics, you don't have any tools –'

Smeek pulls open a drawer in the table. There
are three sharp wooden-handled knives. 'I have no
choice, Doyle!' he says. 'Carbonet's going to die if

105

I don't do anything. We need to find a way of boiling some of the water and we need something to use as thread for stitching . . . HELP ME!'

'Keep your hair on!' says Doyle and then, seeing how completely bald his once-hairy cellmate now is, he laughs. 'Your hair!' he says. 'We could weave the strands to make thread. Now, what about a needle?'

They frantically search the shack trying to find anything and everything that might possibly play a part – however tiny – in increasing the chances of saving Carbonet's life.

Smeek finds the old teddy bear under an upturned tin bath in a corner. He holds it up triumphantly. 'Just what we need to help him keep his body shape!' he announces.

The operation takes fourteen hours. Doyle spends some of the time assisting Smeek, some of it being sick outside, some of it trying to sleep and to keep warm as the night-time temperatures drop even further, and some of it trying to keep cool. The details of the surgery itself are gory and Smeek's skills under such near-impossible conditions are incredible. At first working by light from the old hurricane lamp (also used to heat the knives and boil the water), now hanging from a crossbeam, and later from the glaring sun, filtered through a hessian-sack curtain covering the one window, he cuts, stitches, cauterises, sets and generally repairs Carbonet's internal organs, skin and bone, somehow holding the man together inside a padded suit made from the teddy bear, making the man and the material one.

'Mr Maggs saved your life,' says Le Fay when Duffel has finished telling them of this extraordinary operation.

'He did,' he says quietly, turning away, but Fergal clearly sees the tears seeping out from beneath Duffel's glass eyes. 'Once I'd recovered enough and we reached civilisation, he did further operations to make me as you see me today . . . I was horribly mutilated when I came through the Doughnut and something went wrong. Now I don't know where the teddy bear ends and I begin. It's unlikely anyone else could have done what Mr Maggs, as you know him, did. He was a remarkable scientist and surgeon and a true friend.' Le Fay goes over to Duffel and gives him a hug. Somehow, it seems an okay thing to do to a teddy bear without asking.

'What did you do?' asks Jackie. Her words sound harsh.

'Do?' sniffs Duffel.

'What did you do – *will* you do, or whatever – to end up sharing a cell with Mr Maggs as a high-risk prisoner? What was your crime?'

'That's the awful thing,' says Duffel, somehow managing to look more forlorn than any of the McNallys have seen him in the brief time they've known him. 'I was a government plant . . . I was working undercover, pretending to be a prisoner, in order to befriend Smeek and to find out as much about him as possible.'

'Then why didn't you stop him jumping through the Doughnut?'

'Because, by then, I was on his side. I *wanted* him to escape. After months of spending time

108

together before the escape, I came to believe that what we were doing to him was wrong . . . especially when I realised what kind of alien he really was.'

'What planet was he from?' asks an excited twin. (It's hard to tell which one. They both look so similar.)

'Earth,' says Duffel.

'You mean –?'

'Yes,' says Duffel. 'He was not only from your future but from my future too . . . from ahead of *my* time. The Mr Maggs you met was not human in the sense that he wasn't standard *Homo sapiens sapiens* like you or I. He was a member of the next stage of evolution . . . he is what we will become.'

At exactly the same moment that Duffel is making this startling revelation, Count Medoc Silverman is driving his Bentley into the garage next to the stable block of his home, and the garage door is automatically closing slowly behind him. To any casual observer, the chairman and owner of Tap 'n' Type looks as smooth and unruffled as always. But inside? Inside he's a very worried man.

Since Duffel came to see him – or Carbonet as he'll always think of him, however much a dreadful freak he's become since Smeek put him back together – Medoc has been afraid.

Duffel had talked wildly and passionately about how important it is that they go back to their own time. About how their presence here is causing 'rips' – the outbreak of holes – because they've somehow messed with the Space Time Continuum. But what does he know?

Medoc had wanted to know how their going back might help to put things right. Duffel's answer had been unimpressively vague: 'It's not so much putting things right as stopping making things worse,' he'd said. 'Every little thing we do in this time is changing history. It's wrong. If we can get back to our own time at least we won't be making things even more *wrong*.'

Medoc walks out of the side door of the garage and towards the house. Go back? The little freak must be joking. Back in his own time, Count Medoc Silverman was nothing more than a man in a slate-grey jump-suit with **DOYLE** printed above his breast pocket, and nothing to look forward to except an endless prison sentence for a series of frauds involving missing government gold – boy, does he love gold – and computers.

Here, on the other hand, he is a success. A free man. He isn't harming anyone. Okay, so that isn't strictly true. If he hadn't been here in this time there would never have been a Tap 'n' Type company so there would never have been a Tap 'n'

Type-sponsored competition so that poor kid would never have fallen out of the window . . . but, start making tenuous connections like that, and everyone in the world will find themselves responsible in some way, shape or form for some accident or other. No! Medoc is staying put . . .

Wait a minute. That's not strictly true either.

Medoc lets himself in through his front door, with a gold key, switches off the internal alarm system, and makes his way straight to his vast workshop, which he also has to unlock before entering. Much of the room is taken up with his own version of the Doughnut, put together over the years from the blueprints he'd stolen that day they'd escaped from their cell and jumped through *Doughnut II*. He'd found the plans – the schematics showing every single component of the time machine and how to assemble them – in a drawer when he and the other three had been heaving furniture about to build that barricade against the door. He'd slipped them inside his jump-suit without the others ever noticing . . . and now here are the results of his labour.

Some of the pieces were easy to lay his hands on. Some he bought in hardware stores, some he ordered through his factory, some he had specially made. Money can buy you anything. He smiles to himself. There's Carbonet (or Duffel, or whatever he chooses to call himself these days) thinking that these rips – these holes – are caused by their mere presence in this time. Little does he realise that it's a side effect of him using his very own Doughnut . . . which is why the holes are restricted to this particular country at this particular time. He's just glad that his tests haven't caused the really big flash-bang-wallop that occurred the first time they used *Doughnut II* in a real hurry. That would be most unfortunate. But the holes have only swallowed up a few miles of earth here and there. The odd building and motor vehicle. That's a small price to pay . . .

The Count presses a button and his workshop is suddenly flooded with the sound of jazz, playing from hidden speakers dotted about the room. He starts humming along to the hip-hap-happy tune. Life is *goooooood* and there's work to be done.

Chapter Ten

'So you want us to help you to convince this man Doyle to somehow go back with you to your own time?' says Le Fay, once Duffel has finished explaining his plans.

'Er, yes.'

'And by saying "convince" what you really mean is *force him to* if necessary?'

'Er, yes.'

'And how do you propose to do that?'

'Er, well there are six of us and only one of him . . . and two of you can appear to be vicious dogs – well, a dog and a jackal – if needs be.'

'You talk in a very old-fashioned way for someone from the future,' says Albie.

'Yeah,' says Josh. 'Aren't there a whole load of new words and phrases we've never heard of –'

'– and what do people wear? Silver suits and –'

'You could be putting us in danger,' says Jackie.

'Er, yes,' agrees Duffel, 'but I really think you're my only hope. And if we *don't* do anything, these rips – this outbreak of holes – could end up doing some very serious damage indeed.'

Le Fay, who has been sitting in silence from the sidelines, stands up. 'You haven't said *how* you intend to get you and Doyle back to your time.'

'Doyle has somehow managed to build himself a Doughnut but he doesn't know that I know that.'

'You have been a busy bear,' says Le Fay. 'Jackie, why don't –'

She's interrupted by Albie, but not by one of his quick quips or joky jokes. He groans and falls forward off an old office chair. As he hits the cold bakery floor, he starts to grow; not just his arm but all of him. His clothes, everything. He's getting bigger and bigger all over, before their very eyes. As he grows, his body lets off a strange rumbling sound, like the worst collywobbles anyone's tummy has ever had. In less than fifteen seconds the rumbling has stopped and so has Albie's growing. He gets to his (extra large) knees, then to his (extra large) feet and stands up. He's over twenty feet – over six metres – tall. If this was an ordinary room, not a vast empty bakery, there's no way he'd be able to stand to his full height.

Everyone is flabbergasted. Fergal does a

frightened-doggy widdle – there's a Bumbo side to him, remember – Duffel sits down with a bump that must hurt him, padding or no padding, and Jackie and Le Fay gawk, but it is Josh who is most stunned. All of his life, he and his twin have looked almost identical. It's been near impossible to tell them apart. And now there's no doubt who's who. Albie is the twenty-foot-tall one. Josh finds himself crying.

Albie leans forward to take his twin's hand. 'IT'S OKAY, JOSH,' he says. 'I'M OKAY.' He's startled by the loud booming of his own voice. He wasn't planning on speaking louder, but with his huge chest and lungs, that's just the way it came out. Josh's hand looks tiny in his.

Five, four, three, two, one. Jump! We're back in time again (depending on one's starting point of course). As Melvyn Gottlieb will so neatly put it (one day): 'When you're dealing in time travel, the terms backwards and forwards are little more than matters of opinion.'

We're in a room. It's very small and very neat and tidy. There's a woman in the room, sitting by a window, looking out to the street below. In one arm, she holds a baby boy. In the other she holds another boy, the same age and almost identical to the other. She is talking to the one on her right.

'And now I must name you, little one,' she says with that unique love in her voice that only a mother can have for her child. 'And your name will be the only clue to the power that I can see you'll one day hold.'

There's a squeak as a doorhandle turns, followed by a creak as the door opens. In steps the dashing, uniformed figure of a young sea captain.

'Rufus!' beams the woman.

'Hello, Freya,' says the man, bending forward and kissing his wife on the forehead. If love were light, this room would be flooded in brilliant sunshine. 'The twins not asleep yet?'

'Today's the day I'm naming them,' Freya McNally explains. 'This is Joshua,' she says.

'Hello, Joshua,' says Captain Rufus, tickling his son under the chin. Joshua is kind enough to give him a smile in return. 'And what name have you given this other fine chap?' he asks, turning to the other.

'I was about to tell this little one that his name is Albion,' she says.

'Josh and Albie,' smiles Rufus.

'Albion and Joshua,' smiles Freya.

'Can I go and tell Jackie and Le Fay their brothers' names?' asks Captain McNally, excitedly.

'Of course,' says Freya.

It is only when her husband has left the room that she turns back to Albie. 'I have named you after Albion, son of Neptune. Giant among men,' she says. But, of course, he is far too young to understand a word his mum is saying.

'Googa,' gurgles Albie.

'Gaga,' gurgles Josh.

'WHAT DO I DO, JACKS?' pleads Albie, his voice echoing around the abandoned bakery.

'Try whispering, for a start,' says Jackie, trying to calm him down. 'There's no need to panic.'

'SORRY,' says Albie, lowering his tone. 'HOW DO I GET BACK TO MY NORMAL SIZE?'

'How should she know?' says Josh, still staring up at his enormous twin in disbelief.

'HOW DO YOU GET BACK TO BEING A HUMAN SHAPE WHEN YOU'RE A JACKAL?'

'I've told you loads of times,' says Jackie. 'I just think it.'

'SO I SHOULD THINK MYSELF BACK INTO BEING SMALL?' asks Albie.

'Give it a go,' says Jackie. 'Once you've got the hang of it, I'm sure you'll find it easier and easier.'

Albie frowns a giant frown across his giant forehead and really concentrates.

Fergal jumps up in front of him, barking. What he's trying to say is: *You may look different, but you still smell just the same!*

'IT'S NOT WOR-king!' Albie cries but, by the time he's finished saying it, he's back to being exactly the same size as Josh, and the twins give each other a big hug.

'Now think big,' says Le Fay.

'What?' asks Albie.

'See if you can think yourself into your giant form,' says Le Fay.

'Okay,' says Albie and, seconds later he's growing again.

Now he's got the hang of it he GROWS and shrinks back to normal, GROWS and shrinks back to normal, GROWS –

'That's enough!' laughs Le Fay. 'We've got to get on!'

'I knew that you McNallys were right for this task!' says Duffel. 'That new-found talent of yours could come in very handy.'

All fears of Albie's sudden discovery and transformation are forgotten and are replaced with a feeling of excitement and possibility.

'You know what this means, don't you?' Albie says to Josh.

'What?'

'That your secret power will probably be revealed soon. I mean, we're the same age and everything. It's more than likely.'

'I suppose,' says Josh, 'but I'll probably turn out

to be able to shrink to the size of a mouse, and one of you will tread on me by mistake.' He doesn't want to be jealous. He really doesn't. It's just that not only has his brother beaten him to finding out his secret power, but it's also a really *cool* one. He can't hope to compete with that! 'What puzzles me is what your name has to do with being able to grow really big,' he says. 'I thought the names Mum gave us were supposed to be clues. At least Jacqueline with her jackal-in her makes sense. But *Albion*?'

'Let's save this until later,' says Le Fay.

Albion, son of Neptune. Giant amongst men.

The next surprise is that Duffel has got hold of a car from somewhere and has made some very basic conversions to it so that he can drive it (by adding blocks to the brake, clutch and accelerator/gas pedals so that his short legs can reach them. That kind of thing). But the surprises don't end there. You'd probably get a bit of a shock if you were in a car – waiting at some traffic lights, say – and you glanced across at the car next to you to see that it's being driven by a teddy bear. So Duffel has got around this by wearing a disguise whenever he's out on the road, comprised of what looks like a yellow clown-wig and a pair of women's dark glasses.

The car is hidden over on the other side of the disused bakery, by a big roll-up/roll-down garage door. Duffel keeps the disguise on the back seat, so he leans in, takes it out and puts it on: first the wig, then the glasses.

He's about to ask the McNallys what they think of it but there's no need. Their reaction to his 'new look' says it all. Fergal has his head thrown back and is howling; the twins are convulsed with laughter, hugging each other with glee; Le Fay is actually clutching her side – yes, clutching her side – the laughter hurts so much and is pleading with him to 'Take it off! Take it off!'; and even Jackie, who likes to be polite whenever possible and is doing her best *not* to laugh, has tears in her eyes.

'Okay, okay . . .' says Duffel. 'But can you drive, Jackie?' The others are too young to ask.

Jackie shakes her head. 'I'm afraid not.'

'Perhaps my secret power is to be a Formula One driver?' says Josh.

'I don't think we'll take a chance on that one!' says the teddy bear in the yellow wig and dark glasses. 'Which means I'll have to drive –'

121

'– which means you'll have to wear the disguise –' says Albie.

'– and we'll have to try to stop laughing,' says Josh.

'You've got it,' nods Duffel. The truth be told, he doesn't mind the laughter one bit. They not only have a tough task ahead of them but, should it work, he'll be going somewhere where there won't be much to laugh about.

'Everybody in,' he says. 'We must go and confront Doyle before he causes a rip to open up that does some even more serious harm.'

As he drives the McNallys out of town, on possibly their most unlikely exploit of all, Duffel tells them the name that Doyle is now using. He never expected the reaction it gets.

'*Medoc Silverman?*' says Jackie in amazement, from the front passenger seat.

'Wasn't he the guy –'

'– at the Tap 'n' Type competition?' say the twins.

'Woof!' says Fergal (which is hardly surprising).

'He's Malcolm Kent's boss!' gasps Le Fay.

'You know him?' asks Duffel, from under his wig and glasses.

'Not *know* exactly,' says Le Fay, 'but his company sponsored a typing competition I won. He opened

122

the grand finals . . . That was the evening that Fergal fell out of the window.'

'That can't be a coincidence,' says Duffel.

'How do you mean?' asks Jackie.

'I first saw you because, of all the brains Mulch could have stolen, he stole Fergal's from the Sacred Heart Hospital. That brought you into contact with me and Mr Maggs, two of the three survivors who jumped through the Doughnut . . . but the fact that you'd also been in the presence of – in some way involved with – the third and only other survivor, Doyle-Silverman, too, surely means that it *can't* be a coincidence.'

'Are you suggesting that this was somehow planned?' asks Le Fay, leaning forward from the back seat, holding onto the back of Duffel's seat.

'Part of the great scheme of things?' says Duffel, his eyes on the road ahead. 'Not exactly.'

'Good,' says Albie. 'I don't like the idea of us having been born with these powers of ours for some –'

'– particular quest,' adds Josh. 'I never like stories with quests in them. They're always –'

'– the same, and always have people with names like Tharg, who speak –'

'– in riddles,' says Josh. 'And they always have very complicated plots. I don't like too much plot!'

'I was thinking more that the Laws of Nature

might have a way of evening things out. If we play around with Time, treating the past like another country and coming visiting, Nature might find a way of redressing the balance.'

'Undressing the what?' asks Albie.

'Putting things right,' says Jackie.

'And you think that we might be a part of this not-exactly-great-scheme of things?' asks Le Fay.

Fergal, who is on her lap in the back, breaks doggy wind. (That's a polite way of saying f-a-r-t-s.)

'Oh, Fergal!' groan the twins. 'Smell-eeeee!' Josh unwinds a window.

'Woof!' says Fergal. *Sorry.*

'I'd like to think that putting right the Laws of Nature was left in better hands,' Le Fay comments.

'I disagree,' says Duffel. 'Me, Smeek and Doyle all decided to change our names – to take on new identities – but do you know how I ended up being called Duffel, and Smeek became Mr Maggs?'

'How?' asks Le Fay.

'Because those were the names *you* called us, Le Fay,' says Duffel. 'You met us both long before you ever came to Fishbone Hall.'

Another time. Another place. Le Fay McNally is standing in a room. Much of it is in shadow. Something about the perspective seems a little strange: a little *off*. The walls don't quite meet the floor at right angles. The ceiling and the floor aren't quite parallel. Everything is shades of grey. The window – yes, there's a window, though she hadn't noticed it before – is not quite square. It's as though she's on some arty set in a black and white movie; a cross between a Salvador Dali painting and a 1950s cartoon which exaggerates and distorts everyday objects.

In a corner stands Smeek. His head is large, bald and pumpkinlike, since his hair fell out as a side effect from escaping through the Doughnut; most of it removed with a little help, and one big yank, from Doyle. His teeth are like shark's teeth. He looks up from whatever it is that he's doing.

'Who are you?' he asks in the familiar voice Le Fay thought that she'd never hear again.

'It's me, Le Fay McNally, Mr Maggs,' she says.

'What did you call me?' Smeek demands. *This is delicate work. How did she get in here?*

'Mr Maggs,' she repeats.

'And why do you call me that?' Smeek wonders. *Is she confusing me with someone else. And where's Doyle?*

'Because that's the name you insisted I call you,' says Le Fay, stepping closer to him across the bare grey floorboards. 'With the Mister and everything.'

'When –?' begins Smeek. 'Oh,' his expression changes. 'I think I understand.' *I'm in a different time. A different place now. Maybe we've already met in a different future.*

'Mr Maggs,' says Smeek, slowly rolling the words around his mouth, trying out the new name for size. He grins in the shadows. 'I like that . . . You say we've met?'

'Yes,' Le Fay nods. 'In Fishbone Forest. I was the girl looking – er – for her dog. Don't you remember? You had a fall . . . We all thought you were dead.'

'And what was I doing in this Fishbone Forest?'

'You were planning to implement your *Manifesto of Change* . . .' Le Fay is really close to him now.

Smeek smiles. 'A manifesto of change? What an

excellent idea. Our meeting like this is most fortuitous, Le Fay McNally. Really most fortuitous . . .' *I like the idea of a manifesto*, thinks Smeek. *What kind of changes could I include in it? I'd change the order of the letters of the alphabet for a start!*

'How did you get out?' she asks.

'Out?'

'Of the hole?'

'Mr Maggs . . . Fishbone Forest . . . *Manifesto of Change* . . . The hole,' says Smeek. *By hole she must mean a rip caused by someone using the Doughnut. One day, I'll meet this girl Le Fay McNally again, and by then I'll be calling myself Mr Maggs. What useful information.*

'I wish I understood what's happening,' Le Fay says. 'Everything is so strange.'

Smeek stares intently into her eyes. *There's certainly something strange about you*, he muses. *How did you get here? What time are you from?* 'You work it out,' he says. *I must finish what I'm doing. Almost done.*

Le Fay looks down to see what he was working on when she came into the room. Her eyes widen. She screams. If this were a dream she'd wake up now.

But this isn't a dream. There on the table lies a bloodied half-man half-teddy bear.

'Duffel!' she cries.

Chapter Eleven

'You're telling me that I was in the hut in the Australian Desert where Smeek – Mr Maggs – was putting you back together when you were still Carbonet . . . on the very day you all came through the Doughnut and ended up in 1993?' says Le Fay. 'I think I'd remember that, don't you, Duffel?'

'But don't you see?' says the teddy bear, doing his best to concentrate on driving. 'You haven't experienced that yet – it hasn't happened to *you* yet – but you will. It's in your future but, because you'll be going back to the past, the past has already been affected. That means that we're going to succeed in getting to use Doyle-Silverman's version of the Doughnut –'

'And that you knew we'd agree to help you before you even asked us,' says Jackie, 'because

128

your knowing that Le Fay met Mr Maggs before he ever ended up in Fishbone Forest means that she must get to use the time machine!'

Duffel nods. 'Exactly,' he says, 'and if you're confused, don't worry about it. That's why we must put a stop to this time-travel business once and for all. It throws up too many inconsistencies, and the Laws of Nature, or the Laws of Physics or whatever you like to call them, don't like inconsistencies.'

'Hence the holes,' says Le Fay.

'Hence the holes . . . another dangerous side effect.'

'But there's a flaw in all of this!' Le Fay protests. 'If, from Mr Maggs's point of view, I'd already met him back in 1993, then why didn't he recognise me when we met again – from his perspective – in Fishbone Forest last year?'

'But he did,' says Duffel. 'He told me so.'

*

'You're a long way from home, little one,' says a voice in the gloom.

Le Fay looks up and gasps at the most extraordinary apparition standing before her. It is a man – at least, she assumes it's a man – clutching a huge teddy bear in one hand and a plastic orange tulip in the other. On top of his pumpkin-shaped head is a hat-cum-umbrella.

'I'm Mr Maggs,' he says softly, smiling a shark's teeth smile. *It is you, isn't it, Le Fay McNally,* he's thinking. *You're the girl I met back in the shack, all that time ago, but no older. How can that be, I wonder?* 'What brings you to my neck of the woods? This is private property. *Very* private property. You're trespassing on the Lyons family estate – well *my* estate now, actually – little girl.' *You somehow looked bigger back then,* he muses. *Still just a girl but more powerful, somehow. Not the bedraggled girl before me now.*

'I'm sorry, sir,' says Le Fay ever so politely as her brain works overtime to come up with an excuse for being in Fishbone Forest.

'Mr Maggs.'

'I beg your pardon?' asks Le Fay.

'Call me Mr Maggs.' *When we met in the past you were very clear how insistent I'd been on being called Mr Maggs, so insistent I must be!*

'I'm sorry, *Mr Maggs*,' says Le Fay.

His mind is already racing. *When I first met you – back in the desert – you told me that I had a manifesto of change . . . and now I do, indeed, have one, Le Fay! I DO. I can hardly wait to tell you all about it!*

There is silence in the car until Le Fay finally breaks it. 'So Mr Maggs must have got to hear about Fishbone Forest from me too?'

'Yes.'

'And found out about Lionel Lyons's fortune as a result?'

'Yes.'

'And Fergal's brain only ended up in Bumbo's body because of his plans to put a brain in Mr Lyons's body?'

'Yes,' says Duffel.

'So, in a roundabout way, that's what saved Fergal!' Le Fay grins.

'I hadn't thought of that!' says Duffel, banging the steering wheel with a paw. 'You're right! That proves what I said about there being no coincidences and the Laws of Nature wanting to balance things out! Doyle-Silverman indirectly brought about Fergal's death . . . and Smeek-Mr Maggs indirectly brought about him coming back to life again. It's a balancing act!'

'Woof! Woof!' says Fergal. None of the others has any idea what he's just said, but he seems happy enough. He's got his head stuck out of the car window. The Bumbo blood pumping through his veins seems to be telling him that this is *just* the way that dogs like to travel.

On the outskirts of the capital is an area called Lockwood, full of very wide tree-lined streets – usually called something 'Avenue' – with some very expensive houses sprawling across green lawns as neatly manicured as the best golf courses. Despite the spate of hot weather which has left much of the rest of the country's grass parched and dry, these lawns are as green as a billiard/snooker/pool table's baize and as smooth. The loving care of privately employed gardeners, with the aid of thousands of gallons of water expelled by lawn sprinklers, has ensured that each garden looks as perfect as the next.

Duffel brings his rather battered car to a halt at the kerb next to the entrance to what little there is left of the wood from which the exclusive Lockwood suburb originally got its name.

'If we park this thing in front of any of the houses, it'll start the net curtains twitching and we'll soon have a private security guard or policeman asking us what it is we're doing,' Duffel explains. 'If we cut through the wood, we come to the back of Doyle-Silverman's property in Cherry Tree Avenue.'

'Does he have private security?' asks Le Fay.

The teddy bear nods. 'But not people. Electronic. He has a whole system of alarms.'

'And how are we going –'

'– to get past them –'

'– without triggering them off?' ask the twins, climbing out of the car onto the pavement.

'They're key operated. If we enter the grounds through the main gate or the side gate, there's a key to deactivate the system,' says Duffel. 'I've tested it out.'

'You happen to have a key?' asks Jackie, stretching her legs. It's been a long drive.

'I do,' says Duffel, still in his wig-and-glasses disguise. 'Let's get under the cover of the trees before we attract any attention.'

Fergal is reading a notice nailed to the trunk of a tree at the entrance to the woods:

'Woof!' he says, pointing at it with his paw and then pointing at his neck.

Le Fay pulls the rolled-up lead out of her pocket and clips it onto her brother's collar. 'Well spotted,' she says, giving him a pat.

In the shade of the trees – a cool relief after a journey in a car jam-packed with McNallys (some hairier than others) – Josh asks Duffel the obvious question: 'How did you get your hands –'

'Paws.'

'How did you get your paws on the key to Count Silverman's alarm system?'

'He kept a spare set hidden in his office in the Tap 'n' Type building. Very well hidden, in fact. They were taped to the underside of one of the drawers of his monstrous desk.'

'So how did you find them?'

'Easy,' he says. 'By a fluke.' (Funnily enough, *Fluke* is the title of a book by the horror writer James Herbert in which the hero finds himself reincarnated as a dog.) 'Silverman stuffed me in a drawer when his secretary came into his office. I could see the set of keys taped to the bottom of the drawer above me.'

'So you took them,' says Le Fay.

'Yes,' says Duffel, removing his disguise and handing the wig and glasses to her. 'Could you carry these, please?' he asks. 'I don't have any pockets.'

'So where did you hide the keys, if you don't have any pockets?'

'I have a split in my side where the stuffing's coming out and my nerves and veins aren't connected up. I put them in there.'

'So, even then, you suspected that Silverman-Doyle wouldn't co-operate and that the keys must be important to him or he wouldn't hide them in the first place?' says Le Fay.

They are moving down the path, through the trees of all shapes and sizes (some of which have fared better in the weather than others). Being public property, no gardeners or sprinklers have been lavished on the woods.

'Of course,' says Duffel. 'Don't forget that I knew you would have to go back in time, to the shack where Mr Maggs saved my life, so I knew that I'd have to enlist your help.'

'Something's been bothering me,' says Jackie, stopping at the back of the group to free her leg from a tangle of brambles growing across the path.

'The plan is to get you and the Count, or Doyle, or whatever you like to call him, back through the Doughnut and then, I assume, you want us to destroy the machine so that no-one else can use it and cause any holes?'

'That's right.'

'So what's my sister doing going through it and ending up back in time?'

'Er,' Duffel stops in his tracks. He turns to face her. 'I have absolutely no idea.'

'The more I think about this plan of yours, the less I like it,' says Jackie.

'We've come this far,' says Le Fay. 'I say there's no turning back now . . . and then there's the matter of Fergal. If Duffel can get back to the time before he and the others escape through the Doughnut, then he can stop them coming through and messing up time. There'll be no Tap 'n' Type, no competition and Fergal will never fall out of that window. He'll be a human brain in a human body and none of this will ever have happened. Things will be back to how they should have been before a bunch of escaped prisoners –' She stops and looks at Duffel '– and an undercover government agent messed it up. Isn't that right?'

'It's a possibility,' admits Duffel. 'But I can't make any promises.'

'And none of us will remember any of this

because it won't have happened after all?' says Albie. 'This is too weird.'

These new thoughts fermenting in their minds, Duffel leads the McNallys off the path and to the western edge of the patch of wood where there's a high wall. They follow it around until they reach a steel-reinforced door with an electronic box set into the brickwork next to it, with a large keyhole in it. A small red light is flashing.

'That means that the alarms to the grounds themselves are activated. They're on.' Rather disconcertingly, the teddy bear puts his left paw through a split in the seam of his body and pulls out a small bunch of keys. He passes them to Le Fay. 'You do it,' he says. 'I find it difficult to grasp with these paws.' Le Fay takes the keys. 'It's the big fat chrome one,' he says. 'I've checked the place out a few times.'

Le Fay puts the key in the electronic box and turns. There's a tiny 'bleep' and the red light stops flashing. She removes the key and is about to hand the bunch back to Duffel.

'No,' he says. 'Use the copper-coloured one to open the gate, and then hang on to them for me.'

Once inside the impressive grounds of *Heyday* – Count Silverman's rather strange choice of name for his home – they edge cautiously towards the house itself. This involves running across an area of lawn and then throwing themselves behind a tree . . . then running across another area of lawn and throwing themselves behind another tree . . . and so on. Fergal and Jackie (back in jackal form) act as scouts, slinking ahead on the look-out for anyone who might spot them. There's no sign of a gardener, security guard, anyone.

When they finally reach the house itself, they find a number of windows wide open to let in the fresh air. It's obvious that someone is in the house and that the inner alarm must, therefore, be switched off. Le Fay holds out Jackie's clothes to her, who clenches them between her jackal's teeth and disappears around the edge of the building, soon re-emerging human-shaped. It occurs to Le Fay that Albie's lucky that his clothes grow to a giant size just as he does, otherwise he'd need a pair of those amazing stretching trousers like the Incredible Hulk wears.

Following a request from Duffel, Josh gets onto Albie's shoulders, climbs through a window and then opens a pair of french windows (glass doors) from the inside. The others now follow him into Heyday. Although they intend to confront Silverman, they need the element of surprise. With that in mind, they cautiously make their way around the house in search of him.

Chapter Twelve

For those of you expecting a picture at the beginning of this chapter, as with all the others, there's no time. We must get on! Silverman, Doyle – call him what you will – is in his workshop when the McNallys burst through the door. They want the element of surprise on their side and that's what they've got.

Jackie comes in first, snarling and behaving in as generally a frightening way that any jackal can without actually biting anybody. Her hackles are up – in other words her fur is sticking out – and her teeth are bared. She is snarling and has her eyes on Count Silverman and Silverman alone.

Next comes Fergal. Now, I'm a big lover of mongrel dogs but, even if you're not, I'm sure you'll agree from the illustrations that he's pretty c-u-t-e. But, as most of you'll know, even the cutest dog can be a bit frightening when it wants to be. With his teeth bared and making his own snarly noises, he too seems far from friendly and, in conjunction with his big sister, does the four-legged contingency of the Duffel/McNally attack team proud.

Next come Duffel and Le Fay, side-by-side and ready for business. Theirs is a different kind of surprise. The Count wasn't expecting to see Duffel again so soon, and Le Fay McNally ever. *Isn't she the girl who won the typing competition last year???*

'What is this?' demands Silverman. 'What's going on here?' He looks frantically about for something to defend himself against the jackal – yes, that's a jackal all right, he knows his animals – and the dog, and the others. Like his office at Tap 'n' Type, the walls of his workshop are covered with gold musical instruments; none of which would make a particularly good weapon. He resorts to the contents of his toolbox, and wields the biggest screwdriver he can find. 'Stay back!' he says, taking a step back himself. 'Don't come any nearer.'

Now the last two remaining McNallys enter the room: the twins, Albie and Josh, looking as harmless as a pair of cuddly bunnies.

'Ha!' says Silverman with a wild look in his eye, singular (more on that in a moment). 'It's Tweedledum and Tweedledee!'

In that instant, Albie thinks big as planned, and grows into his giant self, the rumbling that this causes echoing around the workshop. Silverman looks on in complete and utter disbelief, tilting his head back to watch the boy grow. He drops the screwdriver in amazement.

Fergal bounds forward and picks it up in his mouth.

Jackie-the-jackal launches herself at the stunned Silverman, who stumbles back onto the small stool he was sitting on when tinkering with his machine before their dramatic entrance. Jackie stands guard only inches in front of him. All the fight appears to have gone out of him.

Now they have a chance to take in their surroundings. This is the first time the McNallys have seen any of the Doughnuts, and it's certainly impressive. As for Count Medoc Silverman, he's not like the Count Medoc Silverman the McNallys saw on stage at The Dell hotel at the Tap 'n' Type grand finals last winter, and he's not like the Count Medoc Silverman whom Duffel confronted much more recently at his office. His usually immaculate pinstripe suit is tattered and torn and he's wearing an eye-patch – yup, an eye-patch – over his right eye.

'You've come to take us back, haven't you, Carbonet?' he says to Duffel, his shoulders sagging and his voice more of a moan.

'Yes,' says Duffel. 'Even if we find we can't put right the damage we've done by coming to this time, at least we'll stop making it worse . . . we'll stop changing more history.'

'But I don't want to go back!' says the Count by which, of course, he means going forward to the future they come from.

Duffel looks around at his rag-bag army of . . . of, well, *McNallys*. 'We're not here to give you a choice but to make sure you go.'

'But there's a glitch with my Doughnut,' says Silverman. 'Look at me. Look what it's done.' He certainly looks the worse for wear.

'You've been through the machine?' asks Josh. 'But how could you have been? I mean, you'd have needed *another* machine to go through to get back here.'

'I set the co-ordinates for this room but a week ago. I simply came back through this machine when it was a week younger,' sighs Silverman.

'AMAZING!' says, you guessed it, big, big Albion. He's staying enormous to make sure that the Count stays intimidated.

'And it did this to you?' says Duffel.

'Yes,' says Silverman. 'It felt like being stung by a giant jellyfish or grated by a giant cheese-grater. I - I've lost an eye.' He lifts the eye-patch to reveal a very raw and unpleasant wound. 'You can't take me through there, Carbonet! You could be killing the both of us.'

Le Fay is studying the huge metal ring, much of it made from gold. 'If you can be precise enough to send yourself back to this very place but a week before, you must be able to set the co-ordinates to send yourself to the prison at the precise time and place before you first escaped,' she says.

'It's too risky, I tell you! Too risky!' whines Silverman and, before anyone realises quite what's happening, he's leapt to his feet and is giving Le Fay a desperate shove. She falls backwards through the hole in the Doughnut. He slams the flat palm of his hand against the control pad . . . and she disappears.

'WHAT HAVE YOU DONE?' roars Albie.

Le Fay is falling, falling, falling. She is witnessing a whole variety of events – some familiar, some new, some half-forgotten memories re-awakened – all around her. She's a part of them, intimately involved in all of them yet, at the same time, is somehow distant from them: an observer. There she is in the shack with Mr Maggs . . . with the twins in the park . . . in the first heat of the typing competition . . . crying alone in a room . . . being given a piggyback by Jackie . . . This is nothing like Duffel had described so-called time travel would be!

Of course it isn't, says a voice. Her own voice? It certainly sounds familiar.

Not your voice. My voice.

It is the voice of the fortune-teller she heard at Wandaland before venturing into Fishbone Forest last winter. It is the voice of –

Yes, darling. I am your mother.

Mum? But you're dead.

Am dead. Was dead. Will be dead. We are all these things at some time or other, my sweetheart.

What's going on, Mum?

You're out of Time, Le Fay.

You mean I'm about to die too?

No, you're standing outside time. Few can do it. You are one of the few. I named you after Morgan Le Fay, my clever daughter. Morgan Le Fay was sister to King Arthur. Some called her a sorceress. Some a magician, but these are just titles . . . labels . . . words. She held the secrets to some of the most important magic. She was one of the most powerful people to walk the Earth. So will you be, Le Fay.

Does that mean that I can put things right? That I can stop Fergal falling from the window –

What you can *do and* should *do are not necessarily the same thing. Sometimes what's done is done and should remain so. Aren't you and dear Rufus now happier than you've ever been, Le Fay?*

If we're outside time, Mum, what's that ticking?

145

It's clicking, not ticking.

Clicking?

Of knitting needles.

You're knitting at a time like this?

Yes, two pairs of booties. And we're OUT of Time, remember?

Your voice is fading, Mum! says Le Fay. Don't go! Please don't go!

Remember this above all, cries her mother. *No kind deed is ever wasted.*

'Mum!' Le Fay calls out loud. 'Mum! We all love you! Me, Jackie, the twins. Even little Fergal who never really knew you. We all love you!' She's shouting now, as she spirals past more and more events in her life, slightly distorted and washed of colour.

'I know!' Freya McNally calls back and, in that brief moment, Le Fay can actually see her. Unlike everything around her, she is really there: she is solid flesh and bone, sitting in a simple room of brilliant light, with a huge pair of knitting needles. 'I'm so proud of you all!'

Then there is a loud belching – yup, the deep wet kind – and Le Fay finds herself tumbling out of the Doughnut onto the floor of Silverman's workshop.

'See?' says Silverman, who is lying on the floor, hands tied behind his back with his own tie, with

146

Jackie-the-jackal and Fergal sitting on his chest and stomach. 'It's not working!' Fergal jumps off him and bounds over to Le Fay, jumping up at her in excitement at her safe return, his tail wagging excitedly. The twins (both small and almost identical) run forward. 'Are you okay, Le Fay?'

'I'm . . . I'm fine,' says Le Fay.

'You look different,' says Josh. 'Bigger, somehow.'

'Powerful!' says Albie. 'That's what it is . . . What happened to you?'

'I discovered my secret power,' she says. 'I'll explain later. Right now there's work to be done.' She turns to Duffel who is punching codes into the keypad on the Doughnut.

'Take Doyle back to your own time, Duffel, but don't try to put right what you've done to this one. That's our history now. It's happened, so you could just end up making things worse . . . By changing history, you've already changed the future . . . What you go back to won't be the same as the future you escaped from anyway,' she says. 'Who knows what you might find.'

'This really is a mess, isn't it?' says Duffel. 'What happened to you in there?'

'I'm just a kid,' she shrugs. 'What do I know?'

The teddy bear stares at the small freckle-faced girl with the wiry red hair and the gappy teeth. 'A lot more than you'll ever tell, Le Fay,' he says. 'I always knew that you were the right ones to come to.' He turns to Silverman. 'Come on, Doyle. We've got an important appointment to keep.' The others help the dishevelled Count to his feet. Jackie takes the opportunity to nip behind a workbench and soon reappears as a fully-dressed sister.

Duffel punches in a final code and the Doughnut begins to hum again.

'Well, goodbye, everybody,' he says. 'Thank you . . .' He pauses. 'And please try not to think too badly of any of us. We were in the wrong place at the wrong time, that's all . . . Come on, Doyle.'

Count Medoc Silverman has his eyes downcast. He won't look at them. 'I'm sorry . . .' he says. Together, they step into the ring and are gone.

'Goodbye, Duffel,' says Le Fay in almost a whisper, knowing that it is too late for him to hear the words anyway. 'Good luck.'

'Now what?' asks Jackie.

'We destroy this thing before it does any more damage. Somewhere, some new holes will already have opened up because we just used it.'

'Shall I grow to my giant size and stamp on it?' asks Albie eagerly.

'Woof,' says Fergal. *Great idea*.

'No, we'll let Josh do it,' says Le Fay.

'Woof,' says Fergal. *How come?*

'Because I know his secret –'

'You can understand Fergal's barks!' Jackie interrupts.

'Oh yes,' says Le Fay, surprised. 'I suppose I can . . . now I know my power, it's been unlocked.'

'You can talk to animals?' asks Albie.

'You know *my* power?' asks Josh excitedly.

'Oh, yes,' says Le Fay. She knows most things now. She is most powerful, whatever label you may choose to give her.

'What is it? What is it?'

Le Fay dashes over to the nearest wall and pulls a beautiful gold trumpet from its brackets; just one of the many instruments lining the room. 'Take this,' she says. 'And everybody out. Hurry. We must destroy that machine right now.'

They leave the workshop and hurry out into the garden.

'Blow,' says Le Fay.

'What?' asks Josh.

'Blow that trumpet,' says Le Fay.

Josh puts the mouthpiece of the trumpet to his lips and blows. A fantastically loud note blasts out of the instrument.

'You're a natural!' laughs Le Fay. 'Play us a tune.'

'But I don't now how –' Josh protests.

'Just do it!' says Le Fay.

And Josh starts playing. Brilliantly. And loudly. And the ground starts to tremor and the house starts to rumble and shake.

'I think we should run!' says Jackie and everyone takes their big sister's advice. They've just reached the gate through to the wood when Silverman's house collapses in a pile of rubble. All eyes are on the twin.

150

'Nice one, Josh,' says Le Fay. 'It seems Mum named you after Joshua in the Bible. The Joshua who ordered his army to blow trumpets that led to the collapse of the walls of Jericho. I think you'll find that you can play just about any instrument and each will have a different effect!'

'Like I can charm snakes and . . . and . . .?'

'And that kind of thing,' nods Le Fay.

'Cooooool, brother!' says Albie. Josh can't wait to put his new-found talents to the test.

Le Fay unlocks the gate and they pile out into the wood. As they walk down the path back towards the car, Jackie has a worrying thought. 'Uho! I think we're in a bit of a fix,' she says.

'What do you mean?' says Le Fay.

'We never thought about how we'd get back home! We don't have Duffel to drive us!'

Le Fay gives her a toothy grin. 'No problem, Jacks, I'll drive.'

'You can drive all of a sudden?' asks Jackie as they all clamber into the car.

Le Fay gets into the driver's seat. 'I can do lots of things now.'

There are people in the street dashing here, there and everywhere as a result of the collapse of the house in Cherry Tree Avenue. No one is giving the out-of-place McNallys a second glance.

'The emergency services are on their way!' one

neighbour shouts to another.

'I'll bet it was one of those holes,' a third neighbour speculates. 'Opened right up under the Count's house!'

The McNallys know better, of course. They've put an end to the holes.

There's a wail of distant sirens.

Le Fay turns the key in the ignition and the car engine comes to life.

'Wait a minute!' says Albie. 'You're just a kid. We could be pulled over by the police.'

'You don't mean?' says Le Fay hesitantly.

'Yup!' says Josh. 'You must –'

'PUT ON THE DISGUISE!' they shout as one, followed by fits of laughter and barking.

Le Fay reaches for the wig and glasses in her pocket.

Chapter Thirteen

Now our final leap forward. Not a big one. There, it's done. At last Lionel Lyons's money is being used the way the real Lionel Lyons would have wanted it to have been: helping others. Tom Dwyer, now the brains inside his body, is ensuring that the huge fortune is put to very good use indeed, as described in the wishes expressed in Lionel's writings, first jotted down as an eight-year-old after that little talk his father gave him on his knee. And, do you know what, it's made Dwyer a happy man too. For him, helping others beats teaching French any day.

With the able and unique assistance of the McNally siblings – bound to him by their knowledge of his secret and his of theirs – the money not only goes to help the big causes (famine relief, war aid and the fight against disease, for example) but also to help the small individual causes that can make such a difference (a teddy bear for a child who's never had one; a pet for an old people's home; a holiday for those who've never been away from home before; help for an injured badger). I'm sure you can think of examples of your own.

Charlie 'Twinkle-Toes' Tweedy has proved very useful tracking down worthy recipients, and Malcolm Kent is excellent at publicising the work of the charity. People have been helped far and wide but, as Jackie pointed out, 'charity begins at home'.

Noble drives a breakdown truck for a living. He enjoys his work because he likes helping people, and most motorists are very glad to see a breakdown truck if their car won't go and they're stuck at the side of the road. He has a big oily tool-kit in the back of the truck and will only tow a car away if he fails to fix the fault at the roadside, or if the car is beyond repair.

Noble's head looks a lot like a large turnip and, if you don't know what a turnip is, it's a big round root vegetable that looks a lot like Noble's head. I'm not being rude. Noble is the first to admit that he's 'no oil painting'. But what does he care? He loves his job. He loves his wife and three boys, and they love him right back.

If you were to ask Noble about some of the most significant events in his life, he's unlikely to include the time he gave a ride to four members of the McNally family last winter. Sure, he remembers it. Who wouldn't? You don't see two almost-identical twins every day, nor a boy (Fergal) dressed in a nappy, just so that he'd been able to travel on a coach free-of-charge. And then there'd been the young woman who was with them; their big sister Jackie. She'd been most appreciative of him driving them into town and dropping them off near The Dell hotel where, Noble strongly suspects, they were planning to stay w-i-t-h-o-u-t p-a-y-i-n-g.

But would Noble have seen giving the McNallys a ride in his breakdown truck as a truly significant event? Most probably not. The significant events in Noble's life were when he first laid eyes on the future Mrs Noble (who was called Maggie Jupp back then) across a crowded pig-pen on her father's farm; or the day he married her; or the days when each of their boys – Pug, Gamble and Benjy – were born. That kind of thing. Giving the McNallys a ride up in the cab of his truck has been just one of Noble's many acts of kindness. Which just goes to show, you never know where a good deed might lead.

★

Wednesday morning begins like any other Wednesday morning in the Noble family but then the oldest son, Pug, pulls open the curtains in the box room and sees what is out in the yard. Soon everyone is outside, except for Noble himself who, blissfully unaware of anything being out of the ordinary, is in the bathroom going through his morning routine. He's had his bath and washed his hair and is in the process of shaving when he hears a cry.

'Dad!' Benjy, the youngest, shouts up to Noble from the bottom of the stairs. 'Daaaaaaaaad!' Assuming that if it is *that* important then Benjy will come upstairs and tell him what he wants, Noble chooses to ignore his youngest.

'Daaaaaaaaaaaaaaaaaaaaad!' Benjy shouts again, *really* loudly this time.

Noble, who is shaving with an old cut-throat razor in front of the cracked bathroom mirror, carefully runs the blade under the tap and folds it shut. 'What is it, Benjy?' he asks emerging onto the landing.

'Come look!' says Benjy. 'Come quick.'

Noble can hear the excitement in the boy's voice. He sounds like he does on Christmas morning. Noble runs grinning down the stairs two at a time, his face still covered with foam. 'What is it, Benjy?' he repeats, now clearly intrigued.

Benjy grabs his dad's wrist and 'pulls' him – leads him more like – through the kitchen, past the pantry office, out through the open back door and into the yard.

Noble stops and stares.

STOPS and STARES.

There.

Slow down.

This is a big moment.

You read about people's eyes opening wide in amazement. You read about people's jaws dropping. Well, the eyes in Noble's turnip-like head don't get any wider. The jaw of his turnip-like head doesn't drop. He simply stops and stares.

There in his back yard, next to the old and battered breakdown truck he's had for many, many years, is a brand-spanking-new one. It is bigger. It is better. And there down the side, in gleaming red letters outlined in gold, are the words: **NOBLE'S BREAKDOWNS**, which are the very words he hand-painted (rather badly) on his old truck many years before.

On the top of the cab of the truck is an enormous red bow, reminding Noble of a helicopter rotor blade. (He sometimes helps out at Fairwick Airport and has even worked on a helicopter engine.) In the truck sit Pug and their middle son Gamble. Pug is at the steering wheel, pretending to drive. He sees Noble come outside. 'This is great, Dad!'

'Brilliant!' agrees Gamble at his side. He does a big thumbs-up.

Still clutching his father's wrist, Benjy is jumping up and down in uncontrollable excitement. 'See!' he shouts. 'See!'

Noble walks over to his wife who is staring at the new truck in disbelief. He puts his arm around her shoulder. 'It's beautiful, Jon,' she says. 'But where did it come from?'

'I don't know,' Noble confesses. His mind is already racing ahead with possibilities. Is this really for him?

It has **NOBLE'S BREAKDOWNS** on the side.

It *must* be.

Has Maggie finally won the State Lottery after all these years of trying, and is simply pretending not to know where the truck came from?

His mind is already racing. With *two* trucks he could handle twice as much work if he hires a second driver. Bob Lesley. That's it! He could hire his friend Bob Lesley to drive the other one. Bob isn't much of a mechanic since he had his accident and lost his job, but Noble could send him out to tow away the car wrecks that are beyond repair. He could pay Bob's wages out of the extra money the extra work would bring in. That'd be good: more work for Noble's Breakdowns and a job for Bob . . . if this truck is somehow really his.

Noble walks over to the cab, climbs up onto the running board and pulls open the driver's door. 'Shift over, boys,' he says and they shunt along the bench seat so that their dad can sit behind the wheel.

'Me! Me!' Benjy shouts from the ground, and his mother passes him up to Noble who sits him on his knee.

'This was in the glove compartment, Dad,' says Gamble, passing Noble a gold envelope.

Noble tears it open.

'This is like one of those award ceremonies on the telly,' says Pug. 'And the winner is . . .'

'Whassit say? Whassit say?' demands Benjy, looking at the card his father is pulling from the envelope. (He is too young to read.)

No kind deed
is ever wasted.

Noble reads out the words.

'Who's it from, Jon?' asks Maggie Noble.

He passes her down the card through the open cab door. 'I've no idea, love,' he says. 'Does that lion symbol at the bottom mean anything to you?'

Mrs Noble digs her hand in her apron pocket and pulls out a pair of old black-framed reading glasses which she proceeds to perch on the end of her nose and squint through at the card. She makes a face. 'Nothing,' she says. 'Do you really think this truck is ours to keep?'

'I most certainly do,' says Noble. He's found what else is in the envelope: all the ownership, tax, insurance and registration documents required in this particular country at this particular time to show that the brand-spanking-new breakdown truck belongs to Mr Jon Noble and is licensed to drive on the roads.

Noble lifts Benjy off his lap, and steps back out onto the running board, placing him directly in front of the steering wheel. Benjy whoops with joy and grabs it with both hands, making engine noises.

Noble jumps to the ground with a crunch of gravel and hugs and kisses his wife. When they finally let go of each other, both of them seem to have shaving-foam beards.

Hidden by a nearby bush, a dog watches the delighted Nobles circling their new truck. He has a lolling tongue and a happy expression on his face. His tail bangs on the ground with obvious delight. If I had to attribute human emotions to him, I'd suggest that he might be thinking: 'Mission accomplished. A job well done.'

He turns and heads for home, where his loving and happy family is waiting for him.

THE END
of this, the final, exploit

Epilogue

Dear Ralphie,

Thank you for the human brain. It was much more suitable than the juvenile brain my idiot assistant provided for the task, and was a perfect fit.

I'm so glad you made it through the Doughnut before my arrest.

Here's hoping we can get together sometime.

Your loving cousin,

'Maggs'

The Philip Ardagh Club

COLLECT some fantastic **Philip Ardagh** merchandise.

WHAT YOU HAVE TO DO:
You'll find numbered tokens to collect in all Philip Ardagh's fiction books published after 01/04/05. There are 2 tokens in each hardback and 1 token in each paperback. Cut them out and send them to us complete with the form below (or a photocopy of the form) and you'll get these great gifts:

> **2 tokens** = a Philip Ardagh poster
> **3 tokens** = a Philip Ardagh mousemat
> **4 tokens** = a Philip Ardagh pencil case and stationery set

Please send the form, together with your tokens or photocopies of them, to:

Philip Ardagh promotion, Faber and Faber Ltd, 3 Queen Square, London, WC1N 3AU.

Please ensure that each token has a different number.

1. This offer can not be used in conjunction with any other offer and is non transferable. 2. No cash alternative is offered. 3. If under 18 please get permission and help from a parent or guardian to enter. 4. Please allow at least 28 days delivery. 5. No responsibility can be taken for items lost in the post. 6. This offer will close on 31/04/07. 7. Offer open to readers in the UK and Ireland ONLY.

Name: ....
Address: ....
....
....
Town: ....
Postcode: ....
Age & Date of Birth: ....
Girl or boy: ....

Philip Ardagh Club
token number 1

For more infomation and competitions join the Philip Ardagh Club on-line.
Visit www.philipardagh.com

Heir of Mystery

or

Four Legs Good

Bestselling author Philip Ardagh is probably best known for the Eddie Dickens Trilogy, which started life as a series of letters to his nephew, Ben, but has since been translated into 20 different languages, receiving both critical and popular acclaim. *Heir of Mystery* is the second in his new series Unlikely Exploits, which began with *The Fall of Fergal* and continues the exploits of the downtrodden McNally family. When neither writing nor planning what to write next, Philip Ardagh thinks about the food he's not supposed to have now that he's 'eating sensibly'.

UNLIKELY EXPLOITS 2

HEIR OF MYSTERY

or

Four Legs Good

PHILIP ARDAGH

illustrated by David Roberts

faber and faber

First published in 2003
by Faber and Faber Limited
3 Queen Square, London WC1N 3AU
This paperback edition first published in 2004

Typeset by Faber and Faber Limited
Printed in England by Mackays of Chatham plc, Chatham, Kent

© Philip Ardagh, 2003
Illustrations © David Roberts, 2003

Philip Ardagh is hereby identified as author of this work in accordance
with Section 77 of the Copyright, Designs and Patents Act 1988

Me and My Teddy Bear
Words by Jack Winters
Music by Fred J. Coots
© 1950 Chappell & Co. Inc. and Leo Talent Inc., USA
Ascherberg Hopwood & Crew Ltd, London W6 8BS
Reproduced by permission of International Music Publications Ltd

A CIP record for this book
is available from the British Library

ISBN 978–0–571–21094–7

4 6 8 10 9 7 5

*To Tim and Bradley
of the East Sussex Ambulance Service,
and to the doctors, nurses and auxiliary staff
of the Coronary Care Unit
at the Conquest Hospital,
all of whose acquaintance I unexpectedly
made when reaching the closing stages
of this book.*

A heart-felt thank you.

A Word to the Wise

There are more good people in this world than bad. You may not think so, but it's true. The bad ones make a lot of noise and cause a lot of trouble, so they're the ones we see on the news and portrayed in books and films, but your average human being is a good human being. And that's a fact.

Although it's always important to be careful in life, from whom to trust to what time you walk home on your own, it's also important to remember this. Sure, the guy who saves you from drowning *might* be planning to shave your hair off and sell it as a wig but, more likely than not, he's simply trying to save your life. If most people were bad, nothing would ever get done. There would be no such thing as society. So be alert, yes. Be sensible, yes. But try not to be afraid. If you're afraid, you're letting the bad guys win.

PHILIP ARDAGH

'Anything awful makes me laugh. I misbehaved once at a funeral.'

From a letter dated 9 August 1815
by Charles Lamb

Prologue

THINGS TO DO TODAY

Get up √
Wash, and brush teeth √
Get dressed √
Feed cats √
Empty dishwasher √
Have 1st cup of coffee √
Read mail √
Check answerphone for messages √
Check e-mails √
Have 2nd cup of coffee √
Write HEIR OF MYSTERY
Watch telly   MUST DO!!!!
Feed cats
Have supper
Wash, and brush teeth
Go to bed

Chapter One

First and foremost, this is a book about death. Okay, so it doesn't start with an actual death like the unlikely exploit which precedes it (with young Fergal McNally hurtling out of an open window, the wind whistling past his sticky-out ears), but you'll find a lot of it about. Life's like that, though, I'm afraid. Then again, if we didn't have death, this little planet which we call home would be a very overcrowded place. Not only that, most buildings would be old people's homes and entire continents would be taken up with retirement village after retirement village, populated by some very old and very wrinkled people indeed. On your birthday, you wouldn't only get a card from your grandparents but also your great-grandparents, and great-great-grandparents and so on and so on, all the way back to some couple (looking suspiciously like close relatives of apes, if Charlie Darwin is to be believed) whose idea of a fun day out is hunting and gathering, and whose idea of a card might be a particularly interesting leaf, folded in half, with a sooty smudge on the front. If you thought your gran's moustache tickled, just imagine one of them trying to plant a slobbering kiss on you. So death is not only the opposite of life, it's also an important part of it . . . or, to be more accurate, an important part of the circle of life, which is more than just a theme in Walt Disney's *The Lion King*. People are born. People grow up. People have children. People grow old. People die. People's children grow up and have children and *they* die, and so the big wheel keeps on turning. The sad part is when the circle is interrupted. Fergal McNally didn't even finish the growing-up stage, which understandably upset his sisters Jackie and Le Fay, and his brothers Albion and Joshua (aka Albie and Josh, or the twins) . . . and a significant number of people in *this* exploit don't reach the growing old stage. I'm sorry, but there it is. As I began by saying, just three hundred and fifty-one words ago, first and foremost this book is about death.

In addition to death, you're also about to encounter a lot of rain. Like death, rain has its uses. Without rain, most – if not all – plant life would die, there'd be one long drought, and eventually all the animals and humans would die too, so we should be offering a great big cheery THANK YOU to our local rain gods or to the God of Everything, or to Mother Nature (or whichever, if any, deity handles these things). That doesn't mean to say we have to like rain. (I'm glad we have electricity – it's very useful – but I don't particularly want to hug it. Hug a big piece of electricity and it'll burn you to a crisp.) I like the different seasons. I like summer to be sunny and winter to be snowy. I like the crispy golden leaves of autumn and fresh green shoots of spring. I feel sorry for people who live in brilliant sunshine all the year round. B-O-R-I-N-G! Rain plays its part in making the seasons individual. But the rain in this book is a merciless rain. It's torrential – which is why it comes down in torrents – and it's cold and seemingly never-ending.

*

The night this particular unlikely exploit began it was raining in Fishbone Forest; a forest that gets its name from the shape of its trees. Huge, pineless firs, they look like the skeletons of long-dead fishes, their noses to the ground. Wrought iron railings run all the way around the huge forest, with four great gateways, one at each of the four main points of the compass. The gates are always locked. These have always been a puzzle to the local people, who believe that no one in their right mind would want to go into the forest anyway. What they don't realise is that they're there to keep *things* in, not people out.

And the rain? This was the kind of rain that would have to be painted with great slashes across a canvas with lashings of paint. This was the kind of rain that soaked your clothes into a soggy mass in under a minute and then continued to beat down on you. This was the kind of rain which made you think that it had something *personal* against you!

It was through this downpour that an old van, the colour of English mustard, was driving up to the West Gate of Fishbone Forest. At the wheel was a small man. He was a very small man. In fact, he was as small as the small masked burglar at the end of the first unlikely exploit. Okay, okay, so he *was* the small masked burglar at the end of the first unlikely exploit; which means the first time we met him he was stealing a human brain in a jar of pickling vinegar from the Sacred Heart Hospital.

The small masked burglar was no longer masked but he was still small and did have a name. That name was Stefan Multachan, which sounds rather grand but, because he wasn't, everyone who knew him called him 'Mulch'. The only time he was ever addressed as Mr Multachan was when he was sent junk mail – 'Dear Mr Multachan, You're already halfway towards winning a holiday of a life time'; 'You're a guaranteed winner' – or when he was caught doing a burglary: 'Stefan Multachan, we find you guilty of stealing the bag of newts from Wilf's Fish Emporium and sentence you to two weeks' hard labour and ban you from keeping amphibians for six months . . .' You get the picture.

The human brain Mulch had stolen was still in its jar of pickling vinegar, now wrapped up in brown parcel paper – the good thick stuff – and was sitting on the passenger seat beside him. Brains weren't usually kept in pickling vinegar at the Sacred Heart. They were usually kept in formaldehyde or a formaldehyde solution but, for reasons far too time-consuming to relate now, this particular brain ended up in pickling vinegar from the nearby Ma's Pickling Store. (The 'Ma' in question was actually one Mrs Edna Bloinstein and, unusually for a 'ma', I'd say, she'd never had any children.) This particular brain belonged to Fergal McNally, whom I mentioned earlier.

Well, the brain couldn't really belong to Fergal McNally because Fergal McNally was dead. What I meant to say was that it had been Fergal's brain. It was the brain *of* the dead Fergal. If you could see through the darkness, through the rain, through the side of the English-mustard-coloured van and through the brown parcel paper – the good thick stuff – you would see the word 'JUVENILE' written on the label beneath Fergal's name. That's because Fergal was just a little kid when he fell out of a fourteenth storey window and landed splat on the pavement below.

Of course, Fergal's family had no idea that Fergal's brain had been removed from his dead body – though it's standard procedure for a post mortem, carried out to try to find the cause of death – let alone put in a jar of pickling vinegar, let alone stolen by Mulch, wrapped in brown paper and driven to the West Gate of Fishbone Forest. In fact, the dead boy's two sisters (Jackie and Le Fay, remember) and two twin brothers (Joshua and Albion, need I remind you) were, at that very moment, being driven home to their father to break the news of the terrible accident.

Mulch drew the van to a halt and managed to struggle into a bright yellow plastic raincoat and matching hat before opening the door to the rain. The sound of the rain on the plastic sounded like he was being hit with a million tiny ping-pong balls, and the water ran off the brim of the hat like a waterfall. Mulch's hands were soaked as he produced a large, old-fashioned key from his pocket and put it in the lock of the gate. The mechanism was well oiled and the key turned with ease.

Mulch pulled both gates open wide, the rain splashing in his face making it hard to see, and leapt back into the van. He drove into the forest, parked again and dashed out to close and lock the West Gate behind him. There was a flash of sheet lightning; in other words not the forked lightning of horror movies, which often hit branches and set them alight, but the type of lightning which seems to light up the whole sky with one bright flash.

What very few people know (but you're about to be one of them) is that Fishbone Forest is not a natural forest. By that I mean that it was actually planted by a member of the ancient Lyons family many hundreds of years ago (when they weren't quite so ancient), rather than having taken root naturally, like the ancient woodlands to the north.

A grand house, Fishbone Hall, had been built in the middle, surrounded by an equally grand garden with lakes and fountains and terraces and statues, with the forest surrounding that. Over time, people on the outside forgot about the house and garden on the inside, and assumed that it was forest through and through. The house and garden were still there in the centre, but could no longer be described as grand. Grotesque might be a better word for them, though somewhat harder to spell.

The ornamental ponds had dried up, their fountains long-since silent and still, and the lake was more foul-smelling thick green slime than water. The statues had crumbled, becoming faceless or even headless stone freaks. And the house itself? The house had become so overgrown with ivy, *inside* and out, that it looked more like some giant rock formation than a human-made structure. The whole place had a feeling of decay about it. It seemed unnatural. It seemed that the boundary of human-made and natural had somehow blurred. Some indefinable line had been crossed. There was something *wrong* at the very heart of Fishbone Forest.

Lights shone from many of the glassless windows as Mulch drove up towards the Hall along a slippery path which wound like a great snake through the hideous, bone-like trees.

At last, the path turned into a sweeping driveway and Mulch steered the van through the neglected garden, past crumbling balustrades, ivy-choked statues and weed-clogged flowerbeds of long-dead roses. He pulled the English-mustard-coloured van to a halt as near to a door at the side of the house as possible. Picking up Fergal's brain in the wrapped jar, he tucked it under his arm, opened the driver's door and made the short dash from the vehicle to the dryness of the house.

He stood in the bright light of the kitchen, rain dripping from his yellow plastic mac and hat.

'Any luck?' asked a bored-looking teenage boy who'd obviously only recently got in from the rain himself and was drying his clothes in front of a roaring open fire. He was wearing an old blue towelling dressing-gown.

'Yup,' nodded Mulch, putting the brown paper

parcel on the kitchen table before proceeding to pull off the coat and hat.

The boy snatched up the parcel and shook it.

'Careful!' pleaded Mulch. 'You might damage it!'

The boy was holding the parcel to his ear. 'It sounds brainy to me!' he laughed. He liked teasing Mulch, who was so much smaller than him.

'Toby! Put that down!'

The order was like a whip-crack through the air. The stupid grin froze on the boy's face and he returned the jar to the table.

'Good,' said the being who had entered the room. I'd like to be able to call him a man, but that would be stretching the definition a little. There was a lot about him that suggested that he was a male human being: the head, the arms, the legs, but put them all together and you got something altogether *different*.

This frightening apparition was clutching an outsized, roughly stitched teddy bear which should have made him look, at the very least, *slightly* endearing. In truth, it made him seem all the more strange. The bear was furless – worn with love – and its limbs floppy, but its glass eyes were as shiny and clear as real eyeballs. 'You have selected a brain, Mulch?'

'Well, selected might be a bit of an exaggeration, master,' he said. 'There was only this one and no others to choose from.' Mulch handed him the parcel.

The being – the master – who went by the name of Mr Maggs, tucked his teddy under one arm and tore off the brown paper to reveal the brain in the jar. He sniffed the air, catching the faintest whiff of pickling vinegar. 'It's rather small,' he said, and then he caught sight of the label. 'This is a child's brain, you fool!'

'It was the only one there!' Mulch protested.

'Then you should have left it and gone back another night!' fumed Mr Maggs.

'But you said you wanted one tonight!'

'An adult brain. Not a child's!' groaned Mr Maggs, banging the jar down on the table, Fergal's brain glooping around in the vinegar. Brains in fluid are inclined to gloop.

'I could always go back tomorrow night, or the

11

next . . .' Mulch said, defensively.

'You could have if you'd left this brain where it was,' snarled Mr Maggs, 'but now you've stolen this one, every hospital in the city will be on 24-hour brain watch. Buffoon!'

'Nincompoop!' added Toby, with a cheeky grin.

Mulch stuck his tongue out at the boy when Mr Maggs wasn't looking.

Toby picked up the jar, 'So what shall I do with this, then, Mr Maggs? Put it out with the rubbish?' He was joking, of course. There was no rubbish collection from this long-forgotten ramshackle house.

'No!' said Mr Maggs, snatching the brain. 'Time is running out. For my little plan to work, Lionel Lyons needs to be alive and well . . . and for him to be alive and well, he must have a brain.' He glanced back at the label. 'Young Fergal McNally's will have to do. Toby. Go and prepare the operating theatre.'

'Can't I get a drink?' Toby protested.

'GO!' said Mr Maggs. 'But do put some clothes on first!'

Chapter Two

Let's leave Fergal McNally's brain for the time being, and pay a visit to the rest of him. You'll find this story doing this kind of thing a lot; switching between the two main theatres of events. I'm not absolutely sure 'theatres of events' is quite the right technical term – I didn't go to writing classes – but what I mean by it is straightforward enough. There are two main strands to this exploit: one involving Jackie, Le Fay, Albie and Josh McNally and the other involving the people – er, the *beings* – in Fishbone Forest. I don't think I'd be giving too much away by saying that, sooner or later, events collide and these 'theatres' become one. (The picture on the cover's a bit of a give away on that score, isn't it?) So let's skip forward in time, and to a different location, to drop in on Fergal's funeral.

It was a small affair. At the graveside that wet, wet morning was his father, Captain Rufus McNally, a war hero, and his four surviving children. Their mother, who'd been the one to name Fergal and his siblings – which is an important plot point *so don't you forget it* – had long-since died and, for years, Captain Rufus had drunk far too much of what one should really only drink a little of. He'd become a bitter man who spent too much time alone with bottles and his split wooden leg.

Jackie and the others had feared that Fergal's death would bring yet more rage from their father. Instead, it brought his feelings back to him and, after years of neglecting his children, the McNallys suddenly began to feel like a family again. Fergal's death had also reunited their father with Charlie 'Twinkle-Toes' Tweedy, who now held an umbrella over his old friend's head in the rain.

Tweedy had been the chief house detective at The Dell hotel from which Fergal had fallen to his death. Before that, he'd been a policeman, finishing his career on the force – they wanted to call it the police *service*, but he always saw it as the police force – as a very well respected captain, famous for two major character traits. Firstly, he never ever took a bribe or turned a blind eye to wrong-doing. Secondly, he danced beautifully whenever he solved a case, which is how he'd earned the name 'Twinkle-Toes'. Before that, he'd fought in the same war that Captain Rufus McNally had, also in the navy . . . and the then young and brave Captain Rufus had saved his life.

The man standing next to Tweedy at the graveside in the rain was called Malcolm Kent. He had come from The Dell with the McNally children, to break the news of poor little Fergal's death to their father, and had returned for the funeral. Although I describe them as 'children', there are two things I should say about Jackie:

Number one, she was old enough to be her brothers' and sister's mother. Number two, she sometimes turned into a jackal. Yup, that's right: a jackal. That may come as a bit of a surprise (especially if you haven't read the first exploit) but to the McNallys it was no big deal. They were used to it. For as long as they could remember, their big sister had always been able to turn into a jackal, so it never seemed particularly strange or impressive. It was just what Jackie did. But it was agreed that it was something they should never discuss with outsiders.

Like most things in life, being able to transmogrify/metamorph/shape-shift into a howling beast had a downside as well as an upside. Sometimes Jackie couldn't control the change, which could be a little annoying and inconvenient, but it was jolly useful if she needed to be somewhere in a hurry!

But back to the graveside. At this stage, neither Charlie 'Twinkle-Toes' Tweedy nor Malcolm Kent knew of her secret. Though Malcolm had come from the hotel, in the back of the hotel minibus with the McNallys, he didn't work for The Dell. As those of you who are o-so-lucky-enough to have read *The Fall of Fergal* will remember, he worked for Tap 'n' Type (a company which held a typing competition at the hotel which little Le Fay McNally had just won).

The McNallys were a poor family, and winning the competition was one of the most exciting moments in their lives . . . until Fergal had his appointment with the sidewalk/pavement/ground, and then everything had changed.

The three other people at the graveside were Simon – a friend of Le Fay's in particular – and his parents Doug and Lenny (which may sound like a man's name but she was, most definitely a woman).

If the McNallys, with their leaky, draughty apartment, were poor, then Simon and his parents were *dirt* poor. They lived in an abandoned greenhouse near the edge of Fishbone Forest. There, it's that place again. They lived there

16

because no one with any sense or money would go within the shadow of the trees.

So there it was: Simon and his parents, Captain Rufus and his children, Twinkle-Toes Tweedy and Malcolm Kent. Apart from them, there was just the priest.

In that country, at that time, if you were of that particular branch of that particular faith, the priests sometimes wore a hat which looked rather like a cross between those worn by matadors (bull fighters) and those worn by members of the Mickey Mouse Club (but with less pronounced ears).

If the occasion had been anything other than Fergal's funeral, it's more than likely that the twins, Albie and Josh, would have been nudging each other and giggling at it. Instead, they hardly noticed it and their tears mingled with the drizzling rain. I'm sorry this is so sad, but that's the nature of a funeral, despite the word being an anagram of 'real fun'.

The priest spoke a few words over the small, child-sized coffin before Twinkle-Toes Tweedy and Malcolm Kent gently lowered it into the ground. Fergal's father, Captain Rufus, stepped forward and, scooping a handful of soil from the top of the pile by the grave, tossed it down on to the coffin. It was Jackie's turn next; she stepped forward and –

letting out a howl like the jackal she sometimes was – she tossed a single red rose into the hole. She then stepped back and put a supporting arm around her sister Le Fay. In her hands she clasped a beautiful golden envelope. It had contained a voucher for the prize she'd won in the Tap 'n' Type competition at The Dell hotel, but now it contained a message for Fergal.

She lent over the freshly dug grave and dropped the envelope into the hole. It landed on the brass plaque with Fergal's name on it, screwed into the lid of the coffin. Both it and the coffin had been paid for by the hotel management.

Finally, Albie and Josh stepped forward as one. Josh pulled a small rubber ball out of his pocket and he and Albie held it in their hands together – Albie clasping Josh's right hand with his left. It was their most treasured possession and, I can tell you, they didn't have many possessions, treasured or otherwise. They dropped it into the hole.

It hit the coffin lid, bounced out of the grave and hit the priest – SMACK! – on the nose.

To her shame, it was Jackie who laughed first, but she was swiftly followed by Albie and Josh *and* Le Fay . . . and soon their father was laughing too. Then Twinkle-Toes Tweedy couldn't hold back any longer and burst out into such a silly laugh that he set the others off even more. The suppressed giggles of Simon and his parents soon turned into frantic guffaws.

Malcolm, who was a very nice man, was trying to comfort the priest, whose nose was now bleeding, and only started to laugh when he realised that the priest – the victim of the accident – was shaking with laughter too! Tears of laughter streamed down *all* their faces. They hugged each other. They wiped their tears. They laughed some more. Jackie was now laughing so much her sides hurt. Twinkle-Toes Tweedy was bent over double. The priest retrieved the rubber ball from amongst the floral tributes – flowers, to you and me – and handed it to Josh.

Together, he and Albie knelt down and leaned into the grave, dropping the ball on the coffin from a far lesser height, so there was less bounce. The laughter subsided and soon the service was over.

As they walked away from the graveside, Rufus McNally couldn't help himself and started laughing again, which triggered yet more hysterics from the others.

'It was the funniest funeral I've ever been to,' the priest later told his housekeeper as she put an ice pack on his swollen nose. 'They were such nice people.'

Back at the McNallys' apartment, which was up a flight of wide concrete stairs, on the second floor from the ground, the mourners gathered for a meagre meal of sandwiches and crisps. To the McNallys, it was quite a spread but they weren't hungry. To Simon and his parents, it was a FEAST. They usually lived off the fruit and veg which fell from the fruit stalls, or was thrown to the ground by the stall holders at the daily market in the nearby square. When the market packed up and went home, Simon, his dad Doug and his mum Lenny moved in, scavenging the discarded boxes. They weren't alone. Other human scavengers were on similar missions.

Lenny became very good at making excellent vegetable stews and vegetable soups, and they ate plenty of fresh fruit. They didn't care about a few splits and bruises, but there wasn't a great deal of *variety*. Bloater paste sandwiches may not be your or my idea of a luxury repast, but Simon and his parents tucked in. As for what some call crisps and others call potato chips, Simon couldn't believe his eyes . . . but felt very guilty at the loud crunching noises he was making when no one else was eating.

Jackie smiled at him. 'Tuck in,' she said. 'It'd be a terrible waste not to eat it, just because *we're* not hungry.'

On the table by the window was a photograph of Captain Rufus and Mrs McNally, proudly holding Fergal as a baby. It was one of only two pictures they had of Fergal. The other hung in 'the back room' (which was really at the side). Fergal was wearing a nappy. The weird thing was, he'd been wearing a nappy the day before he died . . . but that had been to disguise him as a baby so that he could travel for nothing on a coach trip! Fate, or someone up there, can play cruel tricks sometimes.

'I wonder what his power was?' said Le Fay in a hushed voice, touching Fergal's face in the photo. 'His secret ability?'

'We'll never know now,' said Jackie.

By 'power' Le Fay meant the thing that made each of them different. Jackie already knew her power, of course. That was becoming the jackal. Le Fay, Albie and Josh were yet to discover theirs. They had no idea what they might be. Being almost identical twins, would Albie and Josh have almost identical powers, or two totally separate ones? And what about Le Fay?

Somehow their mother had always known what special 'power' each of her children would have and had named them accordingly, or so she claimed. Their father, Rufus, had had no say in the matter and had been as surprised as Jackie herself the first time she turned all four-legged and furry and started to howl at the moon.

'The clues are in your names,' Mrs McNally had told her children, but would say no more. 'You must find the powers within yourselves.'

Looking at that photo after the funeral, Le Fay wished that Fergal had been named 'Lazarus', then at least there might have been the chance that he would have come back to life somehow. But no such luck, his body was well-and-truly dead and buried now.

But what Le Fay didn't know about – what *none* of them knew about – was the brain: the one with the faint whiff of pickling vinegar.

Chapter Three

I don't know about you but, despite my warning, all this talk of death, funerals and wakes has still managed to make me feel a touch on the gloomy side, and I didn't intend to write this – and I doubt that you're reading this – in the hope that we'll all end up feeling thoroughly miserable.

My books are generally thought to be a barrel of laughs, not a barrel of tears . . . not that I've ever *heard* of a barrel of tears and not that I've ever actually seen a barrel of laughs, but people do talk about them. I wonder where the idea came from? Perhaps you could toddle off to your local library and look it up in *The Big Book of Answers*. You can't expect me to do everything for you.

Back already? Good. I hope it was a nice break from all that weeping and wailing and gnashing of teeth. Okay, so we haven't actually had any gnashing of teeth yet, but there's still time *and* it gives me the opportunity to tell you a story about the McNally children's grandmother – Captain Rufus's mum – back in the days when she was still alive. I've heard a different version of this story told about somebody else, but I like the Granny McNally version, so I'm sticking to it. She was an old lady by the time of the incident I'm about to relate and never bothered to wear false teeth, even though all her *real* teeth had long since fallen out.

One day, Granny McNally was sitting in the front pew of her local church, like she did every Sunday, eagerly awaiting the sermon from the nice young preacher with the centre parting, when someone she'd never laid eyes on strode into the pulpit and started preaching about Fire and Brimstone and the Horrors of Hell. Now, there's nothing wrong with preaching Fire and Brimstone and the Horrors of Hell if you seriously believe that your fellow human beings are going to end up in Hell unless you do your best to save them. In fact, that would probably be the only right and proper thing to do.

The problem was, the people at the church Granny McNally went to had rather a different idea about religion. *Their* religion had more to do with the nice things people could do to help one another; lending a helping hand and being kind, honest and true. Devils prodding you with pitchforks in the fiery depths of hell (which they thought of with a small 'h' if they thought of it at all) didn't really come into it. Giving shelter to the homeless, food to the hungry and books to the poor didn't leave much time to worry about much else.

This meant that the congregation at St James the Lessser (with three 's's due to an error by the sign painter over 150 years before) were a bit puzzled and even uncomfortable when this visiting preacher was talking about the truly horrendous things that would happen to them if they didn't 'repent' and, thus, ended up in Hell.

'There will be weeping!' cried the preacher, throwing his arms wide. 'There will be wailing!' and he made the word 'wailing' sound like a long, lamenting wail. 'There will be gnashing of teeth!'

Granny McNally put her hand up, like a kid in class. The visiting preacher was stunned. No one had ever interrupted one of his Fire-and-Brimstone sermons with a question before.

'Yes? What is it?' he spluttered.

'Are you saying I could go to hell?' she asked.

'We could *all* go to Hell!' nodded the preacher fervently.

'And I'll weep and I'll wail and I'll gnash my teeth?'

The preacher nodded. He was certainly getting through to some of these people.

'But what if you don't have any teeth?' she asked, grinning a toothless grin to reveal that her mouth contained her tongue and not much else.

The visiting preacher was staring into a gaping black hole, like the entrance to Hell itself! He began to tremble.

'Teeth,' he whimpered, 'will be provided.'

With that, he fled the pulpit *and* the church and never came back to St James the Lessser (with three 's's) again. The next time the Reverend Norris – the nice young preacher with the centre parting – was off sick, a different preacher took his place; one who didn't once mention Hell – with or without a capital 'H' – and usually stuck to safe topics, such as 'being kind to animals' or 'a funny thing which happened to him on the way to the

27

church that morning' . . . especially if he saw Granny McNally in the front row, waiting to pounce.

And so, from my favourite Granny McNally anecdote, we return to the younger McNallys and the days immediately following Fergal's funeral. They were some of the hardest they ever had to face and, rest assured, there were still some pretty hard ones to come. With the funeral coming up, Jackie, Le Fay, Albie and Josh had had something to focus on; an event to get through. Now that it had come and gone, there seemed to be simply nothing more than the-whole-of-the-rest-of-their-lives-without-Fergal to focus on.

Then there was the guilt. When someone dies there is always guilt: guilt at what one should have said and done, but never got round to saying or doing . . . and now it was too late.

Fortunately for us and for the McNallys, events were soon to overtake them, or take them over. Soon there was to be little time for sitting around and feeling sorry for themselves. This was a time for action. It began with Le Fay deciding that she, Jackie and the twins, Albie and Josh, must go to visit 'Wandaland'. What made her decide? She had no idea at the time, but there were forces at work and all will be revealed. What you can be sure of, though, is it *wasn't* 'just one of those things'.

So what was this Wandaland that Le Fay was so keen for them to visit that particular rainy day amongst all the other rainy days? It may sound like Wonderland – I'm sure that was intentional – but that's where any similarities cease.

It's hard to imagine anything less wonderful than Wandaland, I can assure you. In the interest of research I've been there and, let me state categorically, whatever the opposite of wonderful is, that's what Wandaland has by the bucketload.

As most of you in a guessing mood will have guessed, Wandaland was named after a person called Wanda. (Or should that be 'called after a person named Wanda'? Take your pick.) That person was a very old, large black lady named Wanda de Vere and she'd built Wandaland all by herself many decades ago. Back then, Wandaland didn't have to compete with TV sets in most houses or computer games and the like. Back then, paint that was now faded or flaking – or faded *and* flaking – was fresh and brightly coloured. But even then, it was far from wonderful.

The story goes that Wanda de Vere was descended from slaves. Her grandparents, or great-grandparents (there are different versions) had been bought and 'belonged' to a white man in a country a long way from their original home, but they had escaped via something called 'the underground railway' – which wasn't really underground and wasn't really a railway – and ended up settling in the town where the McNallys now lived. It's shocking to think that there was a time and a place where 'owning' people was considered to be an okay thing to do. It's easy to be dismissive about something like that because it's 'nothing to do with us' but – if I could put on my serious hat for a moment, and step outside the action of the story – it's up to us to make sure things like this never happen again.

Now, back to Wanda. When she was twenty-one, and still called Wanda Smith, she married a man named Vernon de Vere who had made a fortune selling safety matches. There was a time when matches were far from safe and they'd rub against each other in your trouser pocket as you walked along – if you wore trousers – and set fire to your leg . . . or they'd rub against each other in someone else's trouser pocket as they walked and set fire to *their* leg. So safety matches were very much in demand when they came along. And come along they did in wagons (and later trucks) with DE VERE MATCHES emblazoned on the sides in fiery orange letters.

Wanda and Vern de Vere (as he liked to be called) were very happy together but, sadly, he was killed in the war. (It doesn't really matter which war, it was simply one of those wars referred to as 'the war' once it was over, because it was the freshest war in people's minds until the next, and even more dreadful, one came along.)

To encourage people to enlist – sign up to join the army and fight – recruitment offices were set up in church halls, town halls and empty shops across the land. Large temporary signs were put up outside these offices, with patriotic slogans designed to encourage all right-thinking young[ish] men to sign up, then and there, to fight.

It was one such sign that fell on Vern de Vere's head as he was innocently walking past a temporary recruitment office near one of his factories. I'm led to believe that the wording on it was: REAL MEN DON'T WAIT TO BE ASKED TO FIGHT FOR WHAT'S RIGHT.

Because Vern de Vere had been a well-known and well-respected businessman, and because it was an army sign that had flattened him on the pavement, the government decided to pay Wanda a war widow's pension as a mark of respect.

Following his final wishes to the letter, she had her late husband's coffin made like a giant DE VERE matchbox and cremated (burnt), even though most people preferred to be buried back then. But, if matches are your business, you're going to want to be burnt, aren't you?

His ashes were placed in a bronze urn shaped like a giant safety match, especially commissioned and sculpted by the (then) famous artist Hans Gobble (as in the noise turkeys are supposed to make).

Wanda was never quite the same after Vern de Vere died. She took a further turn for the worse when, in the 1950s, Hans Gobble statues became so sought-after that her late husband's urn (with her late husband's ashes still inside) was stolen to order for a corrupt art dealer. It was around about then that Wanda gave up all interest in the match factories and turned her attention to Wandaland.

She built an entire high street, or main street (call it what you will) in which the houses that lined it on either side most resembled one-room garden sheds. This was in the days before one could buy self-assembly sheds, so that in itself was quite unusual. Then Wanda painted them in bright colours – and I mean BRIGHT – sometimes creating new shades by mixing the various colours together.

Often when guide books talk about a person 'building' a place they mean that the person came up with the idea, or designed the plans or just paid for it to be built but, more often than not, they didn't physically build it all themselves (brick by brick, plank by plank, stone by stone). They were simply in charge and put their names to it. Not so with Wanda. Come rain or shine, it was her out there doing the sawing, hammering or painting, with just her dog for company.

People with opinions (and such people are easy to find) were of the opinion that Mrs de Vere was creating Wandaland as a therapy and the general consensus was – in other words *most* of these opinionated people agreed – that this was a bad thing. It was good that she was occupying her time with something new but a bad thing that this 'thing' was erecting and painting rows of shacks. Shouldn't a rich widow be taking her mind off her husband's death by throwing herself into charitable works, not building some crazy make-believe world?

But, like most truly sensible people, Wanda

didn't really care what people like that thought. They were welcome to their opinions and she was welcome to hers. When her self-built shanty town was complete, she got the son of the man who'd come up with the original lettering for DE VERE MATCHES to paint a great big sign which read 'WELCOME TO WANDALAND'. She charged a nominal – very small – entry fee and, in those early days, people flocked to see it. Even most of them who'd tut-tutted came along for a look-see. Everyone wanted to know what Mrs de Vere had been up to, and what was inside those sheds.

Back then, she gave groups guided tours in person. Later, people were left to wander around on their own and she left hand-written notices pinned up here, there and everywhere to explain to visitors what was what. Some made sense: 'This shed represents a ship on the Sea of Life. The blue at the bottom is the sea. The blue at the top is the sky. One of you step inside while another lifts the lever up and down. This movement represents the waves.'

Other notices were more abstract or (as someone less charitable once put it) 'plain weird'. These included: 'This shed represents the shed-shaped air excluded from this space because the shed itself is taking it up' and 'Just because I bothered to write this notice doesn't mean you should bother to read it.' There is the distinct possibility, of course, that Wanda de Vere had a wicked sense of humour!

Wandaland was a very strange place indeed. It wasn't built by a woman with a single vision, but one with lots of *different* visions and most people left very confused. Wanda de Vere seemed to spend most of her time in a little toll booth by the entrance, taking the money, with a faithful dog curled up at her feet. As the years passed, the nominal fee got more and more nominal until, one day, she stopped charging altogether but, by then, few people visited Wandaland anyway . . . but Mrs de Vere still sat in her toll booth, meeting and greeting anyone who should pass by.

The dogs changed over the years, though. When one of her much-loved companions died, she would bury it in her dog cemetery at the far end of the one and only street in Wandaland, and then go and choose a puppy from the dogs' home on Dillington Street – Dillington Street Dog Shelter – and this would become her new companion. It would sleep at her feet in the booth for much of each and every day until they went home to her grand apartment in the 'no pets' building where the doorman and concierge politely turned a blind eye.

When Jackie, Le Fay, Albie and Josh McNally arrived at Wandaland, trying to huddle under one tatty umbrella, Wanda de Vere had been taking her current dog, Nimmo, for a rather wet 'walkies' and was just leading him back into the booth on the piece of fraying twine she used as a leash. She smiled at Jackie and the children.

'A warm welcome to Wandaland,' she said, which was pretty much what she always said to everyone, rain or shine.

Whereas the sheds had originally been empty – apart from the strange objects and furniture Wanda might have placed in them for aesthetic reasons – nowadays they were sometimes used by carnival folk as places to stage minor entertainments. Instead of pitching a tent, they hung a banner or hand-written sign outside a shed such as: 'PALMS READ', 'HOT DOGS',

'CRYSTAL BALL FORTUNE TELLING', 'ROAST CHESTNUTS', 'TEA LEAVES READ HERE', 'I GUESS YOUR WEIGHT', 'YOUR FORTUNE IN THE STARS', 'BEARDED FISHES AND OTHER WONDERS'. The rows of sheds had become the place of business of the biggest collection of so-called clairvoyants in town.

It was a shrewd move that each fortune teller had his or her own particular talent. More often than not, a fortune teller will offer a wide range of services from tarot card to crystal ball readings. Here in Wandaland, everyone stuck to his or her own speciality so, if you wanted your tea leaves read *and* a palm reading, you had to visit two different sheds with two different fortune tellers and cross two different palms with silver (in other words, you had to pay them both).

It also encouraged any visitor into fortune telling to put the fortune tellers to the test, by seeing if each one, with their own method, came up with similar predictions. It was a clever money-making enterprise.

'We're here now, so now what?' asked Albie, feeling very cold and very wet.

'What now?' asked Josh.

'Exactly,' said Jackie, looking at Le Fay through the steady drizzle.

'I'm not sure,' said Le Fay, honestly. 'It's just that I really felt we should come.'

'I wouldn't mind a hot dog,' said Albie.

'Or half a hot dog,' Josh added hurriedly, seeing the expression on Jackie's face.

'We don't have money to waste on hot dogs –' she sighed.

'Or fortune tellers,' admitted Le Fay.

'If we went to all of these, they'd cost a fortune too!' grinned Josh.

'So what shall we do?' asked Albie.

'Let's look at the dog cemetery,' Le Fay suggested.

'But that's a sad place,' said Albie.

'No it isn't,' said Le Fay, marching off down Wandaland's one and only street, its potholes filled with rainwater. 'At least, it shouldn't be. If you were a dog, wouldn't you want to be one that's loved so much that your owner buries your ashes in a special place with a tombstone and everything?'

Jackie caught up with her sister and gripped her hand. 'Perhaps it's too early to be visiting a dogs' graveyard after . . . after Fergal's funeral,' she whispered.

Le Fay hesitated. Remembering that Jackie sometimes turned into a jackal – who could forget? – and that jackals come from the dog family, Le Fay wondered whether her big sister would find a dog cemetery an even sadder place than others might. What on Earth had possessed her to insist the others come to this place anyhow? And in the rain?

Then she saw the sign: FREE FORTUNE TELLING TODAY ONLY. It was over the door of one of the tattiest sheds, once painted in bright green paint that had faded to little more than a greenish tint on the grain, and the door was wide open. 'Look!' she pointed.

Seeing the word 'FREE' Josh and Albie were inside that shed before you could say, 'Which-twin's-which?' Le Fay and Jackie followed.

The inside can be described in two words (or three if you include 'and'): small and dark. It was a tight squeeze and what little daylight there was filtered through a small window ingrained with years of grime.

They blinked to adjust to the lack of light. At the right-hand end of the shed, steeped in shadow, sat a fortune teller. The top of his head was swathed in red turban (which had definitely seen better days) and his nose, mouth and chin were hidden by a scarf made out of the same material.

You'd probably see people in more impressive costumes at any amateur dramatics production, or at any fancy dress party, or could make a better costume using bits and bobs from any half-decent dressing-up box, but the McNally children – not that Jackie was a child any more – had neither seen an amateur dramatics production *nor* been to a fancy dress party *nor* had a dressing-up box, so the Fortune Teller looked pretty exotic to them.

All they could see of his face were his eyes.

'Which one of you has come to have their fortune foretold?' asked the Fortune Teller, his voice disappointingly high and quavering.

Jackie pushed Le Fay forward. 'It was your idea to come here,' she reminded her.

'M-Me,' said Le Fay, suddenly feeling nervous. 'My name is –'

The Fortune Teller held up a hand to stop her

40

from going any further. The mottled skin looked like old parchment – which was what one looks for in a wise old mystic – but his watch strap was made of yellow plastic, and his sleeves were frayed, which somewhat lessened the effect. 'Sit,' he commanded.

Le Fay sat on a small three-legged stool facing him. The other three crowded behind her. The Fortune Teller took Le Fay's right hand and, the moment they touched, he jolted back, eyes widening, as if he'd been given a nasty burn or an electric shock, but he tightened his grip rather than letting go. 'Powerful forces are at work here!' he said, in a squeaky voice.

'I'll bet you say that to everyone,' Albie whispered. He was clearly unimpressed.

Josh nudged him in the ribs and tried not to giggle.

The Fortune Teller's gaze came to rest upon the almost-identical twins. 'The giant killer and the musician, I see,' he said, the tone of his voice changing and a look of confusion passing across his face, clearly visible in the only part of it that the others could see: his eyes.

'Huh?' said Albie.

'The name's Josh, not Jack,' said his brother, assuming that this fraud had been referring to 'Jack the Giant-Killer', the hero of a fairy tale that Jackie had told them about when they were younger.

'He should stick to the "powerful forces" script,' Albie muttered.

'Quiet!' said Jackie, who was always very insistent that they be polite. The shed smelled of damp McNallys.

The Fortune Teller's manner had noticeably changed. He turned Le Fay's hand palm up and leant forward to study it. 'Of late you have experienced great joy and great sadness. Though poor in possessions you are rich in the heart and the love of your family . . . You . . . You . . .'

He sat bolt upright, the long flowing scarf falling from his face. His eyes grew wider still and he stared with the look of a blind man.

When he spoke again, they could see his mouth now but the voice was completely different. It was a woman's voice: 'You have buried Fergal but not his brain,' it said.

The McNally children gasped as one.

'You have buried Fergal but not his brain!' the voice repeated.

Le Fay pulled her hand away. 'What is this? Some kind of joke?' she demanded, her anger overcoming any timid feelings she might have had. 'Well, it's not funny.'

'Find the boy's brain,' said the voice coming from the old man's mouth.

'Wh-Wh-Where is it?' stammered Jackie, her

hand gripping Le Fay's shoulder. 'Where can we find it?'

'Fishbone Forest,' said the voice. The Fortune Teller toppled backwards and hit his head against the shed wall. Le Fay jumped up to help him, knocking over her stool in the process.

'No!' snapped Jackie. 'Outside!'

The McNallys tumbled out into the rain. Jackie was holding the closed umbrella but was far too distracted to open it.

'How did that old fraud know Fergal's name?' asked Josh, clearly shaken by the experience but doing his best not to let it show (and his best wasn't good enough).

It was Jackie who was the one who was physically shaking, though. 'Mum . . .' she said.

'What is it, Jacks?' asked Le Fay.

'That was Mum's voice,' she said. 'We must go to Fishbone Forest . . . It was Mum who made you make us come here, Le Fay. And it was Mum speaking to us through that man . . .'

Chapter Four

Now I couldn't blame some of you for muttering, 'What a jolly book this has turned out to be. NOT!' but I did warn you, remember? Look back at page one. I wasn't kidding, now, was I? As well as Fergal's funeral, we've had plenty about dogs dying (and a dogs' cemetery) we've had talk of gnashing of teeth in Hell (with a capital 'H'), someone being cremated in a giant matchbox after being killed by a falling sign (only to have his remains stolen) and we've even touched, for the briefest of moments, on the horrors of slavery, but – on the surface – few things can be as shocking as the McNallys learning from their long-dead mother that their recently deceased brother's brain wasn't buried along with the rest of him but was somewhere in the creepiest forest around!!!!!! (My editor had better not remove any of these exclamation marks, even though there are six of them. A statement like that needs each and every one of them. Less than half a dozen just won't do.) And where did the McNallys learn this shocking news? Shut in a shed with a fortune teller. Well, one thing's for sure, you don't get to hear about these kinds of exploits every day.

Jackie, Le Fay and the twins headed for the exit, umbrella still down. They hurried as one past the handful of other stragglers who'd decided to visit the extraordinarily unwonderful Wandaland on such a grey, wet day.

'Are you sure it was Mum's voice?' asked Le Fay.

'Do you think I could ever forget it?' asked Jackie. Being so much older than the others, she had so many more memories of their mother, who had died when Fergal had been born.

'But *how* could she speak to us?' demanded Albie. 'I don't believe in ghosts!'

'Shouldn't we stay and talk to that guy?' said Josh, meaning the Fortune Teller. 'He might know some more.'

'I doubt it,' said Albie. 'He had you down as Jack the Giant-Killer and me as a rock star!'

The twins both gave a half-hearted laugh.

'It *was* Mum and she wants us to save Fergal's brain,' said Jackie.

'That still doesn't explain how –'

Jackie stopped in her tracks and snarled. 'I think you're forgetting something,' and the others came to a standstill beside her. 'We're not like other people. We're different. I turn into a jackal and all three of you have special powers too, it's just that we don't know what they are yet. We got those from our mother. How? Because she was special too. Now, I'm not saying that Mum is still alive in some other form in some other place, I'm simply saying that her power lives on *through us*. Maybe that means that in times of real importance, such as NOW, we can hear her speak to us. It's not her in person . . . it's her in essence . . . in spirit . . . and, no, I don't mean the spooky white-sheet-ghost-rattling-chains kind of spirit . . . Do you see what I'm saying?'

The rain pitter-pattered down on their soaking wet hair.

'It's the source of our powers telling us that we must find Fergal's brain?' asked Albie.

'Like it was somehow the power inside me that made me insist we all come here today?' said Le Fay, deep in thought.

'Exactly,' said Jackie. 'There has to be some reason to it all.'

'But how did Fergal's brain end up in Fishbone Forest?' Le Fay shuddered because, unlike you and me, she had no idea about it being put in a jar of pickling vinegar at the Sacred Heart Hospital or being stolen by Mulch and taken back to that teddy bear-hugging being Mr Maggs. 'That's one of the last places I'd want to go.'

'Name a *good* place for a brain hunt,' said Josh.

'Good point,' said Jackie. They headed for the exit. They passed the toll booth with Nimmo curled up, out of sight, at Wanda de Vere's feet. 'Have a nice day!' she called after the McNallys as they left Wandaland behind them.

★

Following Mr Maggs's instructions, Toby was preparing the operating theatre, deep in the basement of the ruinous Fishbone Hall. If you're imagining something out of a *Frankenstein* movie, with different coloured chemicals bubbling and smoking inside glass beakers and test-tubes, a huge wooden operating table with straps to hold the patient down and an enormous wall-mounted lever for switching on the electric current, you couldn't be much further from the truth.

This was one of the few rooms in the entire building that was ultra modern and ultra clean, like a high-tech operating theatre in an expensive private hospital (not that there were many of those in that particular country at that particular time).

Every surface and every surgical instrument was already gleaming, but Toby knew not to argue with his master. He'd been told to prepare the operating theatre and that included cleaning everything, so cleaning everything he was. He even placed the gleaming surgical instruments – everything from razor-sharp scalpels to metal tongs and tweezers – in a stainless-steel dish which he lowered into a special sterilising machine and, whilst they heated up, he washed down the surfaces with disinfectant from a spray bottle.

Toby had a Discman clipped to the waistband of his jeans, and was listening to heavy metal as he worked, singing out loud; not that he could hear his own voice too well above the sound of *Death Throws* pumping through the headphones.

'*Spirits of the dead!*' he shouted, following the chorus of his favourite song by the band: 'Walking With Skeletons'. As you may have guessed by now, Toby was, in many ways, what many people consider 'a typical teenager'. If you have a teenage brother, you'll know exactly what I mean. He was the kind of guy whose feet would stink in his trainers/sneakers/gym-shoes if Mr Maggs hadn't had such strict rules about everything. And even young Toby wasn't stupid enough to deliberately get on the wrong side of Mr Maggs.

As he scrubbed and cleaned and sang to himself, he was unaware that the aforementioned Mr Maggs had entered the room. Mr Maggs moved surprisingly quietly for such a large being. (I nearly said 'man' but, for reasons already outlined, you know just how wrong that would have been.) It wasn't simply that he was 'light on his feet' – he could have been as noisy as he'd liked in this instance, and Toby still wouldn't have heard him – but he had a way of seeming to melt into place – no, *fade* into place – out of nowhere, but that wasn't possible, was it? It's just that he was very good at being there when one least expected it . . . but it wasn't sudden. There was a sense that he'd somehow been there all the time, but one hadn't noticed him until then. Actually, it's very hard to explain, which is why I'm not doing such a great job, but I hope you get the idea: even Mr Maggs's entrances and exits were strange.

Toby looked up, and there the master was. 'Ready?' Mr Maggs mouthed, having pulled down the surgical paper mask which had been covering his mouth.

'Ready!' Toby nodded, throwing the cloth he'd been using into a bin lined with a yellow refuse sack marked: WASTE FOR INCINERATION. He pulled off the disposable gloves he'd been wearing and threw them in too, then clicked off his Discman.

'Excellent,' said Mr Maggs. 'Would you be kind enough to have Lionel Lyons join us?'

Toby hurried across the operating theatre to a large stainless-steel door set into the far wall at waist height. He grasped its handle and it opened with a hiss to reveal the end of a large drawer. He slid out the drawer, on which lay an elderly gentleman about to suck an orange-flavoured ice-cream, frozen solid. It wasn't just the ice-cream which was frozen solid, but the gentleman too.

'Bother!' muttered Toby under his breath.

'What is it?' demanded Mr Maggs.

'Er . . . There must be something wrong with the temperature control. He's supposed to have thawed out by now and –'

'Be nicely chilled out and ready for the

operation,' said Mr Maggs, striding across the room, his outsized teddy clutched to him. He took one look at Lionel Lyons and groaned. 'Am I surrounded by buffoons?'

'I could put him in the microwave,' Toby suggested, hoping beyond hope that Mr Maggs wouldn't explode into one of his rages.

'How many times have I told you not to call it that?' his master demanded. 'It's not a cooker!'

Try telling that to Mulch, Toby thought, thinking back to the many times he'd seen the little man heat his meat pies in the giant thawing machine; but he said nothing.

51

Toby slid the very frozen Lionel Lyons off the drawer and on to a gurney/trolley/stretcher-on-wheels-thingy and wheeled him over to what he and Mulch thought of as the giant microwave (one of Mr Maggs's own designs). He opened the huge door and slid the frozen man (with frozen ice-cream) inside, and shut the door.

'Set the heat to slow thaw and the timer to three hours,' said Mr Maggs. 'We must damage as little tissue as possible . . . Yet another delay. Why must I always suffer delays? Where's the brain?'

'I thought you had it,' said Toby.

Mr Maggs hit him with his teddy.

Approximately two and a half hours later, there was a knock at the door of Mr Maggs's study, which was a strange half-indoor/half-outdoor room, with ivy growing all over one side of the massive oak desk, behind which Mr Maggs now sat.

He assumed it was Toby come to report that Lionel Lyons had fully thawed. 'Enter!' he boomed.

It was, however, Mulch who opened the door, and came through the doorway, with a large package under one arm. This was a matter of courtesy because he could just as easily have stepped through any number of large gaping holes in the various inner walls.

It was still raining hard in that part of the study open to the sky, and the over-stuffed chairs were getting soggier and soggier and turning a darker shade of beige.

'What is it?' asked Mr Maggs, stroking his teddy bear's head between the ears.

'Excellent news, master,' said Mulch, with a kind of fawning bow. (That's a bow as in bending your head, not a bow as in something you fire an arrow with or wear in your hair.)

'What is it?'

'An adult brain! We have an adult brain!' said Mulch, barely able to contain his excitement.

Mr Maggs suddenly seemed even bigger as he leant forward and asked, 'Where? Show me! Show me.'

Mulch placed the package on the desk. He took the lid off a plastic box and there, packed in ice, was indeed an adult human brain.

Tears sprang to the master's eyes. 'Where did you get it?' he wanted to know.

'It was delivered,' Mulch explained. 'The card that came with it says: *From a grateful donor, Cousin Ralphie*,' he read.

'You can always rely on family,' Mr Maggs sighed happily, looking even more like a grinning pumpkin than Mulch had ever seen.

'So what shall I do with the juvenile's brain?'

asked Mulch, relieved to be out of a tight spot and to see his master happy at last.

'I have no use for it now,' said Mr Maggs with the wave of a hand. 'Get rid of it.'

Oh dear, oh dear, oh dear.

Chapter Five

'Why don't you want us to tell Dad about Fishbone Forest?' asked Le Fay. 'He seems so much better . . . so much *nicer* since Fergal died.'

'Yeah,' agreed Josh. 'Nowadays he doesn't just talk to us when he's telling us to get him something, or *not* to do this or *not* to do that.'

'Until lately, I'd forgotten he could talk without shouting,' added Albie.

It was true. Captain McNally really did seem a different man: a *caring* dad.

'That's as maybe,' said Jackie, sounding very grown up, because 'that's as maybe' is the kind of phrase that grown-ups use. 'But what do we tell him? That Mum, or the power-of-Mum, spoke to us through some pretend fortune teller at Wandaland and told us that Fergal's brain isn't

55

buried with the rest of him but is somewhere in Fishbone Forest?' said her sister.

'I know it sounds crazy, but so does you turning into a jackal . . . and he's used to that. He knows that we all have special powers, and *that's* because Mum used to have them too, so why shouldn't he believe us?' Le Fay reasoned.

It was still raining but they'd wanted to talk away from the apartment so they were up a tree in the local park. To call it a park was a bit grand, the truth be told, though it appeared on maps as 'GARLAND PARK'. There were no flowers or anything. It was more a large patch of grass, with a single tree right in the centre. Near the tree was a large hole (about the size of an Olympic swimming pool) which had opened up without warning a month before. It was now roped off to discourage people from falling into it. This was just one of a series of holes which had started appearing right across the country eighteen months or so previously. No one seemed to know what had caused this outbreak (or breakout) of holes and no one seemed to know how to stop them. Some experts thought that their cause was geological; some thought that their cause was supernatural; others were convinced that they were created by extraterrestrials. Most people simply got used to them, in the same way that people get used to living with volcanoes or earthquakes or bombing from enemy planes. The holes were okay so long as you, your family, your friends or your home didn't fall into one.

Years ago, some kids had put a sheet of corrugated iron in the top branches of the tree to act as a kind of roof, and the McNallys (and others) often used the tree in Garland Park as a sort of floorless tree-house, sitting or standing on the branches. If you couldn't afford to hang out in one of the cafés or burger places where you had to buy something to sit there, you could literally hang out of the tree.

Now, Albie and Josh were standing in the highest branches, directly above the seated Le Fay and Jackie (who felt that she was far too old to be climbing trees, and that it was undignified for a part-time member of the dog family, what with being a jackal and that, when it was *cats* that were natural tree-climbers).

'We could ask Mr Tweedy for help,' Albie suggested. 'What with him being a detective and all.'

'I can't see the point in going after the brain anyway,' said Josh, his voice little more than a whisper.

'What?' demanded Jackie.

'Nothing,' said Josh, guiltily.

'No, go on,' said Jackie. 'We must all have our say.'

57

'Well, even if we do find Fergal's brain, it's not going to bring him back, is it?'

'That's true,' said Jackie, 'but don't you think it should be buried with the rest of him?'

'Fergal won't miss it,' said Albie, coming to his twin's defence.

'That's also true but it's important to Mum –'

'Or the power-of-Mum,' Le Fay interrupted.

'– that we find it, and that ought to be reason enough. Shall we take a vote?' asked Jackie.

'There's no need,' said Josh. 'Of course we're all in this together. I was only thinking out loud, that's all.'

'Then, tomorrow, it's Fishbone Forest here we come!' said Le Fay, raising her voice to be heard above the rain beating down on the corrugated iron. Despite the effort, she didn't sound very enthusiastic.

★

When Lionel Lyons had finally thawed out, Mr Maggs set to work placing the brain so kindly donated by Mr Maggs's Cousin Ralphie inside his skull, connecting all the relevant bits here and there. (That may sound a bit wishy-washy and lacking in medical terms but I've left it this vague for three reasons. Firstly, because to the lay – that means 'non-expert' – reader, none of these technical terms will mean a great deal; secondly, if I say much more than 'he peeled back the skin off the top of the head, sawed off the top skull, removed the damaged brain putting the 'donated' brain in its place, connected it all up, then put the head back together again', it's bound to put some of you off your breakfast, lunch, tea or supper; and, thirdly, if I put in too much detail it might encourage the odd reader – and I mean *odd* – to try out a little DIY brain surgery him (or her) self ... and my name could come up in the court case, with the defence lawyer stating, 'My client used Philip Ardagh's *Heir of Mystery* as an instruction manual during the brain surgery, therefore it must be Mr Ardagh's, and not my client's, fault that the patient died.' See what I mean?)

Suffice it to say that it was an extremely long and complicated operation and, requiring both hands, meant that Mr Maggs's teddy had to be tied to his waist with the cord of his operating gown.

Toby, meanwhile, acted as his theatre nurse, handing him all the relevant surgical implements, swabs, bandages and the like, but Mulch was banished to the other side of the glass. He had assisted the master in earlier practice attempts at what he called 'reanimation' but had been a little clumsy on more than one occasion, which had thrown Mr Maggs into a violent rage. Fortunately, Mr Maggs had been violent towards various items of furniture in the room, rather than towards Mulch in person, but the damage was done. This was why Mulch was now given the supposedly more simple tasks, such as breaking into the Sacred Heart Hospital to steal a brain. And look how displeased Mr Maggs had been with the result of *that*.

Watching Mr Maggs now as he glued the sawn-off top of the skull back in place and pulled the skin back down into position and nimbly sewed a line of stitches, Mulch thought how unfair it was that Toby was the one in there with him. Mulch had worked for the master for years, but Toby was just a kid and he got to be taking part in one of Mr Maggs's most dramatic projects yet . . . for not only was the surgery itself so remarkable but having a version of Lionel Lyons up and about was of vital importance too. This man was crucial to Mr Maggs's future. The master had plans and these plans required massive funding; funding which L. Lyons Esquire could supply.

Mulch stared through the glass, wishing that there was some way to prove his worth to Mr Maggs. He so wanted his respect.

The operation complete, Lionel-Lyons-with-someone-else's-brain (or should that be someone-else's-brain-with-Lionel-Lyons's-body because, after all, it's the brain that does the thinking and it's the thinking part of you that *mostly* makes you who you are) was wheeled into the 'recuperation room' just off the operating theatre, and wired up to a number of monitors that would set off various alarms around the crumbling Fishbone Hall should the patient's 'vital signs' – whatever they might be – become dangerously abnormal.

Exhausted from his work, Mr Maggs and his teddy went for a sleep in the enormous four-poster bed in his bedroom, or 'bed chamber' as he preferred to call it. Like the desk in his study, much of this massive bed was overgrown with ivy. It was fortunate that the bed had a canopy because, again like his study, part of the room was open to the elements and the rain came pouring in.

Mr Maggs lay on his back staring up at the canopy, his teddy clasped to his chest, face up. Despite his tiredness he couldn't sleep; there was such a mixture of excitement, triumph and the fear that things may still not succeed. If this reanimation worked . . . if he could pass off the once-dead Lionel Lyons as an alive and kicking 'I've-never-felt-so-good' Lionel Lyons, then Phase II of his plan could come into effect. He would be able to implement his *Manifesto of Change* . . . and the world wouldn't know what had hit it.

As his master lay in his bed, thinking of the future, Mulch struggled on with his raincoat and dashed out to his van the colour of English mustard. He pulled out the choke, put his foot on the clutch and turned the key in the ignition. The engine was cold and wet, and it took a number of false starts before the little van's engine spluttered to life. He released the handbrake and the car lurched forward.

No sooner had he started off down the drive than the rain seemed to get much worse. The windscreen wipers were fighting a losing battle and Mulch could see next to nothing. He wasn't too bothered, just so long as he could stay on the path that led to one of the gates out of there. It wasn't as if this was a public road and he was in danger of hitting another vehicle or human being. There were no other people crazy enough to set foot in Fishbone Forest except for Mr Maggs and Toby. No, scratch that. That should, of course, just be Toby. Mr Maggs didn't quite meet all the criteria to fit in the 'people' category.

*

Wanda de Vere was upset to say the least. Bumbo had gone missing. Bumbo may seem a slightly strange name for a dog – even a bumbling one – but, as anyone who takes the time to read the dogs' names carved on the tombstones in Wandaland's dog cemetery will know, for some reason, Wanda gave all her dogs names ending in the letter 'o'. You may recall that, for example, the dog Wanda had with her at the ticket booth back on page 36 was called Nimmo. In fact, Nimmo was a replacement for Bumbo, who has only just gone missing in this strand of the story. In other words, he came *after* Bumbo in the whole scheme of things but got mentioned *before* him. How and why? Remind me to explain it all a little later on.

When Wanda spoke to the doorman and concierge at her building, they assured her that they hadn't seen the dog slip out on its own, and they were both sure that at least one of them would have noticed because the hallway was never left unattended.

'But what if your back was turned and he slipped out behind another tenant who'd opened the door for himself?' she asked the concierge.

'I've worked here for seventeen years, Mrs de Vere,' he said, respectfully, 'and in all that time, I've only ever seen one person open the door for him or herself, and that's you.'

Wanda lived in a very expensive apartment block occupied by very rich people who weren't used to doing things for themselves. The richest people in the country generally had homes in the capital (where The Dell hotel was located, from which Fergal fell from the window) but quite a few lived in the McNallys home town. This was because it was once a busy river port and many families had made their fortunes from shipping and import and export in the eighteenth and nineteenth centuries.

People from such families, such as those in Wanda de Vere's building, had cooks to cook for them, housekeepers to keep house for them, butlers to butler or butle for them (both terms are correct and I, personally, prefer 'butle', not that I have a butler) along with a whole host of general servants to generally serve them. Some of them even had people to help them dress in the morning. About the only thing they did all on their own, in addition to going to the toilet, of course, was to blow their own noses. The reason for this was because, no matter how rich and lazy you are, you don't want to be reminded of the time your mum took a hanky out of her handbag and, in front of all your friends when you were trying to act cool, pressed it up against your nose and said 'blow'. Wanda had to admit that she couldn't imagine any of them actually *opening the door* for themselves.

'But what about the tradespersons' entrance?' she asked the doorman. That was the entrance and exit at the back of the building, used by anyone who wasn't actually a tenant or accompanying a tenant. (In other words, your butler could use the front entrance if he was with you but not on his own.) There was no doorman or concierge there, just a security guard ready to sign for packages delivered by post/mail/courier and to make sure no 'undesirable' came in to shelter from the rain, or to find some shade, or to be a general nuisance or steal something. People were coming in and out of those doors all the time.

'If your dog somehow got out of your apartment and down to the ground floor, Mrs de Vere, then there is the possibility that it got out of the tradespeople's entrance, I grant you,' he said. 'But I'm sure someone would have noticed. This is a no-pets building. A dog on the loose would be something out of the ordinary. Everybody would notice.'

The concierge then checked with the security guard sitting behind a small desk at the tradespersons' entrance. 'Sure I saw a dog,' said the security guard. His name was Jimmy Spleen and it was his first week on the job. The usual security guard was off sick. 'I don't know how it got in here in the first place but I had it out of that door and out on the street before anyone could shout blue murder.'

He saw the look of horror on the concierge's face.

'I know how strict they are about the no-pets rule here,' he added. 'Did I do something wrong?'

'No, Jimmy,' said the concierge, kindly. It wasn't the young security guard's fault. But what was he going to tell Mrs de Vere?

★

Mulch took the corner too fast in the wet and the little van slew across the track in a spray of mud. Steering into the skid and then out again, he kept in control of the vehicle and out of the trees, and was feeling relieved . . . until, seconds later, he hit something with a terrible THUD.

Mulch stopped the van and clambered out into the pouring rain and looked back down the track. He could make out a mound of wet fur in the roadway. He hurried back to it.

He'd knocked down a dog.

Mulch let out a groan of despair. He loved animals. He carefully lifted up the whimpering dog in his arms and carried him to the van. Laying the injured animal on the passenger seat, he found a place to turn the van round and headed back to the crumbling mansion as fast as he dared drive in the wet.

Chapter Six

'Can you sit up?' Mr Maggs asked 'the patient', as he chose to call Lionel Lyons's body with the new brain.

The patient opened his eyes and stared up at the strange-looking being who'd performed the operation. He smiled. '*Bonjour, mes amis, comment ça va?*' he said, his voice croaky (no doubt as a result of his vocal cords being frozen and unused for some time).

'It worked, master!' Toby whooped with delight. 'You're a genius!' He did a little victory lap around the bed in the recuperation room. It wasn't up to Twinkle-Toes Tweedy's standards, but it was nice to see none the less. 'This is incredible . . . I'm a part of history in the making.'

Mr Maggs gave Toby one of his dagger-in-the-eyes stares. 'Did you ever doubt me?' he demanded.

'N-N-No, of course not, Mr Maggs,' said Toby. 'You're the man! The . . . er . . .' He couldn't come up with the right word, so quickly switched to: 'You're amazing!'

'This is just the beginning,' Mr Maggs whispered, almost glowing with obvious pride. 'But what's he saying?'

'Je m'apelle Jean. Est-ce que vous voulez sortir avec moi?' The patient looked around.

'The man is babbling like an idiot!' Mr Maggs roared. The fleeting sense of achievement had quickly turned to rage and incomprehension. 'And will you stand still?'

'Sorry,' said Toby, stopping in his tracks. 'But it's early days, master, and you've achieved the impossible. The successful reanimation of a human being . . . Genius, Mr Maggs! Genius!'

'Ma mere n'est pas à la maison . . .' said the patient, still smiling, but looking less sure of himself now.

'What's he saying?' Mr Maggs demanded.

'How should I know?' asked Toby, leaning over the patient. 'I think he might be French.'

'WHAT???' bellowed Mr Maggs.

'You know, French. From France.'

'I know what French is, you fool,' said Mr Maggs. 'But *why*?'

'Don't look at me, master,' said a more nervous

Toby. 'Mulch said your Cousin Ralphie sent you his brain. Was your cousin French?'

'It wasn't his *own* brain, you idiot! It was a brain my Cousin Ralphie had . . . had *acquired*. But why would he provide me with a French brain?'

'How should I know?' Toby said once again, this time with an actual shrug. 'Can you tell the nationality of a brain just by looking at it?'

Mr Maggs pushed the teenager to one side and leant right over the patient. 'C-a-n y-o-u s-p-e-a-k E-n-g-l-i-s-h?' he asked very slowly and clearly, as though talking to an idiot.

'*Je crois vous ne m'avez pas rendu juste.*' The patient frowned. He sat up suddenly – almost hitting Mr Maggs's head with his own – and swung his legs over the edge of the bed. Then he seemed to notice his hands for the first time, and held them up, as if to study them, with a mixture of surprise and fascination. '*Plume de ma tante!*' he gasped.

'His co-ordination seems excellent!' said Toby, clearly impressed by the way the patient had sat up and swivelled so abruptly. Mr Maggs had instructed him to make observations of the man's behaviour.

'Great,' said Mr Maggs, as though 'great' was the last thing he was feeling. 'I have a well-co-ordinated patient who has to pretend to be Lionel

Lyons in the next few days, and he doesn't even understand English! Marvellous!' He punched the pillow on the bed. A single feather fluttered free. 'Wonderful!' He made that last word sound about as wonderful as Wandaland.

'Perhaps it's the medication you gave him? The drugs?' Toby suggested, doubtfully. 'You said that they, as well as the operation itself, might cause confusion, lack of co-ordination and depression even . . .' Soothing the master was an important role in his duties around Fishbone Hall. Being around an unhappy Mr Maggs was not a pleasant experience.

'Why would the drugs make him speak French, you BUFFOON?' wailed Mr Maggs. 'Do you think they were made in France? Do you think that could have made any difference?'

Toby was about to say 'How should I know?' for the third time, when he thought better of it. 'You're the genius, Mr Maggs, not me,' he pointed out.

Mr Maggs clutched his teddy bear to him and gave him an extra loving squeeze. 'I don't need to be reminded of that,' he said.

The patient stood up, took two unsteady paces and then fell to the floor on his back, his legs still 'walking' in mid-air. 'No sniggering at the back!' he snapped. 'And open your text books on page twenty-two.'

72

Mr Maggs looked at Toby and Toby looked at Mr Maggs. They both smiled as realisation dawned.

'Start translating from line eight, Jones,' said the patient, still pumping his legs back and forth, 'beginning with *Madame Mustard est malade*.'

'He's not French!' said Toby.

'He's a French *teacher*,' said he and Mr Maggs and Toby together.

Things were looking up.

Now it's time to take a short pause to take stock of what exactly happened when, as this latest unlikely exploit unfolded, because I don't want anyone getting all confused and then blaming me; especially when the McNallys and the occupants of Fishbone Manor are about to meet.

Stefan Multachan – Mulch to you and me – stole the Fergal-brain-in-a-jar and arrived at Fishbone Forest on the day that Fergal died, with the reanimation of Lionel Lyons's body and the French teacher's brain happening soon after ...

... but much of what the McNallys have been up to didn't happen until after Fergal's funeral, a week or so later, in fact. So now that we're getting close to the part where Jackie, Albie, Josh and Le Fay finally come face-to-face with Mr Maggs, Toby and Mulch, don't forget that a good number of days must have passed since the patient sat up and started babbling away in

French. It doesn't help that it rained non-stop throughout this story so it's hard to tell one dull wet day from another.

Now, I'm fully aware that you could have worked this out for yourselves, and some of you probably already have, without really even thinking about it, but I want to make things nice and straightforward for you. There's no need to thank me. It's what I'm here for.

The walk from the McNally house to the north gate of Fishbone Forest wasn't a short one at the best of times but, in the pouring rain, seemed to take for ever. It would have taken about an hour on the bus but there was no way the McNallys could afford the fares. Instead they went by what their family called 'Shank's pony', which is another way of saying 'their own two feet'. It's interesting how you can make the most mundane thing sound more interesting, just by giving it a different name. Simon's parents, Doug and Lenny, called water 'Adam's Ale' (it being about the only thing they ever drank, apart from juice squeezed from old fruit), which made it sound extra cool and refreshing.

Living, as they did, in an old greenhouse, they got their Adam's Ale from a collection of old water butts. When the torrential rain started, they were glad because it meant that they'd be sure of a good supply later in the year, when there might be no rain at all. After a week, though, with all the water butts full and the greenhouse beginning to spring leaks in yet more places, like everyone else, they wished that it would stop.

The greenhouse was near the north gate of Fishbone Forest and it was here that Jackie, Le Fay and the twins were heading.

Wet and tired from their walk, they finally made it. Le Fay knocked on the door, which had soggy bits of wood and cardboard filling the frames where panes of glass had long since been broken and gone.

It was Simon who opened it. He was alone.

'Hi,' he said, clearly pleased and surprised. 'Come on in out of the wet.'

He and his parents had obviously done the best they could to make the old greenhouse into a home, using things they'd found – many of which other people had thrown away – or, on rare occasions, had been given.

The greenhouse had been divided into various different 'rooms' with 'walls' made from strung-up blankets and curtains and, in one instance, from the wood of old fruit crates from the market nailed to a frame.

There were shelves made from proper planks of wood, separated by bricks, one on top of the other, and a table made from what looked like a giant cotton reel – but had once had telegraph wire coiled around it – lying on its side. There were two old wooden chairs and an old armchair Simon's mum, Lenny, had found in a skip the previous summer and had dragged all the way across town.

'It's very cosy here,' said Jackie politely, once they'd taken off their coats. Simon insisted that she sit in the armchair because she was the grown-up. She'd never been to his home before because he'd been more a friend of Le Fay's and Fergal's.

'I could make a fire to dry you off if you like,' said Simon. His father had made a wood-burning stove out of an old oil drum, which he'd cut a door into (so they could put wood inside) with a length of metal drainpipe as a chimney (disappearing through a hole in the greenhouse roof).

Jackie knew how precious fuel must be and was quick to say, 'No thank you.'

'We'll be going out again soon,' she added. 'We need your help.'

'Sure,' grinned Simon. 'What with?'

'We want to get into the forest,' said Le Fay.

The corners of Simon's mouth dropped so quickly you'd never have guessed that a smile had been there in the first place. 'I'm not going in there,' he said.

'We're not asking you to,' said Albie.

'*We're* the ones who have to get in,' said Josh.

'You guys are crazy,' said Simon. 'No one goes into the forest.'

'Are you telling me that you've never been inside? Not even just a few feet to collect firewood?' asked Le Fay. 'It'd be a great place to collect wood, and it's right on your doorstep.'

Simon shook his head. 'No way,' he said.

Everyone in the town had tales to tell about Fishbone Forest and the nearer people lived to the place the more people seemed to be frightened of it. They ranged from stories about hearing strange cries at night or seeing strange coloured lights in the sky above it, to the tale of a group of teenagers who'd been foolish enough to climb over the railings for a dare and only two or three of them were ever seen again, found wandering the streets foaming at the mouth and ranting like madmen. The story went that these 'survivors' were hidden away in some lunatic asylum somewhere and that the authorities had tried to hush the whole thing up.

One story which definitely was true was that a man had once tried to set fire to the forest by tossing a can of petrol, with a flaming rag in the end, over the railings. The fire was mysteriously put out and, two nights later, the man's own house was burnt to the ground. Fortunately, he hadn't been in it at the time. He moved to a different area. (The 'putting out' had been down to Mulch. The revenge fire had been one of the jobs Mr Maggs had entrusted to Toby because he'd been worried that Mulch would mess it up. The instructions had been to 'teach the man a lesson' . . . but 'no injuries'. How charmingly considerate.)

Jackie looked straight at Simon. 'You have been inside, though, haven't you?' she said. 'We're definitely going in, with or without your help, but if you can tell us how to get in without us having to climb up and over the railings, we'd really appreciate it.'

'It'd save us slipping in the wet and stabbing

ourselves on one of the spikes,' said Josh.

'Impaling,' said Le Fay. 'That's what people do on spiked railings, they get impaled.'

'Like Vlad the Impaler who deliberately spiked people –' said Josh.

'I get the picture,' said Simon. 'But why do you have to get into the forest?'

'We –' began Albie.

'– can't –' said Josh.

'– tell you –' added Le Fay.

'– that,' finished Jackie. 'It's family business, Simon. You understand.'

'Very important, but very private,' said Le Fay.

'I understand,' said Simon. Sometimes it's best not to ask such things. 'There's a break in the railings where a truck hit them a few years back. It's only small and low down so you'll have to crawl through,' he explained. 'The others should fit through no problem, but you might be a bit too big,' he told Jackie.

'Don't worry about me,' said Jackie. 'I'll find a way.'

'Have you been through the gap?' asked Le Fay.

'Only once,' said Simon, 'and don't you dare ever tell Mum or Dad.'

'We won't,' Le Fay promised.

'I heard what sounded like an animal in pain – a badger or something – and crawled inside to see if I could find it and help it . . . I was only in there a few minutes but found nothing but trees. It was scary.'

'I'll bet,' said Jackie. 'Will you tell us where this gap is?'

'I'll show you,' said Simon.

'We need to go now,' said Le Fay.

'Then let's go,' said Simon. He disappeared behind one of the curtain walls and reappeared wearing a home-made cape around his neck, made from an old piece of tarpaulin. His mum, Lenny, had made it for him to keep the rain off.

Le Fay picked up the duffel bag she'd put at her feet. 'I almost forgot,' she said. 'We meant to give you these after the funeral.' She opened the bag and pulled out a few clothes, including a raincoat. 'They were Fergal's,' she said.

To most of us, these clothes would probably have seemed too worn and tatty to give to a charity shop or to a jumble sale, but these had been some of Fergal's best clothes (not that he'd been the first to wear them by any means) and they were far better than anything Simon was wearing.

Simon accepted the pile and put them on the table before holding up the raincoat. 'Are you sure you don't want them?' he asked.

'Fergal doesn't need them any more,' said Le Fay.

'No . . .' said Simon. 'I suppose not.' He took off his tarpaulin cape and put on Fergal's raincoat. 'I've never had a coat before,' he said. He did up the belt. 'Thank you,' he said. He couldn't have been happier if someone had given him a brand-new one with a designer label and a buckle made of solid gold. 'Thank you very much.'

He gave Le Fay a hug.

Le Fay never considered the McNallys to be poor because she considered Simon and *his* family to be poor. Little did she know that Simon didn't consider himself to be badly off either because he had two parents who loved him and *he* knew people who didn't even have a roof over their heads.

It's at times like these I like to remind myself how lucky I am. I think I'll just nip downstairs and tell the cats how much I love them.

(I'm back. I met my wife on the stairs, so I thought I might as well tell her how much I love her too. Now, where exactly was I?)

Simon and the McNally children set off in the rain and followed the railings around the edge of the forest until Simon came to a stop.

'Here,' he said, crouching down and parting the branches of a bush growing through the railings at waist level. He revealed a spot where, sure enough, the railings had buckled, making a gap wide enough for all of them but Jackie in her current form to fit through.

'Thanks,' said Le Fay.

'How are you going to find your way back once you've done whatever it is you have to do?' asked Simon, watching the raindrops being repelled by the waterproof material of his new (to him) raincoat.

'We've thought of that,' said Albie.

'It was our idea,' said Josh.

'Together,' said Albie.

'We got it from a book full of myths and legends. It had lots of weird stuff in it,' said Josh.

'Like people hiding in a large hollow wooden –'

'Cow called Marjorie?' asked Simon, who'd once found a discarded paperback book with a weird hollow cow in it.

'Horse,' said Albie. 'A large hollow wooden horse.'

'The Trojan horse,' said Josh. 'Full of Trojan soldiers.'

'Greek soldiers, actually,' said Le Fay.

'And there was a story about a beast named the Minotaur who was half man –' began Albie.

'– and half bull,' said Josh.

'He lived in a big maze –'

'– called the Labyrinth.'

'Get to the point, boys,' Jackie insisted. 'There's a job to be done.'

Albie and Josh combined glares to give her one big one. 'In the legend, the hero finds his way to the middle of the maze, where the beast is, with a magic ball of string which unrolls in front of him, leading him straight to the creature's lair. Then he follows the unwound string back through the maze to the entrance, and escapes.'

Josh put his hand in the duffel bag and pulled out the biggest ball of string Simon had ever seen. It wasn't made up of one long piece but of lots of different pieces of different lengths, thickness and colours – from fat, brown, hairy and made from hemp to thin, blue, smooth and made from nylon – all knotted together.

The McNallys had been collecting string for years. You never know when such things might come in handy. Like then, for example.

'This will help us find our way back here –' said Albie.

'– if we tie one end to the railings and unravel it as we go,' said Le Fay, getting a word in before Josh had a chance to finish his twin's sentence for him.

The rain was getting even harder now. 'It really is time we went in there,' said Jackie.

Simon was eyeing the small break in the railings. 'I still can't see how you're going to get through, Jackie,' he said.

'Don't worry about me,' Jackie grinned. 'I'm quite a contortionist. Now you'd better head back home and leave us to it.'

Le Fay gave Simon a hug. The twins said thanks.

'Thanks again for the raincoat,' said Simon, turning to go. He paused. He looked as though he was torn between a reluctance to leave the McNallys to their secret mission and a desire to put a significant distance between himself and Fishbone Forest.

'Go!' said Jackie.

He went.

When he was gone, Jackie looked around to

make sure no one else was watching, and then quickly turned into a jackal. Even if you've seen that kind of thing on films and TV, done with computer special effects, it's nothing like seeing it happen in real life: the skeleton beneath the flesh changing shape and the smooth human skin turning to a hairy jackal's pelt.

There was the funny side too. Because she was in a potentially public place, Jackie had kept her clothes on during her transformation . . . and human clothes don't fit a jackal too well! Le Fay and the twins quickly pulled them off her, once she'd transformed, and stuffed them in the duffel bag.

Now all four McNallys were ready to slip into Fishbone Forest, in the search for Fergal's brain.

Chapter Seven

I want you to put yourselves in the McNallys'
shoes for a moment. Not literally, of course,
particularly when Jackie wasn't wearing any on her
four paws. (Her shoes were in the duffel bag, left
by the railing with the string tied to it, marking
their exit.) No, what I mean is that I want you to
imagine yourselves in Jackie, Le Fay, Albie and
Josh's position. They've just snuck inside Fishbone
Forest in search of a missing brain, not knowing
what might lie ahead . . . and, after making their
way through the trees for a while, with not even
the slightest hint of what lay around the next
corner, do you know what they saw?

Go on. Guess.

No, seriously. Have a guess.

Fishbone Hall?

No.

The ivy-choked statues and slimy green pond?

No. Have another guess.

Mr Maggs and his big teddy?

No.

Jackie, Le Fay, Joshua and Albion had gone in search of a missing brain and there, standing on the path in front of them, stood a small man WITH A BRAIN IN A JAR.

It felt like going on a treasure hunt on a desert island and finding the treasure not half an hour from the shore: not much of an adventure, but fantastic news if it's a chest full of gold coins you're after rather than hours of action-packed excitement.

The McNallys eyed Mulch through the pouring rain. Mulch eyed the McNallys. It's hard to say who was more surprised.

No one ever dared venture into Fishbone Forest, yet here were three children – two of whom looked almost identical – and the weirdest dog Mulch had ever seen (having never seen a jackal).

A dog! That was it. A thought flashed through Mulch's mind. These children must be looking for the dog that had strayed into the forest a week or so previously. The one he'd knocked down. Poor mutt . . . poor kids. Only a hunt for a missing pet would make anyone in their right mind venture within the walls of this dreadful forest. And even then they'd have to be terribly brave or terribly stupid. He must get them out of the forest before Mr Maggs caught sight of them.

Jackie, Le Fay, Josh and Albie, meanwhile, were still recovering from the shock of coming face to face with what they took to be Fergal's brain in a jar. Of course it must be Fergal's brain, they reasoned. They were told by powerful forces that Fergal's brain was in the forest, so who else's was it likely to be? The place was unlikely to be full of people casually wandering around in the rain with stolen brains, now, wasn't it?

'GIVE THAT HERE!' said Le Fay, recovering from the shock and launching herself at the strange little man. Mulch pulled back, hugging the jar to his chest. Le Fay landed face down in a muddy puddle, with an 'Ooof!' She'd winded herself and the gritty soil stung her hands.

The kids wouldn't have bothered Mulch that much if it wasn't for that mangy dog they had with them. He looked at Jackie – although, of course, he didn't *know* that's who he was looking at – who was baring her teeth at him with an impressive snarl.

'Clear off!' he snapped. 'Didn't your mummy and daddy warn you about this place? Fishbone Forest is no place for children.'

'You have something that doesn't belong to you –' began Josh.

'– and we want it back,' said Albie.

I was right, thought Mulch. They've come for that dog I ran over.

'I won't tell you again,' said Mulch. 'Every second you're in here you're in danger. Now get out of it, for your own good.'

Jackie sunk her teeth into the bottom of Mulch's trouser leg. Mulch almost dropped the jar and everyone – including the hairy beast by his foot – held his or her breath as he fumbled to regain his grip. The lid rattled, the brain glooped, and there was the faintest whiff of pickling vinegar.

Jackie let go of his trouser leg.

'Now look what you nearly made me go and do!' Mulch whined. 'Control that beast!'

'Here, Jacks!' said Le Fay innocently, in a little-girl-calling-her-pet-dog voice. Her big sister played her part and bounded over to her side, but then quickly turned and fixed her jackal stare on the man with the brain. Le Fay was covered in mud from her fall. They all looked wet, but she looked wet *and* dirty.

Mulch decided to try another approach. 'Listen, kids,' he said, his tone more friendly. 'My boss is around here someplace and if he catches you here he'll be angry . . . and I guarantee that, if you knew him like I know him, you wouldn't want to make him angry.'

89

'Fine, said Le Fay, bravely stepping forward. 'Then give us the brain and we'll go.'

Mulch hadn't been expecting this. 'The *brain*?' he said. 'What do you want with a brain?'

'More to the point –' said Josh.

'– what do *you* want with a brain?' demanded Albie.

For some reason, Mulch looked flustered; guilty. 'I . . . er . . . That's none of your business,' he said.

Le Fay stepped forward, Jackie the jackal trotting alongside her on padded paws. 'Give us the brain and we'll go,' she repeated.

'I've had enough of this!' snapped Mulch.

The strange-looking dog – or was it a wolf or something, Mulch wondered – snarled.

Mulch made a decision. He didn't have time to argue and he didn't like the look of the kids' four-legged friend, whatever it was. He turned and ran.

Jackie and the twins set off in hot pursuit. Le Fay tried running but gasped at a pain in her side. She must have hurt a rib or two when she fell. Albie turned to see if she was all right.

'I'm okay!' she shouted. 'Go after him!'

Baaaaaaaad move.

With the others disappearing between the hideous leafless trees, Le Fay now found herself alone in the forest.

Le Fay had always been more sensible than the

twins. Rather than get lost, she would make her way straight back to the gap in the railings and wait there. After all, they might need to make a very speedy exit.

Whether the others caught up with the little man and managed to save the brain or not, they'd eventually find their way back to the exit, string or no string to guide them. Jackie had the senses of a jackal. Even if they split up, Jackie was familiar with their scent and would not only be able to sniff them out and round them all up but also to pick up the trail of their scent all the way back to where they'd got in. If it wasn't for the rain, that is. Rain could wash away the scent and then where would they be? The string was an important backup.

Le Fay hurried back down the path, dodging the bigger puddles, looking for the spot where she'd dropped the ball of string. Her ribs were really beginning to hurt now. She found the ball at the edge of a particularly deep puddle. Head down, she began to follow the already unwound pieces of knotted string that would lead her back to the exit.

'You're far from home, little one,' said a voice in the gloom.

Le Fay looked up and gasped at the most extraordinary apparition standing before her.

There was a flash of sheet lightning and, silhouetted against the trees, stood a man – at least, she assumed it was a man – clutching a huge teddy bear in one hand and a plastic orange tulip (which he appeared to be sniffing) in the other. On top of his pumpkin-shaped head was a hat-cum-umbrella. 'I'm Mr Maggs,' he said softly, smiling a shark's teeth smile. 'What brings you to my neck of the woods? This is private property. *Very* private property. You're trespassing on the Lyons family estate – well *my* estate now, actually – little girl.'

'I'm sorry, sir,' said Le Fay ever so politely as her brain worked overtime to come up with an excuse for being in Fishbone Forest.

'Mr Maggs.'

'I beg your pardon?' asked Le Fay.

'Call me Mr Maggs.'

'I'm sorry, *Mr Maggs*,' said Le Fay. 'My dog got off its leash and through a gap in your railings. He must be in here somewhere.'

'And the other two?' said Mr Maggs, bending down to Le Fay's height. She gave an involuntary shudder. There was something other-worldly and creepy about this newcomer.

'Oh, the twins, you mean?' said Le Fay, realising that Mr Maggs must have spotted them all at some stage, and that a lie involving Albie, Josh and Jackie – and so as near to the truth as possible – was one she was more likely to carry off without slipping up. 'They're my brothers. They've gone off looking for Jackie.'

'Jackie being your dog that got off its leash?' said Mr Maggs.

'Exactly, Mr Maggs,' said Le Fay breezily, trying to make out that she had nothing to hide.

One of the things which was bothering her about Mr Maggs, quite apart from his appearance and the teddy *and* the plastic flower, of course, was that he wasn't behaving like a grown-up. In

93

this situation, a normal grown-up might have threatened her with telling her parents or the police, or demand to know what she was up to, or might ask her how she got muddy, or tell her that she'd catch her death of cold in her soaking clothes.

'A strange doggie, that,' said Mr Maggs. 'I caught a glimpse of it a moment ago when I came around the corner. It looked more like a jackal to me.'

'It's an all-sorts dog,' said Le Fay. 'A mongrel. We got it from the Dillington Street Shelter.' The rain was pouring into her face. Her hair was plastered flat against her head, making it look like it had been drawn on her skin with thick black felt-tip pen.

Mr Maggs ignored her lies, and she felt sure that he could tell they were just that. 'Did you know that in folklore, all over the world, the jackal is associated with the Devil. It is thought of as an *evil* beast.'

Le Fay most certainly did know. When you had a sister who turned into a jackal you found out as much about jackals as you could. Jackals did seem to have a nasty reputation but Jackie had assured her that it was all bunkum and that she never had evil thoughts, even when she was in her jackal form.

'I think that's a load of superstitious nonsense,'

said Le Fay. 'Anyway, I don't believe in the Devil.'

Mr Maggs grinned at her, his face nicely dry under his umbrella hat. 'But what if the Devil believes in you?' he asked.

Le Fay was flummoxed by that. 'Are you going to throw me out or let me help my brothers look for my dog?' she said. 'Either way, I need to shelter from the rain.'

'Which is why you're coming back to the house with me.'

'The house?' asked Le Fay.

'There's a house here in the forest. It was built by the Lyons family. The Lyons were also the ones who planted this forest.'

'Oh . . . I didn't know that,' said Le Fay.

'Well, that's where we're going,' he said. 'It'll take a while.'

'I don't think so,' said Le Fay. 'My father said that I'm not to talk to strangers.'

She felt Mr Maggs grip her arm. 'I'm not *asking* you,' he said. There was an air of menace in his voice for the first time. 'That's where we're going.'

Despite all that wet everywhere, Le Fay's mouth went dry. 'Okay,' she said in a tiny voice.

When they finally reached and entered Fishbone Hall, after a soaking walk amongst the dreadful trees, Toby gave Le Fay an old blue towelling dressing-gown to wear and a towel to dry her hair.

Mr Maggs had said something about having some business to attend to and then left the two of them alone.

'Thank you,' said Le Fay, rubbing her hair with the towel. She stood by an old-fashioned wood-burning stove and looked around the room. A large hole in the ceiling gave her a glimpse into a bedroom above. A hole in the outer wall looked out on to the skeletal trees. 'You live in this ruin?' she asked.

'Sure,' said Toby. 'My room's pretty dry in all weathers.'

'Is Mr Maggs a relative, or something?'

Toby laughed. 'No way. He's the boss . . . or the *master* as he likes to be called.'

'That makes it sound like he owns you,' said Le Fay. She hung the towel around her neck, like a boxer entering the ring, and held her hands in front of the stove. Her ribs still hurt when she moved.

'You should get out of those wet things,' said Toby. 'You're shivering.'

'Well, would you mind leaving the room while I change?' asked Le Fay. 'It's the polite thing to do.'

Toby shook his head. 'Sorry,' he said. 'No can do. I'm not allowed to leave you alone.'

'I'm a prisoner?'

Toby avoided eye contact. He busied himself by

picking up a CD from a small stack of them on a table (which had ivy growing up its legs) and slotting it into the Discman clipped to his belt. 'Mr Maggs would say that you're a guest, but I suppose you are . . . a prisoner, I mean.'

'Then turn around,' said Le Fay.

Toby turned away from her and Le Fay stepped behind a free-standing bookcase for extra cover and slipped out of her wet clothes and into the blue towelling dressing-gown. She also slipped a large glass paperweight into the dressing-gown pocket.

Toby was bigger than her and Mr Maggs was MUCH bigger than her, and she'd never tried hitting anyone with anything, but she felt that tiny bit safer having a weapon of sorts . . . should the time come when she needed one.

Le Fay hung her clothes on the back of a broken wooden chair which she placed in front of the stove. 'You'd better find a way to get me out of here or you're going to wind up in big trouble too,' she said matter-of-factly.

'What do you mean?' asked Toby.

'I mean my dad's a war hero and his best friend is a detective called Charlie Tweedy who is one of the most famous policemen in the country . . .'

'So?' asked Toby, looking unimpressed.

'So when I don't show up at home later on, they're going to come looking for me in the forest and when they find you and Mr Maggs have kidnapped me, you're going to be in big trouble.'

'Somehow I don't think your father and his cop friend know that you're in Fishbone Forest,' sneered Toby. Suddenly he looked a lot less friendly to Le Fay. 'This is just the kind of place that policemen warn little kids away from.'

That had, of course, been the main fault in Le Fay's lie. The fact that Le Fay's father had a wooden leg and that Charlie Tweedy had long

98

since retired from the police force – sorry, service – had been easily glossed over. 'Are you prepared to take that chance?' she challenged.

Toby walked right up to Le Fay, who was standing by an old oval table with a chipped milk jug on it, being used as a vase. It was filled with a bunch of different coloured plastic tulips, like the one Mr Maggs had been carrying outside. She pulled out a yellow flower and twirled the green plastic-coated wire stem between her fingers. 'However much of a fighting man your dad is, and however tough a cop Tweedy is, I'd rather take them on rather than Mr Maggs any day,' he said.

'Has he ever hurt you?' asked Le Fay.

'Me, hurt Toby?' said Mr Maggs, who was suddenly standing at Le Fay's shoulder. Neither Toby nor Le Fay had seen or heard him enter the room. Le Fay jolted with surprise. 'I'm a big pussycat.' He pulled the plastic flower from Le Fay's grasp. 'What do a mad man, a poor man and plastic tulips like these have in common?' he asked, that extraordinary grin of his spreading across his face.

'I-I – er – pardon?' said Le Fay.

'It's one of the master's riddles,' Toby explained. 'He likes a good riddle, now that things have turned out so well.'

'I do indeed,' said Mr Maggs.

'All I want is to find Jackie and my brothers and get out of here,' said Le Fay, digging her hands into the pockets of her borrowed dressing-gown and clutching the hidden glass paperweight for comfort.

'It's what *I* want that matters right now,' said Mr Maggs, tremblings of rage in his voice. 'A mad man, a poor man and plastic tulips such as these . . . I'll give you a clue.' He thrust the fake flower into Le Fay's face. 'Sniff.'

Le Fay was wise enough not to argue. She sniffed. 'I can't smell anything,' she said.

'Exactly,' beamed Mr Maggs.

'It's plastic. It has no scent.'

'Exactly,' Mr Maggs repeated.

'I know! I know!' said Toby excitedly.

'Of course you know, you idiot. I've told you the answer before. But can this one work it out for herself, all on her own?'

'It's a pun!' said Le Fay, strangely pleased that she'd just guessed the answer, despite the circumstances. 'Plastic flowers like these have no scents . . . a poor man has no cents . . .'

'And the MAD MAN?'

'Has no *sense*.'

'Splendid,' said Mr Maggs. Then he sighed. 'What a pity you're the enemy.' Le Fay looked into his eyes. He actually looked sad.

'I'm not your enemy,' Le Fay insisted. 'I'm a kid looking for a dog that got off its leash, that's all . . .'

'If only that were true.'

A moment later the door opened and in marched Albie, Josh and Jackie (back in her human form), followed by Mulch. They dripped water on to the stone-flagged floor.

'Aaaaaaaaaah!' said Mr Maggs, kissing his teddy on the nose. 'The more the merrier!

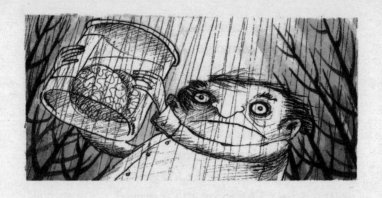

Chapter Eight

Mulch might not have been the brightest person in the world, let alone in Fishbone Forest that day, but, as he ran through the mud and trees in the pouring rain, a thought occurred to him. The almost identical twins, with their fierce-looking dog, seemed to care a great deal about the brain in the jar of pickling vinegar so, rather than running, he would issue them with an ultimatum. Which is why he finally stopped running.

Jackie the jackal bounded forward.

'Call the dog off or I smash the jar here and now!' Mulch commanded.

Albie looked at Josh. Josh looked at Albie. They knew that big sister Jackie would make that decision, but they couldn't tell the man that.

'Here –'

'– Jackie,' they commanded, waiting to see how Jackie might respond.

She obviously took Mulch's threat seriously, because she trotted back to their side.

'Good!' said Mulch, trying to sound as tough as possible. 'Now I want you out of here NOW, or I destroy this brain you seem so interested in.'

'You can't do that,' said Josh.

'Please,' said Albie.

'You're weird, you know that? It ain't healthy two young kids being interested in brains and the like . . . You've put yourself in grave danger.'

On the word 'danger' Jackie dashed off into the trees, her tail held high.

'Jackie!' cried the twins as one. Surely she wasn't going to leave them alone with this strange man? Or had she suddenly got worried about them having left Le Fay on her own?

'I did warn you,' said Mulch. 'But now I'm going to have to let the master decide what we do with you.'

'The master?' asked Albie.

'Is there a school around here or something?' asked Josh. Come to think of it, the man with the jar did remind him a little bit of the caretaker at their school.

'Wait and see,' said Mulch. 'He might even let you keep the brain . . . But, remember, one false move from either of you and I flatten it like an over-cooked cauliflower.'

The boys reluctantly began to follow Mulch. After about ten minutes, Jackie stepped out in front of them, back in human form.

'Not another one of you!' groaned Mulch, for, although Jackie didn't have the same gappy teeth as Albie, Josh and Le Fay, there was no mistaking that she was a relative: her red hair and freckles instantly gave the game away. 'This place is getting busier than Houser Point!' (Which would be like a Londoner saying 'busier than Piccadilly Circus' or a New Yorker saying 'busier than Grand Central Station'.)

'What's going on?' asked Jackie, pretending, of course, that this was the first time she'd come face to face with Mulch rather than simply the first time she'd met him whilst she was in human form.

'You and the boys –' began Mulch.

'Joshua,' said Albie.

'Albion,' said Josh.

'All three of you are coming with me to the hall to meet the master and he'll decide what we're going to do. If you try anything funny, or that dog of yours comes within ten feet of me, I'm tipping this brain out of the jar.'

'We don't want any trouble,' said Jackie calmly. She'd gone back to the spot where they'd come through the railings, turned back into her original form and changed into her clothes from the duffel bag. She'd also found that Le Fay was missing, and that there was a faint scent of her and someone they hadn't run into yet. Someone who smelt very odd indeed. The big problem was the rain, though. It was washing away the scent trails, which meant that Jackie might get as lost as the rest of them . . . so she'd gone back to the twins.

And now all of them were in the relative dry of Fishbone Hall. And there was Le Fay, with the most extraordinary 'man' Jackie'd ever seen, and a goofy teenager in an XXL T-shirt that was much too big for him.

'Look what the Mulch dragged in,' Toby grinned.

★

Le Fay wasn't nearly as frightened now that they were all together, especially when they had one really great trick up their sleeve – a great secret weapon, if you like – and she wasn't thinking of the paperweight in her dressing-gown pocket. What Mr Maggs, Toby and the funny little man they called 'Mulch' didn't know was what Jackie could turn into. They not only outnumbered Mr Maggs and the others four to three, but one of them could become a vicious dog in seconds! If it wasn't for the fact that the McNallys had to get back Fergal's brain, they could probably escape from Fishbone Hall there and then, though getting out of the forest might be harder. Mr Maggs had the distinct advantage of knowing his territory.

Le Fay, Jackie, Albie and Josh sat side-by-side, in that order, on a large old sofa with lumpy cushions and horse-hair stuffing sprouting through worn patches in the arms and back.

Mr Maggs was pacing up and down in front of them, weaving between stone pillars, a roaring fire behind him. 'What am I to do with you?' he mused.

'Simple,' said Jackie. 'Lend us an umbrella and show us a way out of the forest.'

'What about your missing jackal? I beg your pardon . . . your missing *dog*?' asked Mr Maggs.

'All the better if you help us find her,' said Jackie, 'but after the way you've been behaving, I assumed the sooner we were off your property the better.'

Mr Maggs stopped pacing and looked at her. His enormous teddy, tucked under his arm, seemed to look at her too. 'My, you're good,' he said. 'Very clever. What's your name?'

'Sis,' Le Fay blurted out. 'She's called Sis!' She didn't want her sister calling herself 'Jackie' when that was the name she'd told Mr Maggs was the name of their missing dog.

'Hmmm,' hmmmed Mr Maggs.

'Nice place you've got here, Mr M,' said Albie hurriedly.

'Could do with patching up here and there,' said Josh.

'But with a bit of filler and a lick of paint it could be as right as –'

'– rain. Yours, is it?'

Mr Maggs suddenly looked very pleased with himself. 'Yes,' he nodded. He'd obviously been irritated by the twins' chirpy interlude but was now satisfied that the question had given him a chance to show off. 'Yes, it is mine. This forest, the house, and the huge fortune that goes with it has been in the Lyons family for years – *hundreds* of years – but Lionel Lyons was the last of the Lyons line and he died without issue.'

'Without what?' asked Le Fay.

'Without tissues,' said Joshua.

'No, not without tissues, without *issue*,' Mr Maggs corrected him. 'What I mean is that he had no son and heir. He had no one to leave this place to . . . no one to leave the family fortune to. No relative, that is.'

'He died without making a will,' said Mulch, who had been listening at a respectful distance whilst tending to the fire.

'And left everything to me,' beamed Mr Maggs.

Mulch put another log on the fire with a large pair of brass tongs.

'That doesn't make sense,' said Le Fay. 'One minute Mulch says that Lionel Lyons died without a will and the next minute you say that he left you everything.'

'Let's say that he put in a final appearance and made me his heir. It was an . . . an especially arranged appearance.'

Of course, what the McNallys didn't know was that Mr Maggs had deliberately befriended Lionel Lyons; that he had cultivated a friendship with the express purpose of convincing the tired and lonely eccentric old man, living in the middle of the forest, to leave the family fortune to him. And it had all been going so well until Lionel Lyons had simply died of old age when Mr Maggs had been treating him to an ice-cream one day.

What the McNallys didn't know was that Mr Maggs had needed Lionel Lyons alive to make him his heir to the fortune in front of witnesses and, most importantly, go with him to the law firm of Garland & Fudge – always written with a squiggly '&' sign like that, rather than written out a-n-d (which are called 'ampersands', by the way, although it wasn't a Mr Amper who invented them) – who had always dealt with Lyons family business.

What the McNallys didn't know was that Mr Maggs had, therefore, stored the late Lionel Lyons on ice until – after some years of trial and error and much planning – he'd developed a way of apparently 'bringing Lionel Lyons back to life' by placing a fresh brain in his lifeless body (well, *head*, actually), and that Mulch had stolen Fergal's brain for just that purpose, only to have it rejected by Mr Maggs, who settled for the brain of a school teacher (who taught French) provided by his Cousin Ralphie.

What the McNallys didn't know was that Mr Maggs's hare-brained scheme had worked. That, after much confusion and some coaching in his new role, his patient had played his part perfectly. In the eyes of the (hoodwinked) law Mr Maggs was now the rightful owner of Fishbone Forest, Fishbone Hall and, far more importantly to him, the Lyons millions.

'And, after this special final appearance, you somehow ended up with the Lyons fortune?' asked Jackie from the end of the sofa.

'I did.'

'So, if you're now so rich, why are you still living in this dump –'

'– this place?' asked the twins.

Mr Maggs perched himself on the arm of the sofa nearest to Josh and sat his teddy on his knee. 'The money is not to be spent on trivial things such as a roof over my head or fancy meals!' he said. 'I need the money for a far more important project . . . It is for a far higher purpose.'

'What –' said Albie.

'– purpose?' said Josh.

Le Fay thought of Fergal's brain in a jar and remembered the faint whiff of pickling vinegar. 'Yes, Mr Maggs,' asked Le Fay. 'What is it, exactly, that you want?'

Chapter Nine

'What is it, exactly, that I want?' roared Mr Maggs, a terrible grin spreading across his almost human features. He gave his bald teddy a special hug. This was the question he had been waiting for. This was the question he'd been building up to for years of his extraordinary life. 'What I want are *changes*,' he declared. 'Changes!'

As if to punctuate the point, he jumped up off the arm of the sofa and pushed against one of the huge ivy-clad pillars which crumbled and fell on to the cold stone floor in an impressive pile of dust.

'And you shall have them, master,' said Mulch and Toby in unison, like an official response in some bizarre religious ritual, only slightly spoilt by the odd cough and splutter caused by the clouds of pulverised masonry.

The pushing of the pillar had been an impressive

feat, but this was an old house, much of it without so much as a roof and much of it crumbling stone. Le Fay reckoned that if *she'd* pushed that pillar hard enough, she too could have reduced it to rubble. 'What kind of changes?' she demanded, fearing the worst. Le Fay wasn't familiar with the word 'megalomaniac' but, if she had been, she'd have probably used it to describe this *being* standing before them now, half in shadow.

Mr Maggs tucked his teddy under an arm and, with a claw-like hand, reached for a huge leather-bound book lying flat on a stone shelf. Pieces of paper of every conceivable shape and size were sticking out from between its pages, acting as markers: newspaper clippings, old bus tickets, folded paper bags, Post-it notes, torn strips of tissue paper, and even twisted foil once covering exciting chocolate mints. He opened the book just over halfway through, at a place marked by an old label soaked off a jar of marmalade.

'This is my *Manifesto of Change*,' he declared. 'These are my demands . . .' The NcNallys waited with fear in their hearts. What diabolical plan did he have for those around him . . . perhaps for humankind? 'Change Number One,' said Mr Maggs. 'The letter Q shall come later in the alphabet, to appear nearer X, Y and Z.'

There was a period of silence.

Jackie was stunned.

To be honest, she'd been expecting Mr Maggs's demands to be for a limitless supply of slave labour or control over four continents. 'Th-That sounds fair enough,' she said at last.

'Two. A biopic of my life will be made, in which I shall be played by Cary Grant,' said Mr Maggs, turning his face into the light, as though showing his best side to some non-existent camera.

'What's a biopic?' asked Joshua.

'Who's Cary Grant?' asked Albie.

'A biopic is a biographical picture,' said Le Fay. 'A film about someone's life.'

'And Cary Grant was a famous movie star,' explained Jackie. 'The only trouble is he died years ago, Mr Maggs.'

'Change Number Three,' Mr Maggs continued, ignoring them. 'Cary Grant is no longer dead.'

'Oh,' said Jackie. 'And number four?'

'That Christmas trees be drawn accurately on Christmas cards. They're nearly always drawn with the branches growing downwards from the trunk when, in real life, they grow up.'

'I'm not sure what you mean,' confessed Jackie. Mr Maggs turned round the book he was reading from so that she could take a look at an old Christmas card he'd stuck in it. The picture seemed to show a typical Christmas tree, in a snowy wood, its branches growing downwards.

'Does that look right to you?' he glowered, his blackest of black pupils glinting like a bird's in the strange light.

'Y-Yes, I think so,' said Jackie.

'Well, you thought wrong,' said Mr Maggs, and he flipped over the page to show a black and white photograph of a Christmas tree, torn from a newspaper and stuck into his book with old sticking plasters.

Jackie studied the photo. Mr Maggs was right. Whereas the branches in the photo sprouted up like a 'V', the ones in the drawing pointed down like a 'Λ' (whatever that's called). 'Wow!' she said, genuinely impressed. 'I never noticed that before. I wonder why people so often draw them incorrectly?'

'They won't when the master's changes are implemented,' said Mulch, proudly.

Mr Maggs turned back the book his way and turned the page again. 'Change Number Five,' he read. 'Salt and pepper shall no longer be known by the collective term 'cruet'.'

'Cruet?' said Albie. 'I've never heard it called that.' They didn't have salt and pepper pots or shakers back home anyway.

'Me neither,' said Josh.

Le Fay seemed miles away. She was still muttering something about 'Change Number Three.'

'You've never heard the term cruet?' asked Mr Maggs. They all – except Le Fay – shook their heads. 'O, lucky, lucky children!' he said, wiping a tear from his far-from-human eye with his teddy's paw. 'When my changes have been made, we will live in a world where no one will have to hear salt and pepper referred to in that way again.'

Albie leant across to Jackie and whispered in her ear. 'He's quite mad, you know, Jacks.'

Joshua leant across to his big sister and whispered: 'He's nuttier than a bag of nuts with extra nuts in, Jacks.'

Worried that Mr Maggs might overhear the twins' comments and become enraged and do something nasty, she loudly asked what Change Number Six would be.

'Ah,' said Mr Maggs with a contented smile, 'Sums will be easier. All numbers will become even, so that everything divides neatly into the other without complicated remainders and fractions and the like. Three will be an even number, so will seven, nine, eleven and so on . . .'

'But that's ridiculous,' said Le Fay, her mind back on the there and then (which was at the time, of course, the here and now). 'Just because you say something *is*, doesn't make it so!' The minute she said it, she regretted it, but she couldn't take it back.

Mr Maggs was trembling. He was most reminiscent of the early stages of an earthquake or of the initial rumblings of a volcano about to erupt, sending tremors across the stone flagged floor of Fishbone Hall. His teddy bear's floppy limbs trembled under his arm. The book shook in his hands, one or two pieces of paper losing their place and fluttering to the floor. A snarl . . . a roar . . . something was beginning to form in his throat and his eyes somehow grew even wider and even darker.

The McNally children felt afraid, each and every one of them; even Jackie.

'I'm sure she meant no harm, master,' said

Mulch, hurrying to his side, actually stroking one of Mr Maggs's arms in an effort to soothe him.

'N-N-No harm at all,' Le Fay added hurriedly.

'Tell them about Change Number Seven, master,' said Mulch. 'They'll be interested in Number Seven.'

Mr Maggs shook Mulch free of his arm, an act which sent the little man flying across the room, where he crashed into the edge of a table with a terrible crunch and a groan. He gave off a little whimper and touched his head where he'd hit the floor. There was blood on his fingers. Toby giggled. Le Fay felt a pang of guilt. The nasty little man had only been trying to protect them from his master's wrath . . . a wrath caused by her contradicting him.

'Ah, yes, Change Number Seven,' said Mr Maggs, Mulch apparently as forgotten as a swatted fly, and his near-rage down to a simmer, rather than actually boiling over. 'Red wine will taste more like raspberry juice. At the moment it looks so nice but doesn't taste nearly as good as the raspberry juice of my childhood, still warm from the sun.'

'Splendid!' said Le Fay, rather over-enthusiastically, trying to make up for past mistakes.

'Sounds good –'

'– to us,' said Albie and Josh, respectively. Neither had ever drunk red wine *or* raspberry juice but imagined raspberry juice would be rather nice, so it didn't matter to them if red wine tasted that way.

'One of my personal favourites,' said Mulch, getting to his feet, a neatly folded handkerchief pressed over the cut in his forehead.

'I'm rather fond of Number Eight,' sneered Mr Maggs, 'but first let me see if you have been paying attention to the first seven. I'd hate to feel you were being disrespectful and not giving me your full attention. Line up!' He placed the book back on the shelf and hugged his teddy to his chest, the bear staring at the McNallys with his glass eyes.

Jackie, Le Fay, Albie and Josh got to their feet and shuffled into line like a row of students before a teacher.

'Number One?' he demanded, pointing at Jackie.

'To make Q nearer the end of the alphabet, in amongst X, Y and Z.'

'Number Two?' Mr Maggs pointed to the next in line.

'Cary Grant to play you in a movie about your life,' said Le Fay.

'Good. Number Three?'

'Er, to bring Cary Grant back to life?' said Albie.

'Number Four?' demanded Mr Maggs, looming down on Josh.

'Er . . . er . . .' Joshua frantically tried to remember, then, thankfully, the answer popped into his head. 'Trees! Christmas trees must be drawn the right way, with branches pointing up not down!'

'Five?'

'Cruet!' Jackie blurted, having worked out she'd be asked this one and having the answer ready, in the hope of pleasing the master . . . Mr Maggs, that is. He was no master of the McNallys; not if Jackie had anything to do with it.

'Six?'

'No more fractions,' began Albie.

'All numbers even,' began Josh.

'SILENCE!' Mr Maggs demanded. He spoke with such authority that no one dared speak.

'I was asking YOU,' he said, prodding Le Fay

with his teddy's paw, clutched in his long-nailed fingers that looked more a cluster of gnarled twigs than a hand.

'Easier sums,' she announced, keeping her cool in the way she had in the Tap 'n' Type competition at the hotel where Fergal had fallen from the window and died.

'Number Seven?'

'Red wine to taste more like raspberry juice!' said the McNallys as one.

Mr Maggs positively beamed. His grin was as wide as a cartoon grin; much wider than any human being could achieve, showing off his extraordinarily pointed little teeth in all their glory. His head made Le Fay think of a pumpkin with shark's teeth, though not something she'd ever seen in real life.

'And so to Number Eight,' said Mr Maggs. 'Ban beards without moustaches. All beards must be accompanied by a moustache at all times.'

'Great idea,' said Joshua.

'It's got my vote,' said Albie. Neither of them knew what on Earth he was on about.

Mr Maggs patted both the twins on the head, at the same time, in the self-conscious way that no one who's used to children being around ever does. Suddenly he seemed to be behaving like a nice enough person, but the twins weren't fooled.

This teddy-bear-clutching thing was no man, let alone a *nice* one. 'Ahhhhh,' he sighed.

'Mr Maggs?' said Le Fay as cautiously and politely as possible.

'Yes, Le Fay, what is it?' Her name sounded exotic and different coming from his mouth.

'These changes . . . have you done anything to prepare for them . . .' she struggled for the right words, '. . . to make them happen when the time comes?'

'You mean, have I made preparations for implementing them, such as printing alphabet books with the letters in their new order, or –'

'Or looking for ways of bringing that movie star you were talking about –'

'Cary Grant,' said Jackie helpfully.

'Of bringing Cary Grant back to life?' said Le Fay.

The strange and mighty Mr Maggs crouched down and leaned forward so that his sweet breath blew into Le Fay's face as he spoke. 'You are interested in reanimation?' he asked, with obvious interest.

'Reanimation?' said Le Fay.

'Isn't that something to do with drawing?' asked Albie.

'Ssh!' said Jackie with a stern look.

'Reanimation is giving back life to something

that has died,' said Mulch from the shadowy corner of the room he was now occupying, at a safe distance from his master. 'Animation is movement . . . is *life*.'

Mr Maggs ignored his minion. 'When Cary Grant retired, a newspaper reporter was writing a story about him and wanted to check how old he was,' he said. 'So the reporter sent a telegram to Cary Grant's agent. Telegrams were typed messages and you paid by the word, so the message was short. It read: HOW OLD CARY GRANT? Cary Grant himself sent the reply. And do you know what he said? It read, OLD CARY GRANT FINE. HOW YOU?' Mr Maggs threw back his head and laughed. 'Old Cary Grant fine!'

Jackie laughed politely.

'Have you tried to reanimate him . . . to reanimate anyone?' asked Le Fay, once the strange laughter had subsided.

Mr Maggs's face became serious; deadly serious. 'I might have done, but that would be my business, wouldn't it? The kind of business where meddlers may find themselves in serious trouble if they tried to interf–'

Mr Maggs was interrupted by a dog – a very friendly and bedraggled dog – which bounded in from the rain through one of the many gaping holes in the wall of Fishbone Hall.

On seeing the McNallys, he leapt up at Le Fay, causing her to wince with pain where she'd hurt her ribs, and covered her dressing-gown with muddy paw prints; his licky tongue giving her slobbery doggie kisses.

Before Mr Maggs had a chance to speak, Mulch had dashed across the room, past the remains of the crumbled pillar, and grabbed the dog by his collar, pulling him off Le Fay.

The dog yelped and, turning his attention to the twins, wagged his tail furiously.

'I thought I told you that you could only keep the mutt if you kept it out of my sight!' said Mr Maggs. 'Get it out of here.'

Mulch managed to drag the dog from the room, but it took two hands and a great deal of effort.

Chapter Ten

For reasons which will become apparent, I don't know what Mr Maggs had in store for the McNallys. He hadn't asked them to come into Fishbone Forest. That had been their own doing. He hadn't lured them there or tricked them into coming. No one can accuse him of that. It was a twist of fate that had brought them together: he had needed a brain and Mulch had stolen Fergal's for that purpose. You can understand why Mr Maggs didn't want people around when he was busy 'reanimating' Lionel Lyons and tricking the lawyers into giving him the Lyons fortune, but all of this had been achieved before the McNallys arrived, and the evidence – well, *most* of it – destroyed or long gone. So why didn't he simply have Toby or Mulch take Jackie, Le Fay and the twins to one of the exits of Fishbone Forest and tell them never to come back?

Perhaps the answer lies in the way he hugged that teddy bear of his and enjoyed asking riddles. Perhaps what he really craved more than anything in his *Manifesto of Change* was *company*. Was the 'Cousin Ralphie' who sent him the brain of the French teacher – who, incidentally, had died in a boating accident – really his cousin? Did this extraordinary being really have a family? He certainly didn't seem to have any friends. Mulch and Toby were there because they worked for him; and he was a strict master.

And why share his manifesto with complete strangers? After all, he didn't have any idea that it was their dead brother's brain that had led their paths to cross.

Perhaps it wasn't company for company's sake that he craved. Perhaps he needed an audience; an audience to show off to? Because he didn't have family or friends around him, he didn't really have a chance to polish up his social skills. To put it another way: he wasn't very good with people. Not being a person himself no doubt made it all the harder.

If Mr Maggs kept the McNallys in Fishbone Hall at the heart of Fishbone Forest, they could be his captive audience. He could impress them with his manifesto and his riddles as much as he liked. Maybe that was what he intended. As I've said before, we'll never know for sure. Why? Because the holes were active again.

*

In the USA, running all the way from San Francisco to the hills behind Los Angeles, is a geological feature called the San Andreas Fault. It's what geologists call a 'strike-up fault', which means that a fracture in the Earth's crust – way, way, *way* down there – causes vertical movement in the ground near the surface. The San Andreas Fault is nearly always tremoring and twitching (like a dog's legs when it's dreaming about chasing cars or rabbits) but sometimes it causes big, big earthquakes. One of these quakes was so big that it destroyed much of the city of San Francisco in 1906.

Now, the question you might be asking yourself is this: if people know that the fault's there and the damage it can cause to property and lives, why does anyone in their right mind live there? And the answer lies in the fact that we all take chances. Look at it this way: you're more likely to fall out of an aeroplane if you're in an aeroplane in the first place. You're more likely to be killed crossing the road if you crossed roads, but these are chances we're willing to take. To most people, the advantages of flying in aircraft outweigh the disadvantages. If you never cross roads, your movements would be severely restricted. People live and work on the San Andreas Fault for a whole variety of reasons and, though they think about the possibility of earthquakes, they don't think about them all the time; they don't let the earthquakes rule their lives.

It was rather like that in the country where the McNallys lived (and, as I made very clear in the previous exploit, wherever you think that country is, you're wrong). The recent outbreak of holes had started out as big news but, very quickly, became just another of 'those things', to be lived with until it touched your particular lives.

Fergal, Jackie and the twins had encountered a fresh hole when they'd been on their way to The Dell (the hotel from which Fergal eventually fell). If the coach they'd been in had arrived at that spot a few minutes earlier, they'd probably all have ended up in it as it opened up beneath them.

They'd all seen the hole in Garland Park and that was a really big one, but that had been there a few days before the McNallys had come across it, and the authorities had already cordoned it off. Holes touched the edges of their lives, but were never centre stage. Until now.

*

Mulch dragged the dog back out into the rain, around the side of the Hall and into one of the outhouses. This small building had been as ruinous as the main house in places, but Mulch had bricked up the holes in the walls as best he could, and patched the roof with carpet tiles. The truth be told, it was now warmer and drier than his own room. This was where he kept the dog.

Mulch had grown very fond of the mongrel since he'd knocked the poor creature down with his English-mustard-coloured van and then nursed him back to life. He had no way of knowing that he had belonged to Wanda de Vere and was called Bumbo because there'd been no tag on his collar.

He and the animal got on very well after Mulch had done everything possible to put things right and make him well again. He'd even performed surgery. Part of him wanted to tell Mr Maggs; to show off his handiwork and to say, 'Why can't I be the one to help you perform any operations in the future, and not Toby?' But part of him knew that Mr Maggs would be angry if he knew what he'd done. So he kept quiet about the accident and only when the dog was well again did he tell his master that he'd found him loose in the forest and asked to keep him. Mr Maggs had agreed, so long as it never came into the house.

The dog was behaving very oddly. Normally he

was simply pleased to see Mulch and jumped up at him and stared deep into his eyes (though he had never licked him in the way he had licked Le Fay) but now he was struggling to get away from Mulch again.

'Please behave, boy,' said Mulch, 'or you'll get us both into trouble. It's nice and cosy in here and you mustn't upset Mr Maggs.'

It's true. The outhouse was cosy. Mulch had put plenty of dry straw on the floor and there were two big bowls under the window; one filled with water and the other with dried dog food. The only other object in the room was a large jar in the corner. You know the one. It had a brain in it, in pickling vinegar.

The dog still struggled. 'Please don't make me tie you up,' said Mulch. As if he understood, the dog stopped struggling and looked up at Mulch. Mulch rubbed his head between the ears. 'I'll be back later,' he said.

Back in the rain, Mulch pulled the door shut behind him and made sure that the latch was down properly this time, so that the dog couldn't get out again. Then he hurried back into the Hall.

He found Mr Maggs trying to strike a bargain with the McNallys.

'It'll be completely dark soon,' he was saying, 'and you'll never find your way out of Fishbone Forest without my guidance, so I'd like you all to stay the night . . . as my guests.'

The darkness would be no hindrance to Jackie in her jackal form. She could sniff her way out of there. If it wasn't for the rain. The rain changed everything.

'Guests?' said Albie.

'Prisoners more like,' said Josh.

'Our father and Detective Tweedy will already be wondering where we are,' added Le Fay.

'Don't you understand?' said Mr Maggs. 'No one comes into the forest. No one. Missing animals. Missing people. It makes no difference. No one ventures here.'

'We did,' Jackie reminded him.

Mr Maggs paused before answering, idly stroking the back of his teddy bear's head. 'Yes, you four are different, there's no denying . . . and perhaps such different children do have a father different enough to come searching. I think I'll have to –'

And then it happened. We'll never know what Mr Maggs had planned because the whole room started to shake so violently that a number of

131

burning logs rolled out of the fire. Mulch grabbed a pillar but it fell to the floor in great stone chunks.

Jackie instinctively put her arms around Albie and Josh to protect them, whilst Toby ran out of the building into the dark forest and the pouring rain. Le Fay lost her footing and ended up sprawled on the cold flagstones, winded once again and her ribs more painful still.

She watched in horror as the floor directly in front of her began to give way.

Chapter Eleven

As Mr Maggs fell into the gaping void which was the hole that had opened up beneath him, he didn't let out a cry but – unlike poor Fergal McNally who'd made no sound – he began to sing.

Leaning over the edge, with arms outstretched in a futile bid to try to catch him – a reflex action to try to save a fellow living being – Le Fay could hear the words clearly. The others dashed forward. They heard something too. Was it possible? Were they imagining things? No, it really was Mr Maggs's voice they heard as, clutching his beloved teddy to him, he fell to his inevitable death.

His voice was thin and reedy and the words to the old song strangely moving:

'Me and my teddy bear
Have no worries
Have no cares.
Me and my teddy bear
Just play and play
All daaaaaaaaaaaaaaaaaaay!'

Then silence; the terrible silence that follows death. No rumbling. No singing. All was silent and still at the heart of the forest.

'Is everyone okay?' asked Jackie, after what seemed like an eternity. She got to her feet and brushed the dust and grime from her clothes.

Mulch was leaning over the hole, sobbing. 'Poor master . . . Poor, poor master.'

'There's no way he survived that,' said Jackie, no doubt thinking of Fergal's fall, just as the others must have been.

Albie and Josh put an arm around each of Mulch's shoulders and tried to comfort him.

'It sounds to me like he died happy,' said Albie.

'And with his teddy,' said Josh. 'I reckon he'd . . . he'd have wanted that.'

'He wasn't a bad man,' sobbed Mulch, standing up slowly, with head bowed.

'He wasn't a man,' Jackie reminded him, picking Mr Maggs's leather-bound book from the floor, it having narrowly missed the hole by a matter of millimetres. She threw the *Manifesto of Change* into the void after its author. Mulch made no effort to stop her. 'Now he'll never be able to implement his changes.'

'I don't think he would ever have been able to anyway,' said Le Fay. 'Not if he'd lived another hundred years. They'd have been kind of difficult to do.'

'If anyone could, *he* could have,' sobbed Mulch.

Jackie just wanted to get the others home. This was the second death they'd witnessed. There was too much sadness in their short lives.

At that moment there was a barking noise and, for the second time that evening, the dog which had befriended Le Fay bounded through a hole in the wall and into the room. The tremors caused by the hole had not only lifted the door on the outhouse off its latch but also off its hinges.

On seeing Jackie, Le Fay and the twins he yelped with utter delight and wagged his tail like a clockwork toy, leaping up at each of them in turn licking their faces and pawing at them.

'He's not much of a guard dog, is he?' said Le Fay, scratching him between the ears. 'I imagined Mr Maggs would have a pit bull or a German shepherd.'

'He wasn't a guard dog,' said Mulch. 'I don't know where he came from . . . He was loose in the forest and ran straight in front of my van.'

'You knocked him down?' asked Le Fay, looking at the neatly stitched wound on the dog's head as he licked her fingers with his big pink tongue, staring up at her with his big, goo-goo brown eyes.

Mulch nodded.

'Well, the vet's done a good job fixing him up,' said Josh, trying not to think of Mr Maggs lying at the bottom of that hole.

'He seems pretty happy,' agreed Albie.

A look of pride appeared on Mulch's sad face. 'I didn't take him to any vet,' he explained. 'I made him well again.'

'Does he have a name?' asked Le Fay, whose knees were now getting a good clean from the licky dog's licky tongue.

'Fergus,' said Mulch. 'No, that's not right. Fergal. That's it. Fergal.'

Silence.

Have you ever heard the saying that 'the blood froze in someone's veins'? Of course, that's not literally what happens – well, certainly not to Jackie, Le Fay, Albie and Josh – but that's what it felt like. They froze to the spot with a hot and cold tingling sensation all over.

136

They couldn't have been more stunned if someone had stabbed them with an icicle.

Mulch was surprised by the effect that he'd had on them. 'What's wrong?' he demanded.

'Why . . . Why did you call him Fergal?' asked Le Fay, her mouth completely dry. She could hear her own heart thumping in her chest. She watched the dog sit up on his hind legs, thumping his tail with glee at the mention of his name.

'It was the name of the person whose brain I put inside him,' said Mulch at last. 'Fergal McNally, Juvenile,' he explained, remembering the exact wording on the pickling jar.

A moment later, the four McNallys threw themselves at the dog, showering him with hugs and kisses and he, in turn, licked off the tears of joy that were pouring down their faces.

Only Jackie was able to find the words: 'You're coming with us, Fergal,' she said. 'We're taking you home.'

★

It's ironic that the McNally family had so much to thank Stefan Multachan, the masked burglar, for. If he hadn't stolen Fergal's brain in the first place, Fergal – in any way, shape or form – would have remained dead after his fall from The Dell window. If later on, though, Mulch had done as Mr Maggs had ordered they would never have got Fergal back and, let me tell you, a four-legged little brother is better than none at all.

As you'll no doubt recall (if you didn't skip those pages), when Mr Maggs's Cousin Ralphie supplied the French teacher's brain to 'reanimate' Lionel Lyons's body, Mulch was told to 'dispose' of Fergal's unwanted one. It had become redundant. Instead, he'd kept it in the jar, guilty at the thought of throwing away something once-so-precious.

When, after days in which the poor injured dog had got worse and worse and finally died – that's the last death I'll be mentioning in this exploit though, of course, Mr Maggs died after him, chronologically speaking – Mulch'd had the brainwave (no pun intended) of putting the brain from the jar inside the dog, and the dog's old brain in the jar! It had, of course, been Bumbo's old brain he'd been carrying when he'd run into the McNallys in the forest.

Okay, so carrying out the operation had been more to do with wanting the dog back than wanting to preserve the memories of the juvenile human brain with the slight whiff of pickling vinegar but, using his master's techniques, he had, in fact, succeeded in bringing Fergal's mind back to life – full of all its love and feelings and memories right up until he'd hit the ground. *And* Mulch had the decency to name the mutt after him!

It had been a real puzzle for Fergal, of course, because he had no memories of being in a jar. To him, no time had passed since he'd hit the pavement and opened his eyes to find that he was a dog. After he realised that he really had turned into a dog (he didn't know anything about brain implants and reanimation at this stage, of course, though his family later explained everything) he assumed that it must either be his particular special power (turning into a dog when falling out of windows) or to do with reincarnation.

Fergal had read about it once: the belief that when

you die you come back as another animal. The better you were in your previous life, the 'better' the animal you came back as. If you'd led your life like a skunk, you might come back as a skunk was how Fergal had reckoned it worked. Coming back as a dog didn't seem that bad. After all, he could have ended up a dung beetle or something!

The real frustration had been seeing Jackie, Le Fay, Albie and Josh in Fishbone Hall and trying to tell them that he was Fergal and still alive, just in a new body! If only he could have made them understand. He couldn't speak. Sure, he could bark and whimper, but a dog's mouth isn't designed for human speech. It wasn't just that a dog's mouth doesn't have the lips to form the words, no matter how hard Fergal tried, he couldn't form any words in his throat either.

Now that the truth was out and he had his brothers and sisters around him, Fergal found himself doing a very doggy thing. He widdled/peed/weed with excitement. This was something Fergal never would have done and made him realise later, when he had a chance to think about it, that although it was his brain and his memories, it was Bumbo's blood flowing through his veins and Bumbo's heart which was pumping it, so there would always be a little Bumbo in his behaviour.

140

When Fergal was back home with his family, his father, Captain Rufus didn't need much to convince him that this loveable mutt was his youngest boy.

He looked into the dog's eyes and said: 'Welcome home, Fergal,' and then gave him a big bowl of water to drink.

Then came the great discovery.

The only member of the McNally family not pleased to see the return of Fergal or, to be more technically accurate, to see the return of Fergal's brain, with all its memories, inside the body of what had been Bumbo, was Smoky the cat. She took one look at this dog that everyone was so delighted to see and her furry purry body turned to smoke, which drifted away, leaving nothing behind.

'So that's why Mum named her Smoky!' said Jackie. 'Even our cat has hidden powers.'

Of course, Smoky hadn't left. The smoke had re-formed into the big solid cat that she was in the other room, away from the smelly dog. It became Smoky's 'party piece'. Whenever Fergal came into the same room as her, she'd turn into smoke particles and drift off, ready to re-form. Her favourite destination was the top of a big old wardrobe in the bedroom. It was soon thick with cat hairs, like a strange nest!

That was a discovery all right but it wasn't *the* great discovery. The great discovery was that, whenever Jackie turned into a jackal (which, as has been pointed out on more than one occasion, is little more than a kind of wild dog) she and Fergal found that they could communicate without speech. In that state, she could understand his doggy thoughts and later share them with the others.

This made Fergal's happiest times when he and his big sister could run wild on all-fours, chasing each other in the moonlight; nipping at each other's furry tails and howling at the moon. Fergal – the *new* Fergal – was alive again, with all the adventures that life had to offer ahead of him. Which, as I've said on another occasion, about another matter, is all rather unlikely, isn't it?

★

In the middle of deep dark Fishbone Forest, in the remains of Fishbone Hall, there was a deep dark hole and at the bottom of that hole something stirred. It wasn't Mr Maggs. It was a teddy bear, and it began its long crawl upwards towards the light.

THE END
of the second exploit

143

THINGS TO DO TODAY

Get up √
Wash, and brush teeth √
Get dressed √
Feed cats √
Empty dishwasher √
Have 1st cup of coffee √
Read mail √
Check answerphone for messages √
Check e-mails √
Have 2nd cup of coffee √
Write HEIR OF MYSTERY √
Watch telly
Feed cats
Have supper
Wash, and brush teeth
Go to bed

MUST DO!!!! DONE!!

The Philip Ardagh Club

COLLECT some fantastic **Philip Ardagh** merchandise.

WHAT **YOU** HAVE TO DO:

You'll find tokens to collect in all Philip Ardagh's fiction books published after 08/10/02. There are 2 tokens in each hardback and 1 token in each paperback. Cut them out and send them to us complete with the form (below) and you'll get these great gifts:

> **2 tokens** = a sheet of groovy character stickers
> **4 tokens** = an Ardagh pen
> **6 tokens** = an Ardagh rucksack

Please send with your collected tokens and the name & address form to: Philip Ardagh promotion, Faber and Faber Ltd, 3 Queen Square, London, WC1N 3AU.

Name: ....

Address: ....

....

....

Town: ....

Postcode: ....

Age & Date of Birth: ....

Girl or boy: ....

Philip Ardagh Club
token

The Fall of Fergal

or

Not So Dingly In The Dell

When not writing silly books, Philip Ardagh is very serious indeed and frowns a great deal. He also sports a pair of those little round glasses that brainy people often wear. He is best known for the bestselling Eddie Dickens Trilogy, beginning with *Awful End*. *The Fall of Fergal* is the first of his new *Unlikely Exploits* series. He probably lies awake at night thinking: 'Why does no one take me seriously?' His wife is a Doctor of Philosophy, which means that she's far cleverer than he is, but he's bigger than her. So there.

UNLIKELY EXPLOITS 1

THE FALL OF FERGAL

or

Not So Dingly In The Dell

PHILIP ARDAGH

illustrated by David Roberts

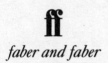

faber and faber

First published in 2002
by Faber and Faber Limited
3 Queen Square, London WC1N 3AU
This paperback edition first published in 2002

Typeset by Faber and Faber Limited
Printed in England by Mackays of Chatham plc, Chatham, Kent

© Philip Ardagh, 2002
Illustrations © David Roberts, 2002
Philip Ardagh is hereby identified as author of this work in accordance
with Section 77 of the Copyright, Designs and Patents Act 1988

A CIP record for this book
is available from the British Library

ISBN 978–0–571–21521–8

8 10 9 7

For Rebecca McNally. No relation.
And for my long-departed Great Aunt Phyllis, who
gave me one of the greatest gifts of all and never even
knew it. Thank you.

A Word to the Wise

There's one thing we need to get straight before any of us get started – me with the writing and you with the reading – and that is this: no matter where you think the events in this book took place, you're wrong. Plain and simple. No room for argument. Just because I have the McNallys speaking English, it doesn't mean they're from an English-speaking country. If you're reading a translated version of the book, it doesn't mean that they actually spoke in the language you're reading either. No. The events in this book took place somewhere none of you has ever been. How can I be sure? Because I'm the author, that's how, and we'll hear no more about it. Discussion closed. And as for the McNallys' names, I know they're strange, but I can't go and change them just to make you happy, now can I? That's what they're called so you'll just have to live with it. In the meantime, I hope you enjoy this, the first of their unlikely exploits.

PHILIP ARDAGH

Marley was dead; to begin with. There is no doubt whatever about that. The register of his burial was signed by the clergyman, the clerk, the undertaker, and the chief mourner . . . Old Marley was as dead as a door nail.

From *A Christmas Carol* by Charles Dickens

Prologue

'Philip!'

What?

'Wake up.'

Huh?

'Wake up! The book's started!'

Started?

'Yes –'

What do you mean, started?

'We've already had the title page, copyright blurb, your "Word to the Wise", the dedication no one ever reads and the quotation.'

You mean . . .?

'Yes, we're on to the story part!'

Blimey.

'You'd better get on with it.'

I'd better.

'Good luck.'

Thanks . . .

Chapter One

The very last words young Fergal McNally heard in his life were: 'Don't lean out of that window!' The very last sounds were probably the air whistling past his sticky-out ears as he fell the fourteen storeys, the honk of traffic horns below (getting nearer and nearer, of course), and – possibly – the 'SP' of the 'SPLAT!' he himself made as he hit the pavement. Fergal certainly wouldn't have heard more than the 'SP', though, because by the time the 'LAT!' part had followed, he would have been well and truly dead.

The person who'd shouted the 'don't-lean-out' warning, good and loud (but far too late), was Fergal's older sister Jackie. Jackie really was an *older*, older sister. Some people (twins, usually) have older sisters just minutes older than them. Lots of people have older sisters a good few years older than them, but Fergal's sister Jackie was old

1

enough to be his mother, which was kind of handy, because he didn't have a real mother. It had been down to Jackie to bring up the rest of them. You know: feed them, clothe them, stop them falling out of windows . . . that kind of thing.

Of course, their father could have brought them up, but he was a useless dad. He even went so far as to get a note from his doctor saying that he was 'excused parenting', and left everything for poor old Jackie to do. He kept himself busy by collecting empty bottles. They were full when he first got them but were certainly empty by the time he'd finished with them. He very rarely spoke to anyone except the man in the bottle shop and to shout at Jackie to tell her how useless she was at everything.

He would hide in what he called 'the back room', though it was more to the side than the back if you counted the front bit of the apartment as being the part that faced the road. He even had his meals in the back room, whilst Jackie fed her brothers and sister (once a day) around a big circular table in the kitchen.

Rufus McNally – that was their father's name – often liked to add to his empty-bottle collection during meal times and would attract Jackie's attention, to bring him another full one, by throwing something at the wall dividing the back

room (which was really a side room) from the
kitchen. Sometimes it'd be a bottle he'd just
emptied. Sometimes it might be a boot. Once he
picked up the cat, but Smoky was no fool and,
with a few swift strokes of the paw and claw, made
it absolutely clear to Captain Rufus that she was
by no means a cat of the throwing-across-the-
room variety.

You see, Smoky was a working cat, not a pet.
She let the McNally children stroke her and she
let them love her, but they didn't feed her. (It's not
that they were mean, it's just that there was barely
enough food for themselves without feeding a cat

as well.) Smoky ate the mice and rats that were unwise enough to stop scuttling behind the skirting and make a break across an open floor.

Once Fergal's dad Rufus threw his own wooden leg at the wall to attract Jackie's attention. He'd looked around for something else to throw but couldn't find anything that wasn't furry and purry, so he'd unscrewed his leg and chucked it with such force that it not only cracked the plaster in the wall but also split the leg itself, right along the grain. Thereafter, it always looked like an overripe fruit with a burst skin.

In the days before any of the children (apart from Jackie) had been born, Rufus McNally had been not only a brilliant sailor but also a war hero. He'd been a happy smiling fellow whom – which is simply a 'who' with an 'm' on the end – everyone had been proud to know. He'd been awarded more gold medals for bravery than he had clean shirts to pin the medals on . . . and then he'd lost his leg.

He didn't lose his leg in the way that people lose umbrellas at busy railway stations. No, Captain Rufus McNally lost his leg in such a way that he couldn't simply go to the 'Lost & Found' and collect it. He didn't lose his leg in an explosion, and he'd been in many of those. He didn't lose it when he was clinging to wreckage in shark-infested waters, and he'd found himself in that predicament on more than one occasion. He lost his leg on the fourth occasion he found himself in a sinking ship. On the previous three occasions he'd done heroic deeds to save others trapped as their vessels went down. On this final occasion it was he who was trapped. His ship had been torpedoed by an enemy submarine and was sinking fast, but he was going nowhere because his leg was caught under a mass of twisted metal.

So Captain Rufus McNally did a very brave thing. As the water poured into the cabin where he was trapped, knowing that if he couldn't free himself he would definitely die, he decided to cut off his own leg. Sorry, but there you are. I'd love to say that the solution was to skip happily with fluffy bunnies with nice music in the background, but this was war. And war is a 'orrible thing. If you don't want to know the details, look away until I tell you that it's safe to carry on reading.

Rufus grabbed a razor-sharp piece of twisted metal (that had once been part of a door frame to the boiler room, if you must know) and cut through his leg – and yes, he did have to hack through his own bone – as the rising water around him reddened with his own blood. At the end of it, he fainted but he floated free, and was rescued by some of his own men who'd made it to a lifeboat. They stemmed the bleeding – people never stop

the bleeding in war stories, they always 'stem' it –
and, fortunately for Rufus, help was close at hand
and he survived.

The down side was that he was a changed man.
What Rufus McNally went through was
unbelievably dreadful – I'd be a liar to tell you
otherwise – but other people have been through
even worse and somehow come out the other side
as decent human beings. Rufus McNally, however,
became bitter, sick and twisted – in that order (he'd
tried twisted, bitter and sick but it didn't suit) –
and it was then that he started to d-r-i-n–

Oh, hang on. I almost forgot:

IT'S OK TO START READING AGAIN, YOU SQUEAMISH ONES.

From being a popular hero, Rufus turned his
back on all his old friends and colleagues and
wanted to be alone. He had his war pension and,
whenever he needed a bit more money, he'd have
his wife (and, after she died, Jackie) sell another of
his many medals. Poor Jackie. That was just
another one of her jobs. No wonder she got a bit
snappy sometimes.

Fergal and the other kids – his twin brothers
Joshua and Albie and his sister Le Fay –
sometimes called Jackie 'Jackal', which may have
seemed a bit mean. Wouldn't you snap and snarl,

6

once in a while, with four younger siblings to look after and no life of your own? Probably. Although there may, of course, have been more to her name than that. Those of you who read on shall see.

But I'm pretty sure they all loved each other. In fact, I'd go so far as to say that I expect Jackie, Joshua, Albie and Le Fay (or, if you'd prefer them in alphabetical order: Albie, Jackie, Joshua and Le Fay) were really upset when their little brother Fergal ended up all dead like that. SPLAT!

The sad thing was that things were looking up for the McNally family at the time Fergal took a nosedive from the window. For a start, it was a hotel window from which Fergal fell and – although Fergal's other sister, Le Fay, was the only person who was supposed to be occupying the hotel room (it was a 'single') – they'd never been in the position before in which even *one* of them could legitimately spend the night in a hotel. And The Dell was quite a posh one. Le Fay had entered a typing competition and had won her local and regional finals. Now she was in the national grand finals and that meant a trip to the capital and a night in The Dell.

What is a typing competition? you may well ask. Well, although I've never actually been in one myself, because I can only type with two fingers, I think you'll find it's a competition to see who can type the fastest, making the fewest mistakes whilst still laying all the words neatly on the page – that kind of thing. Now, it may not sound the most exciting thing to you. You may think that a kick-boxing competition or a fight with laser swords, or a motorbike competition might be more interesting, but it was a typing competition Le Fay had entered and reached the finals in, and there's nothing I can do to change that. Anyhow, her brothers and sister were very proud of her.

Of course, their father wasn't in the least bit proud of her or her typing abilities. (It wasn't the typing part. He wouldn't have been in the least bit proud if Le Fay had run a mile in under one second or performed successful brain surgery on three patients all at once, either. He was excused being a parent, remember. All he cared about was himself.)

When Le Fay asked if she could go to the grand finals – she hadn't told him about the locals or regionals – he said that he didn't care what she did. When Jackie suggested that the rest of them go with Le Fay to give her support, their father said he wasn't going anywhere and, if he wasn't going anywhere, none of the others was going anywhere either.

So Jackie made a stand. She was a grown woman, old enough to be Fergal's mother, and had looked after all of them, including her father, long enough to make an important decision on her own. She took the money she'd been putting aside from her already meagre housekeeping budget each week – the plan had been to save up enough money to buy the others a small present each, come Christmas – and found that she had enough to buy just two return coach tickets to the capital.

Le Fay would be travelling up to town by train at the expense of Tap 'n' Type, the sponsors of the typing competition, but there was no way Jackie could afford to buy two train tickets. The two coach tickets were for her and for Albie and Joshua. The reason why Albie and Joshua only got one ticket between them was that they were almost-identical twins. Jackie hoped that if they kept on the move and took it in turns to hide in the loo, the coach driver would think that they were one and the same person. That left Fergal without a ticket. There were two options here. They could either hide him in their luggage, or dress him up as a baby so that he could travel for nothing.

When the time came, Fergal found himself in the coach on Jackie's lap, with a big nappy (which is a diaper, only spelled n-a-p-p-y instead of d-i-a-p-e-r) on his bottom, and a Sherlock Holmes comic book in his hand.

Sitting next to them, a man with a moustache eyed Fergal's reading material. 'Bright kid,' he said. The moustache said nothing.

Although the coach left two hours before the train, it was due to arrive an hour and a half after it, so Le Fay arranged to meet them at the back of The Dell at three o'clock in the afternoon. There was no way Jackie, Fergal, Albie and Joshua could simply march into the building with their luggage, even if Fergal was pretending to be a baby and Albie and Joshua were pretending to be one and the same person. The management of The Dell would suspect that there was something funny going on (funny peculiar, not funny ha-ha). No,

10

Le Fay would have to find a way of smuggling them up to her room.

Le Fay had been met at the station by a man called Malcolm (which, by the way, is the name of a stuffed stoat in another series of books I wrote, starting with *Awful End*, which I'd be very grateful if you'd rush out and buy). Malcolm Kent was from the publicity department of Tap 'n' Type and it was his job to meet the four finalists off their four respective trains.

'You're the last,' Malcolm explained, taking Le Fay's rather tatty-looking suitcases. Old suitcases in novels are nearly always battered. This was tatty. (The piece of cod the McNallys shared later that evening was definitely battered, though, so you fans of battering have nothing to fear.) 'The other finalists are already back at the hotel.'

Malcolm had a taxi waiting and he held the door open for Le Fay to get into the back. Le Fay had never been in the capital before, had never been in a taxi before and had never stayed in a hotel before. This, she thought, as she settled down in the comfy seat, is going to be a trip to remember. It was, but sadly for the wrong reason. This was going to be the trip where Fergal ended up very squashed and very dead.

Chapter Two

When Malcolm Kent had first laid eyes on Le Fay McNally – which was at the railway/railroad/train station, because he hadn't been at her local or regional heat of the competition – he'd been rather surprised by her appearance.

With the exception of mentioning Fergal's sticky-out ears, I haven't really paid much attention to describing what everyone looked like. You'll see why in a moment. You already know that Dad McNally – Cap'n Rufus – had a wooden leg, and you already know that Albie and Joshua were almost identical, but what you probably didn't know until now is that they all had wiry, untameable gingery-red hair and they all had freckles – hundreds of them in all. And all of them – the McNallys, not the freckles – had two large front teeth with a gap between them except for

Jackie 'the Jackal'. Hers looked more like George Washington's, which, I believe, were actually made of wood. In other words, once you've described one McNally you've just about described them all ... and none of them was about to win any beauty contests; but then again, if you've seen my author photograph, you'll be fully aware that neither am I. Their father looked the most unlike the others because of his big red nose. He hadn't always had a big red nose and it wasn't something that he could pass on to his children. In other words, it wasn't hereditary and had more to do with his trips to the bottle shop.

But it wasn't Le Fay's buck teeth, unmanageable hair and multiple freckles that surprised Malcolm from Tap 'n' Type. It wasn't how shabby her clothes were and how unwashed she looked. (Jackie did her best, but there was no running water in their apartment except for a drip from the ceiling from the apartment upstairs and the condensation on the windows in cold weather.) What shocked Malcolm was how thin and how hungry she looked.

Now, Malcolm wasn't the most caring man in the world. He never gave money to charity, not even to those nice ones that look after unwanted donkeys or retired pit ponies that have been down the mines all their working lives. He didn't always hold doors open for senior citizens and, on more than one occasion, he had smoked in a no-smoking waiting room at a railway station.

Once – and I checked this with his parents, who swear that it is true – he didn't even bother to thank his gran for the socks and aftershave she gave him one Christmas. But when Malcolm first laid eyes on Le Fay McNally, he hoped beyond hope that she would win the grand final of the Tap 'n' Type typing competition.

He thought of the three other finalists: Graham Large, Peggy Snoot and Anna Malting. Graham Large had arrived with three pieces of very expensive-looking matching luggage, and his parents had paid extra so that he could travel down first class and have a whole suite of rooms – separate bedroom, bathroom and sitting room – in The Dell instead of a single room. He'd bossed Malcolm around as though he was a personal servant, not a representative of the sponsors.

Peggy Snoot was nice enough. Very polite, in fact. She seemed a little nervous, but why not? The finals were important to all the contestants.

Anna Malting was a different matter altogether. In the taxi from the station to the hotel she'd gone on and on and on about how her local and regional heats in the competition had been so much harder than everyone else's, and what she was going to do *when* she won the grand prize, not *if*.

Large, Snoot and Malting all looked well dressed, well cared for and well fed. Not Le Fay McNally. Malcolm crossed his fingers and, though he wasn't a religious man, muttered a little prayer to God just in case He (or, of course, She) existed.

Once Malcolm had shown Le Fay to her room, he showed her the itinerary. If you've no idea what an itinerary is, you might imagine that it was a wonderful machine made of gleaming chrome, with horns to shout down and earpieces to listen into. If the truth be told, the itinerary was a piece of paper with type printed on it. Being the itinerary for:

```
          The Grand Finals of
     The Young Typist of the Year
       sponsored by Tap 'n' Type
     Providers of Keyboards to the
   Crowned Heads of Europe & Beyond
```

it was beautifully typed!

Her heart thumping, Le Fay read it quickly to make sure that she'd be able to meet Jackie, Albie, Joshua and Fergal outside The Dell at three o'clock as originally planned. She didn't have a watch. (The McNallys couldn't afford one, and her arms were so thin one would probably have slipped right off over her hand anyway.)

There was to be a 'Meet the Other Finalists' at a 'finger buffet' in the Bellhop Suite at one o'clock. Le Fay knew what a buffet was. There had been a buffet car on the train. A buffet meant food, which suited her fine. If she was really smart, she might come up with a way of snaffling some of the buffet to give to the others when they arrived.

16

It was the 'finger' part that bothered her a bit. Would all the food be fingers? She could think of fish fingers, and there was a plant called ochre, which some people called 'ladies' fingers', but she couldn't think of any other kinds of fingers people might eat. Then she remembered Jackie telling her that there was a delicious pudding called trifle, which had sponge fingers in it. At least those kinds of fingers sounded OK!

The next item on the itinerary was two o'clock, 'Meet the Press', described as being 'A Photo Call with some of the Capital City's Leading Evening Newspapers'.

Le Fay hoped that this wouldn't take more than an hour, because after that it was 'A Free Afternoon for Sightseeing' right up until 'Dinner with our Generous Sponsors in the Sizzle Grill' at eight o'clock . . . which would leave her with plenty of time to spend with her family.

'You don't have to wait until lunch or supper to have some food,' said Malcolm kindly. 'You can use Room Service any time you want.'

'What's that, please?' Le Fay asked politely.

'If you, say, want a chicken sandwich or a mug of hot chocolate,' said Malcolm, 'you pick up that phone, dial 1 and tell them what you want. They bring it to your room and you sign for it, but you don't have to pay. Tap 'n' Type pays. See?'

'I see,' said Le Fay, wide-eyed in wonderment. She imagined people throughout the hotel picking up their phones and ordering chicken and hot chocolate! It was like living in a palace.

This is another example of Malcolm Kent being a very nice man at heart. Room Service was not something officially offered as part of the grand finalists' trip. Of course, Graham Large could dial up and order what he wanted, but Mummy and Daddy would be sent the bill at the end of his stay. Peggy Snoot was far too polite to even think of ringing for Room Service, because Malcolm hadn't told her she could; and when Anna Malting had said: 'I can call down for anything I want, can't I? After all, I've earned it,' Malcolm had replied: 'I'm afraid you will be charged for it, though phone calls home are free.'

'You can ring home too, of course,' Malcolm now told Le Fay. 'You dial 9 for an outside line and then your number.'

'Thank you,' said Le Fay. She didn't want to disappoint the nice man from Tap 'n' Type by telling him that they didn't have a phone at home. They'd used to have one, but the telephone company had got fed up coming to repair the wiring every time her father tore the phone out of the wall and threw it across the back room (which was really at the side).

'Right,' said Malcolm. 'So it's dial 1 for Room Service–'

'And 9 for an outside line,' Le Fay nodded.

'Both the Bellhop Suite and the Sizzle Grill are here in The Dell,' said Malcolm. 'They're both on the first floor. Follow the signs.'

'Thank you.'

'I'll see you at the "Meet the Other Finalists" then, OK?' said Malcolm. 'But feel free to call up Room Service before then if you're hungry.'

'Chicken sandwich and a mug of hot chocolate,' Le Fay nodded. 'Thanks.'

Malcolm went out through the open doorway and closed the door to Le Fay's room behind him. She was alone at last. Now she would have to come up with a way of smuggling the rest of the McNallys inside.

If she'd failed, of course, little Fergal might still be living a normal life today.

Chapter Three

The ambulance man took one look at what was left of Fergal and knew that there would be no driving to the Sacred Heart Hospital at breakneck speed with lights flashing and sirens blaring. The neck-breaking had already happened and, once the doctor had officially declared the poor boy dead – something that anyone with a pair of eyes in his or her head could have done at a glance – he'd simply wait for the police photographer to take a few photographs then scoop the kid into a body bag and take a leisurely drive to the morgue.

The morgue was another name for the mortuary. It was in the basement of the Sacred Heart Hospital, where they put the bodies of those who'd died in the hospital or were brought in dead from outside: accident and murder victims.

The ambulance man, whose name was Morris, idly wondered whether Fergal (though at that stage, of course, he didn't know that the victim's name was Fergal) was the victim of an accident or murder . . . or even suicide? Sometimes people deliberately jumped out of windows. Did this one fall, was he pushed or did he jump?

The doctor – a roundish man who looked, walked and spoke remarkably like a duck – arrived, waddled quacking through the small crowd that had gathered, nodded at one of the uniformed police officers keeping people at a respectful distance, and knelt down next to Fergal.

He whistled through his teeth. 'Fell twelve floors?' he guessed.

'Fourteen,' said the assistant manager of The Dell, a small man with greased-back black hair and a moustache so thin that it looked as if it'd been drawn with one of those extra-fine-nibbed drawing pens. His name was Mr Lesley, spelled the girl's way.

The doctor cursed under his breath. 'I used to be accurate to within one storey,' he muttered, getting to his feet. 'He's dead all right!' he called out to Morris. 'Bag him and tag him.'

Mr Lesley cleared his throat purposefully. It's amazing what message a purposeful clearing of the throat can convey. This one could be instantly translated into: 'Show a bit more respect, doc. The victim's grieving family are within earshot'; and within earshot they certain were.

The moment Fergal had toppled out of the window, Jackie had dashed across the room and leant out, grabbing at thin air. She had let out a cry of 'No!', stretching the 'o' to last a good fifteen seconds, but it's no good me writing it down as 'Noooooooooooooooo!' because that looks as though it rhymes with 'moo' – the noise cartoon cows make – and is the noise Scottish folk make in very bad Hollywood films. This was very definitely a 'no!' to rhyme with 'snow', with the 'ow' long-drawn-out and distraught. It should also be added to the list of the last sounds Fergal probably heard on his way to his squishy death. I'm sorry, I should have thought of it earlier and I hope you don't feel that I've betrayed you as a narrator. Well, at least I've apologised.

Those smart alecs amongst you who are wondering why I didn't mention Fergal's own screaming as he fell fourteen storeys, I simply tell you this: I made no mention of Fergal's scream because he didn't scream or cry as he fell. He fell as silently as a sack of rocks, or potatoes, or something equally silent. Perhaps it was the shock of it all. Perhaps he was about to scream when he came into contact with the solid ground, and all thought of screaming went out of his mind . . .

There, now look what you've made me go and

do: get all involved in the unpleasant side of things again. Where was I? Yes, Jackie had dashed to the window and, seeing that it was too late to catch him, ran straight to the door and out into the corridor.

Le Fay, Albie and Joshua dashed out of the hotel room after their big sister, who'd already reached the lift and was jumping up to press the 'down' button. There were two lifts and, according to the arrow indicator above them, one was on the ninety-third floor and the other on the forty-sixth.

Jackie headed for the main stairs and ran down them at an incredible speed, sobbing as she went, jumping five or six steps at a time. Le Fay, Albie and Joshua somehow managed to keep up, all sobbing their eyes out.

Nothing funny happened at this stage so, if you're hoping for a laugh, we interrupt this story for a joke. Now it's not original, it's not my joke and I'm not claiming it as my own. It's simply the first joke that came into my head when I thought that a little levity might be in order:

Two cannibals are eating a boiled clown. One cannibal turns to the other, between mouthfuls, and says: 'Does this taste funny to you?' Ho ho!

There. Not a side-splitter, but it certainly brought a twitch of a smile to the corners of my mouth and is a nice relief from all those sobbing relatives of Fergal McNally charging downstairs to what was a foregone conclusion: one splatted little brother.

Anyway, I think I'm getting rather ahead of myself again. When we left Le Fay at the end of Chapter Two, she hadn't even smuggled her family into her room, so Fergal can't have had the opportunity to fall out of the window yet. Perhaps we should go back a bit . . .

*

On the back of Le Fay's door were two framed notices, both printed entirely in red ink. One was headed: IN THE EVENT OF HOLES and the other: IN THE EVENT OF FIRE. The one headed: IN THE EVENT OF HOLES was full

24

of doom and gloom and basically said that, if a huge hole opened up under the hotel, there wasn't a great deal you could do except hide under your bed and pray or stand in the doorway. Ideally both: hide under your bed in the doorway and pray. Le Fay was of the opinion that if a big hole opened up under the hotel, no matter what you did, you'd still end up in it.

It was the second notice – IN THE EVENT OF FIRE – in equally red print, that caught her eye. It gave useful tips about not using the lifts and where the 'assembly point' was so that management could do a roll call and try to work out who was still trapped in the building and needed rescuing.

There was a drawing too. It was a plan of the floor of the hotel her room was on and, as well as the main stairs, it showed some back stairs marked: DOWN TO FIRE EXIT. If these stairs led down from her floor to the fire exit, Le Fay reasoned, then they must also lead *up* from the fire exit to her floor! She would go and investigate.

Slipping her room key, with its long metal tag, into the only pocket of her best (but still very drab) dress, she slipped out of her room, along the corridor to the left and slipped through a door marked: FIRE EXIT. (Yup, there was suddenly a lot of slipping, but not of the 'oops!' banana-skin variety.)

It opened on to a cold, dark staircase of uncarpeted concrete steps with a metal handrail set into the wall; a real contrast to the posh plushness of the rest of The Dell. The stairs seemed to go back on themselves in a spiral square – if there is such a thing as a spiral square – for ever and ever (with fire-exit doors from each floor leading on to them); but, finally, Le Fay reached the bottom. There was a set of double doors with a metal bar running across them at average-adult-waist height. EMERGENCY EXIT ONLY, said the sign. PUSH BAR.

It was obvious to Le Fay that there wouldn't be any handles on the outside of the door, which, from the smell of exhaust fumes and honking of car horns, she guessed opened out on to the street, probably at the side of the hotel. This was to stop people doing exactly what Le Fay's family planned to do: sneak in without paying. The only way to get Jackie, Fergal, Albie and Joshua inside this way was to open the door, somehow keep it wedged open, then circle the hotel with them until they found it . . . but what if someone found the exit wedged open first? That's why Le Fay decided she wouldn't open it there and then, but leave it until just before three o'clock, when she'd arranged to meet the others. Le Fay went all the way back up the fourteen storeys via the back stairs.

She could, of course, have slipped out through any of the fire doors and taken the lift up the rest of the way, but she didn't want to arouse suspicion. For all she knew, big hotels such as The Dell hired detectives to be on the lookout for strange goings-on, twenty-four hours a day; and Le Fay was right about that, as you will discover. They're called 'house detectives' and the chief house detective at The Dell was a man named Charlie Tweedy. Charlie was to become interested in the McNally children – very interested indeed.

But Le Fay had no way of knowing that. Not then.

Charlie was an ex-naval man and an ex-policeman and, in all the time he'd been on the force, he'd never let an unsolved case remain unsolved. He was like a terrier, which is one of those dogs that, once it's sunk its teeth into you, won't let go until it's well and truly satisfied it's 'won'.

If you don't believe me, you should see my brother's nose. He bent down to pat a terrier once and to say 'Nice doggie', or whatever it is that brothers say to terriers; but the dog took it to mean 'Let's fight!' When my brother stood up, he had the dog attached to his nose . . . It would probably still be there today if the dog's owner hadn't shown it something more tasty to chew on. My brother does still have a faint scar to remember the occasion, though.

If I told you Charlie had a nickname, you might, therefore, expect it to be along the lines of 'Terrier Tweedy'. That's certainly the name I would have given him. But no, Charlie Tweedy was known in the trade as 'Twinkle-Toes' Tweedy. Stick around long enough, and you'll find out why.

Back inside her room, and a bit out of breath from running down the back stairs and up again, Le Fay looked at the time on the radio alarm clock on the bedside table: 12:18.

Le Fay was feeling very hungry by now, which wasn't unusual, because she was used to having only one (rather small) main meal a day back home, but she wondered whether she should ring Room Service and ask for a chicken sandwich and a mug of hot chocolate. Sure, it was less than three-quarters of an hour until she was supposed to be eating fingers in the Sizzle Grill – or was it the Bellhop Suite? – but the more she thought about plates piled high with fingers, the less appetising the whole 'Meet the Other Finalists' seemed. What if they were monkey fingers? They'd look almost human . . . and would the nails have been taken off, or were you supposed to peel them off yourself? Or was it polite to eat them? They'd be very crunchy.

Le Fay McNally picked up the phone and dialled the number '1'.

'Room Service,' said a cheery voice.

'I'd like a chicken sandwich and a mug of chocolate, please,' said Le Fay.

'Certainly, madam,' said the cheery voice. 'White, brown or rye?'

'A chicken sandwich and a mug of chocolate, please,' Le Fay repeated, a little less sure of herself this time.

'The bread, madam. For the sandwich. Would you like white bread, brown bread or rye bread?'

'Oh!' said Le Fay, relieved. 'White, please.'

'Toasted?'

'Yes. Yes, please. And a mug of hot chocolate.'

'Certainly, madam. One toasted chicken sandwich on white and a mug of hot chocolate for Room 1428. It'll be with you within fifteen minutes,' said the cheery voice.

'Thank you,' said Le Fay. 'Goodbye, then.'

'Goodbye, dear,' said Room Service.

Le Fay put the phone down and sat on the bed.

How had Room Service known which room she was in? she wondered. Were there cameras in all the rooms to make sure that people didn't steal the soap or something? If there were cameras all over the hotel, then she'd have been seen slipping through the fire-exit door and they'd probably want to know why . . .

No, Le Fay told herself. She was just being silly.

There must be some way that the telephone system in Room Service could tell which room you were dialling from. It must light up a number, or something. That's what it must be. She was being stupid. Who'd stay in a hotel with hidden cameras everywhere? All the guests would be embarrassed and go to bed with their clothes on.

Back home, she and Jackie, Fergal, Albie and Joshua often went to bed with their clothes on in the winter, but not because they didn't want people filming them in the nude. They did it because it was far too cold to take their clothes off at night. In fact, they'd often put on extra clothes – including the odd coat or two – before settling down to sleep. Another way of trying to keep warm was all to sleep in the same bed, which is what they did.

Since their mother had died, their father slept in the back room (which was really a side room, remember), but he had the one-bar electric heater on all night in the cold months, so he was fine. The rest of them bundled into what had once been his double bed and snuggled up together as best they could. Le Fay was the one who always felt the cold most and, despite layers of shirts and coats, often kept Jackie awake with her teeth chattering.

Five minutes later, there was a knock at the door.

31

'Room Service!' said a voice.

Le Fay jumped off the bed and opened the door.

It wasn't Room Service at all.

'Are you Le Fay McNally?' asked a complete stranger, with a very unpleasant sneer indeed.

Chapter Four

Framed in the doorway of Room 1428 of The Dell hotel at 12:33 that day was a very large boy wearing a rather tight navy-blue shirt (with monogrammed pocket) and an equally-tight pair of dark blue shorts that reached the tops of his knees. The lower parts of his legs were covered with a pair of white socks, with navy-blue piping, that reached the *bottom* of his knees.

His face was a little podgy and the skin looked so soft that Le Fay imagined that it must have been bathed in twenty-three different lotions and then had thirteen different creams massaged into it with loving care. (She was wrong: it was twenty-four different lotions.) But it was the hair – my God, the hair – that was most shocking of all. Thick, dark brown and swept back into an enormous quiff, it was so stiff that it looked more like spun sugar. How long, Le Fay wondered, did it take to get your hair to look like that each morning? And, even more to the point, *why*? She couldn't take her eyes off the top of his head. She'd never met such a sweet-smelling, softy-skinned, quiffy person in shorts before!

'You must be McNally, the poor girl,' said the boy, pushing past her and walking uninvited into her room. 'I see they've put you in one of the cheapest rooms. More of a closet really, isn't it?' He wrinkled his nose as though he'd just detected a particularly bad smell. 'I'm Graham Large,' he said, which was true. 'I'm the one who's going to beat you all in the competition tomorrow,' he added, sounding rather too sure of himself. 'My father is David Large, owner of Large Lunches. I expect you've heard of him.'

'Er, no,' said Le Fay, politely.

Graham had been looking to see whether Le Fay had brought a typewriter or laptop with her to practise on and, concluding that she'd brought next to nothing with her – let alone a keyboard – turned and stared at her.

If you were to ask Le Fay what colours his eyes were, she wouldn't remember. He may have been glaring directly at her face, but her eyes were still fixed on the h-a-i-r.

'Sponsors always like to have a poor person in the finals of a competition, whatever it's for,' said

34

Graham Large, with that nasty, nasty sneer that came naturally. 'They fix local and regional competitions to make sure it happens. It makes them look a kind, caring company . . . but there's no way the poor kid ever wins. How could you? You didn't get this far on talent or merit. It's just rigged so that you can make up the numbers.'

Le Fay was confused. Firstly, she didn't see herself as being poor and, secondly, she knew that she had excellent keyboard skills.

'We're not poor,' she said, thinking of her friend Simon.

Simon was so poor that he couldn't afford another name. He was simply 'Simon'– as opposed to 'Simple Simon', the guy who met a pie man – and he lived with his family in an old abandoned greenhouse on some wasteland near the edge of Fishbone Forest. (Only someone very poor or completely mad would go anywhere near Fishbone Forest, let alone live near there. It was the sort of place you'd go to if you had absolutely nowhere else to go. Strange things happened in Fishbone Forest – nasty things. The kind of things that people write about in books, such as the next one in this series: *Heir of Mystery*.) Now, Simon and his family were really poor.

Graham Large snorted. It was a contemptuous snort, but don't worry if you're not sure what contemptuous means. It was a piggy snort too. 'If you say so,' he laughed. 'Though why anyone who wasn't poor would turn up dressed in those rags escapes me!'

Now, it was true that Le Fay's dress had been Jackie's dress before she'd grown out of it and that it had been their mother's before Jackie's, but it'd been new when their mother had bought it, so it was less of a handed-down hand-me-down than *some* of the clothes Le Fay wore. It was also true that it'd had a number of alterations and repairs done on it over the years, but Jackie had gone to a great deal of trouble to unpick and re-stitch some of the messier efforts at patching it up, and Le Fay wasn't about to let some perfumed softy make fun of all the hard work her sister had gone to to make her look nice for the competition.

Le Fay had gone red in the face. Her blood was boiling and she was about to . . . about to EXPLODE. What she meant to say next was: 'Get out of my room, Large! I didn't invite you in here!' What she actually said in her spluttering rage was: 'Get out of my room, Lard!' and then spluttered to a halt. Why? Because of the boy's expression the second the word 'Lard' came out.

A look of horror crossed Graham Large's softy, perfumed face. His spun-sugar quiff quivered (quiffs do that sometimes; perhaps that's how they got the name). His eyes – whatever colour they were – moistened. What Le Fay didn't realise was that 'Lard' – her slip of the tongue – was the nickname Graham Large hated most in the whole wide world. It was the name the other boys and girls had used to chant at school before his parents had taken him out of the schooling system and hired a non-teasing, one-on-one private tutor to teach him at home.

'You,' he said, sweeping past Le Fay (with a trail of scent) and striding into the corridor, 'have just made yourself a powerful enemy! A very powerful one!' which was followed by a large sniff.

No sooner had Le Fay shut the door, with some satisfaction, it must be admitted, than there was another knock on it.

'Yes?' she said.

'Room Service!' said a voice.

This time Le Fay went up on tiptoe and looked through the seeing-eye to see who was out there. Through the distorted fish-eye lens, she could see a man in a red uniform with big brass buttons holding a silver tray. She opened the door excitedly.

The young man brought in a delicious-smelling toasted-chicken sandwich on white bread, and a steaming mug of hot chocolate on the tray, which he placed on the bed.

'Thank you,' said Le Fay and, when the man handed her a piece of paper, she signed it with the pen he offered her. 'Thank you very much.'

It was one of the best meals that Le Fay had ever had; and did she feel guilty that she was eating it without Jackie and the others? No, because once she'd smuggled them up there, they could all order as many chicken sandwiches and mugs of hot chocolate as they wanted!

Just before one o'clock, when Le Fay was hurrying to the Bellhop Suite for the first event on the Tap 'n' Type itinerary, Jackie (holding Fergal dressed as a baby) and Albie and Joshua (doing their best to look like one and the same person) were climbing off the coach along with all the other passengers. It wasn't that they'd reached their destination. Far from it. They were on a very, very long fenced road, which appeared to be in the middle of nowhere, with fields on either side, stretching far into the distance, without a single house or turn-off in sight. And there, in front of them, was a hole in the road. A big one.

This wasn't one of those holes in the road that you can drive over and everyone in the car feels funny in the pit of his/her stomach. This was the kind of hole that, if the coach driver attempted to drive over it, he would actually end up driving the coach into, and everyone would end up screaming 'Aaaaargh!' – except, perhaps, for Fergal, who (hindsight tells us) was prone to be as silent as a sack of rocks when falling any great distance – as they plummeted in the general direction of the centre of the Earth, with a capital 'E'.

The coach driver was attempting to lean over the edge of the hole to get an idea of just how deep it was, but was too frightened to get close enough to the edge to get a proper look.

'It weren't there this mornin',' he kept on saying.

The hole in the road can't have been there that long because there wasn't much of a queue of traffic in either direction. The coach was only three vehicles away from it, and there was only a handful of cars the other side of the hole, facing in the opposite direction. A wisp of black smoke drifted out of the hole and hung in the air like a sooty question mark.

'Who do you think made it?' Albie asked Jackie. He'd heard about such holes appearing out of nowhere, but never actually seen one before. He was running around Joshua in circles, in the hope that, if he kept moving, they might have the appearance of being one person with a blurred outline. The actual effect was of one of a pair of almost-identical twins running around the other.

'Who or *what*, my boy,' said the man with the moustache who'd been sitting next to Jackie throughout the journey,

'You mean aliens?' gasped Albie.

'I wish I knew. These holes have been springing up everywhere these past six months. No one seems to know why or how.' Once again, his moustache said nothing.

In keeping with pretending to be a baby, to avoid needing a ticket to travel, Fergal crawled on all-fours to the edge of the gigantic hole and peered into the vast nothingness below.

'Careful!' called Jackie, running after him.

'It's a long way down,' Fergal whispered.

'It weren't there this mornin',' said the coach driver. (I did mention he kept on saying that.)

'How do you propose to get us across, driver?' demanded a grey-haired woman passenger.

'We ain't never gettin' across that, lady,' he said.

'But we've a typing competition to get to!' said Jackie urgently. The man with the moustache eyed her with interest, but said nothing.

'And I am due to be matron of honour at a wedding!' said the grey-haired woman, indignantly.

'Well, it weren't there this mornin',' said the coach driver. If he'd been wearing a cap, I'm sure he'd have taken it off and scratched his head, but he wasn't, so he didn't.

'Then we must get around it,' Fergal blurted out, because he knew how important it was to Le Fay to have her family there to cheer her on.

The man with the moustache appeared at Jackie's side. 'Really bright kid,' he commented.

The driver who'd also heard the super-baby's comment shook his head. 'There's no way that I can get this coach around the edge of the hole,' he said. 'Who knows how soft the earth is in them fields? The whole thing might sink with us in it!'

'We could all wait until you'd driven around it and get back in afterwards,' the grey-haired woman suggested. 'That way the coach would be much lighter.'

'But I still might sink in it,' muttered the driver. 'There ain't no way I'm drivin' around it and that's final, missus!'

'Maybe not,' said the man with the moustache, 'but we can all walk round and try to hitch a ride off the people in the cars the other side. There's nothing they can do except turn back the way they came, anyhow.'

'A brilliant idea!' said Jackie. 'Can you unload our luggage, please, driver?'

While one group of passengers peered into the amazing hole, another argued with the coach driver to let them have their luggage. It wasn't easy.

'I'm only authorised to open the luggage

compartment and release luggage at the end of a journey, see?' he explained, making life difficult for everyone.

'But surely there are special rules for if there's an accident?' asked Jackie.

'Exactly!' said the grey-haired woman. 'Now get on with it, my good man. I've a wedding to attend.'

'But there hasn't been an accident,' the driver protested.

'There would have been if you hadn't stopped in time,' said Jackie.

'But there's nothing in the rules about unloading the luggage if an accident's been avoided,' whined the driver.

'Are there any other circumstances when you're allowed to release the luggage?' asked the man with the moustache, 'apart from when reaching our destination or in the event of an accident, I mean?'

'In the event of a breakdown,' said the driver.

'So, if the coach won't go, then you can let us have our luggage?' asked Albie, coming to a halt in his orbit around Joshua.

'If suitable alternat–' began the driver, but Albie and Joshua weren't listening, they were already sprinting over to the coach.

'Well, technically speaking, what with the queue

of cars now forming behind us and three cars and a huge hole in front, this coach can't go anywhere, now can it?' Jackie McNally asked politely.

'That's as maybe,' said the driver, 'but there's a difference between a car breaking down and—'

'Ah!' said the man with the moustache as a thought suddenly struck him. 'What if the coach was stuck in a patch of mud? The engine was working perfectly and everything, just that the wheels were slipping in the mud and the coach was going nowhere?'

The driver paused, then a smile slowly spread across his face. 'Then I'd probably unload the luggage . . . even though the coach itself ain't reached its destination, been in an accident nor broken down!'

'Exactly!' said the man, triumphantly.

'Which is the same as what's 'appened 'ere!' declared the coach driver.

'Exactly!' said Jackie, the man with the moustache, the grey-haired woman and Fergal-in-his-nappy, all together.

'Then let's get unloading!' declared the driver, striding towards his machine, just as Albie and Joshua McNally appeared from the other side of the coach, looking sheepish.

To anyone viewing Albie and Joshua front on, he or she'd only be able to tell that *Joshua* was looking sheepish, because Albie was standing directly behind him, flat against him, to create the impression of one double-thick human being, requiring just one ticket, rather than that of two almost-identical twins. At least that was the idea.

'You've got a flat tyre, mister,' Joshua told the driver. 'This coach is going nowhere.'

The driver let out a loud and multi-toned groan (surprisingly like the sound a set of half-inflated bagpipes might make if you sat on them, expelling the remaining air) and hurried off to investigate.

When she thought no one was looking, Jackie prodded Joshua in the ribs. 'He was going to unload the luggage anyway,' she said in a harsh whisper.

'But we didn't know that, did we?' came Albie's voice from the back of Joshua's head. 'And it's not as if we did anything to the engine or anything.'

'True,' Jackie agreed and smiled.

Not ten minutes later, Jackie, Albie and Joshua were skirting around the very large, very deep hole with the man with the moustache. Jackie was carrying Fergal, to keep up the pretence for the time being, Joshua and Albie were carrying their trunk between them and, as well as his own small suitcase (which he referred to as his valise), the man with the moustache carried the McNally's other case. The moustache carried nothing.

If something's funny once, it's funny a thousand times – as my Cousin Claire said the day the Iapohani Indians buried her alive to prevent her telling them any more knock-knock jokes – but you'll hear no more jokes about this man-with-a-moustache's moustache! Honestly. Perhaps it would be easier if I gave you his name, and now's an appropriate time because it was just about now that he told it to Jackie.

'My name's Peach, by the way,' he said.

'We're the McNallys,' said Jackie. 'I'm Jackie–'

'And I'm her brother Fergal and I'm not really a baby!' said Fergal, 'so you can put me down now, Jacks.'

Jackie stopped and put her little brother down.

'And we're two almost-identical twins, Albie and Joshua,' said Albie.

'I'm Joshua,' said Albie.

46

'And I'm Albie,' said Joshua. 'And we're not really one and the same person at all.'

'I never doubted it for a second,' said Mr Peach politely.

They continued skirting the edge of the hole. (It was a large one, remember.) Now that she had her hands free, Jackie insisted that she carry her own case, but Peach insisted that he continue to carry it for her.

Fergal dropped back behind the others and peered into the hole again. What on Earth could have made such a thing? Had it been something from above, or something from below? Whatever it was, Fergal was very glad that it hadn't opened up just as the coach had been driving over that very spot. He hoped that no one else had been driving over that spot at the time . . .

Fergal stopped in his tracks. He felt sure that he'd heard something.

'Ssssh!' he said.

Jackie carried on talking to Mr Peach, and Albie to Joshua.

'SHHHH!' he said, in capital letters this time. They SHHHH!-ed.

'Help,' said a strange and tiny voice.

Fergal gasped. 'I think it's coming from down there!' He pointed.

Chapter Five

Mr Peach grinned. It must have been a very large grin, because it even showed under his big moustache.

'Forgive me,' he said. 'I was pulling your leg.'

'What do you mean?' asked Fergal.

'Peter Piper picked a peck of pickled peppers,' said the tiny voice. 'Where's the peck of pickled peppers Peter Piper picked?'

'Huh?' said Fergal. One minute the whoever-whatever in the hole had been calling for help and now he-she-or-it was reciting tongue-twisters!

'There's no one down there, Fergal,' Mr Peach explained. 'I was having a bit of fun with you. I'm a ventriloquist.'

'*You* just said those Piper-pickling words?' gasped Fergal. 'But I didn't see your lips move.'

Mr Peach swelled with pride.

'Hardly surprising with that great big moustache

to hide them behind,' muttered a distinctly unimpressed Joshua.

Mr Peach's cheeks went peach-coloured.

'Don't be rude, Joshua!' snapped Jackie.

The twin muttered an apology.

'Say something else, Mr Peach,' urged Albie.

Mr Peach stopped in his tracks and put the luggage on the ground. He opened his valise and produced – not a ventriloquist's dummy, but a strange glove puppet of a snake, which he proceeded to slip over his left hand.

The snake then opened and closed its mouth as it appeared to recite the following poem:

> *I used to think the world was flat,*
> *Not rounded like a bowler hat,*
> *I used to think the sky was blue,*
> *But I was told 'That's nothing new',*
> *I used to think the sea was wet,*
> *(That's something one should not forget),*
> *I used to wish my poems rhymed,*
> *And still do wish it all the time.*

Fergal was impressed. Even though he ignored the puppet and looked directly at Mr Peach, there was nothing to suggest that the man was really doing the talking. It wasn't just that his lips weren't moving. His Adam's apple in his neck wasn't moving either and there was nothing in his expression to suggest that he was trying to look as if he *wasn't* talking, if you see what I mean. He really seemed to be watching the snake and listening to the poem too.

Moustache or no moustache, there was no denying that Mr Peach was a good ventriloquist. He pulled the snake glove puppet off his hand, stuffed it back into his valise and picked up the luggage. 'Come on!' he said. 'If you want to get to the city, we'd better get moving and try to get that lift.'

Fortunately for the passengers off the coach, quite a crowd had formed the other side of the hole. Those cars not occupied by people wanting to stand and gawp at the hole, marvelling at it, appearing out of nowhere and speculating as to when and where the next one might form, were turning around and heading back the way they came . . . in other words, heading in the direction the coach was supposed to have gone.

Many passengers who, like the McNallys and Mr Peach, ventured around the hole, were given lifts in next to no time. (The grey-haired matron-of-honour-to-be was one of the first.) Because Jackie insisted that she, Albie, Joshua and Fergal (still dressed as an enormous baby) all travelled together, people were unwilling to take them. The obvious excuse was 'no room' but, to be fair, a bunch of freckle-faced McNallys in their strange clothes might not be every driver's first choice of hitch-hiker, even if s/he was driving an empty minibus.

'It's been very kind of you to wait with us, Mr Peach,' said Jackie after yet another driver had refused them a lift, 'but I think you'd be far more likely to get into town on your own.'

'But I hate to leave you like this,' said Mr Peach.

'We quite understand,' said Jackie.

'We can look after ourselves, can't we, Albie?' said Albie, pretending to be Joshua.

'Of course we can, Joshua,' said Joshua, pretending to be Albie.

'Well, if you're sure . . .' said Mr Peach, hesitantly. 'But if you need help once you're in the city, look me up.' He pulled his calling card out of his top pocket. 'Call me if you need me, though I have a feeling we'll be meeting again anyhow!'

'Thank you,' said Jackie, putting the card away carefully.

Not five minutes later the ventriloquist got a lift

51

from a family who'd been planning a trip to an aunt in the country but had now decided to turn around and head for home.

Eventually, Jackie, Joshua, Albie and Fergal did get a lift, not in the back of a truck full of pigs and straw, as usually happens in such stories, but in the cab of a breakdown truck. The driver was a very jolly man called Noble and he was glad of the company. There was one big bench seat, running the width of the cab, and they all squeezed in next to each other, with their luggage fitted in around them.

Noble, whom the McNallys all later agreed looked rather like a giant vegetable – a turnip or a swede – but with hair sprouting out everywhere, was not only Noble by name but noble by nature. When he found out where they wanted to go, he drove them all the way to the back of The Dell hotel. He would have driven them right up to the entrance, of course, but Jackie had specifically asked him not to do that.

On the journey to the city, Noble had them singing car songs. You know the kind: *Ten Green Bottles, Row, Row, Row Your Boat, Old McDonald Had a Farm* and one the McNallys hadn't heard before called *I'll Tickle Thomas.* When it was your turn to sing, you had to think up a new place to tickle Thomas, and then, in the chorus, everyone had to remember – in the correct order – where Thomas had already been tickled. For those of you who hate sing-along-join-in songs, that journey in the breakdown truck would have been a living hell; but Noble and the McNallys had a great time. The twins, of course, wanted to tickle Thomas in rude places but knew that Jackie wouldn't let them, so did a lot of whispering of suggestions and giggling between them. Fergal wanted to tickle Thomas not 'under the chin' or 'on the nose' but 'under the bridge' or 'on the way home', which Noble thought was very clever!

Fergal loved being in the cab looking out at the road in front of them. The windscreen was covered in squashed flies and bugs and could have done with a very good clean, but Fergal didn't care. This was great . . . and he didn't have to pretend to be a baby, for fear of being thrown off. If the truth be told, he was glad that stupid hole had opened up in front of the coach. This was much more fun.

Although they'd lost time on the journey with the coach having broken down and their having to wait so long for a lift, Noble drove his battered breakdown truck much faster than any coach could go, so Jackie and the others weren't that late for their rendezvous with Le Fay. But late is late, and Le Fay was nowhere to be seen.

Noble drove off with a cheery wave from the cab of his truck, but didn't honk his horn. He probably guessed that Jackie and the others planned to stay at the hotel without necessarily telling the management or actually . . . er . . . paying!

★

Whilst the rest of the family were singing *I'll Tickle Thomas* with Noble, Le Fay McNally was putting her plan into action. She'd met the other finalists at the 'Meet the Other Finalists' finger buffet in the Bellhop Suite at one o'clock and, an hour later, she'd met the press at the 'Meet the Press', being 'A Photo Call with some of the Capital City's Leading Evening Newspapers'.

The finger buffet had been a relief to Le Fay. There hadn't been a finger to eat in sight, but nor was there a knife, fork or spoon, so she deduced what a finger buffet must be: a buffet where you didn't eat fingers but ate *with* your fingers! All the food was pretty much bite-size. It tasted good, but she was really glad that she'd eaten that chicken sandwich and drunk that hot chocolate up in her room. That'd been the best sandwich – and the best chicken – Le Fay had ever tasted. (Apologies to any vegetarian readers for going on about it.)

Le Fay now got to meet the two other finalists she hadn't already met, and liked them. Graham 'Lard' Large, whose dad owned Large Lunches, kept his distance, glaring at her whenever their eyes met by chance. Peggy Snoot was very polite and said 'How-do-you-do?' and shook Le Fay's hand. She asked her where she lived and whether she'd had a nice journey. When Le Fay got all excited about the train and the taxi ride, Peggy listened politely and didn't say anything boastful or nasty when Le Fay explained she'd never been on a train or in a taxi before.

Anna Malting explained that she'd been in the toughest heats to get this far in the competition so, by rights, she should have won already . . . but Le Fay could see that she was really nervous underneath and, by the end of the buffet, they were chatting together happily about animals. Anna had three gerbils, two hamsters and a guinea pig, but wasn't allowed a cat. Le Fay told her about Smoky, but didn't mention that he wasn't a pet but a rat-catcher, because she imagined gerbils, hamsters and guinea pigs were probably a bit like rats, so it might upset her.

'Why's he called Smoky?' asked Anna.

'Mum gave him that name,' said Le Fay. 'She named all of us.'

'I wish I had a cat,' said Anna, and the two girls found they'd become firm friends.

The 'Photo Call with some of the Capital City's Leading Evening Newspapers' wasn't quite what Le Fay had expected. She wasn't sure *what* she'd expected, but it wasn't three very young and bored-looking men in crumpled suits. Two had cameras with flash bulbs. The third had a notepad and a pen.

Malcolm from Tap 'n' Type made a short speech, as though talking to a room full of people, with the four finalists lined up behind him. The photographers took plenty of photos, and the man with the notepad sucked the end of his pen and didn't write anything down.

When the 'photo call' was finished, Malcolm passed a piece of paper headed PRESS RELEASE to him. The man muttered his thanks and stuffed it in a pocket of his jacket.

Just then, the door burst open and in came a man wearing an electric-blue suit, with a gleaming chrome camera around his neck.

'I'm sorry I'm late!' he said, sounding flustered.

'That's fine,' said Malcolm, stepping forward. 'Which paper are you from?'

'*Large Lunch Latest*,' said the man in the blue suit, walking straight past him.

'I . . . er . . .' Malcolm had obviously never heard of it.

'It's a newspaper for people who work in my father's company,' said Graham Large, stepping forward grandly. 'My father thought his workers would like to see a picture of me on the front page of the next issue.' He then turned his attention to the photographer. 'I was beginning to think you weren't coming!' he snapped.

'S-Sorry, Master Large,' said the man. He proceeded to take a series of stomach-churning pictures of Graham Large preening himself like a peacock. I expect that if the poor employees of Large Lunches ever saw the final full-colour photo on the front of their company newspaper, it put them off work for the rest of the day.

Le Fay didn't hang around to watch the one-boy photo session. This was the part of the itinerary where she had 'A Free Afternoon for Sightseeing'. In other words, she needed to go and wedge open the fire door at the side of the hotel, then meet Jackie, Fergal, Albie and Joshua around the back.

She took the lift back up to her room and took a box of tissues from the en suite bathroom. This would be thick enough to keep the door open, and thin enough not to make it too obvious. Making her way back down the now familiar route of the drab fire-exit stairs, her tummy had never felt so full in her life. She couldn't wait to get the rest of the family – except for grumpy old Captain Rufus, of course – up to her room to order them chicken sandwiches and chocolate.

At the foot of the stairs at last, Le Fay pushed the bar to the fire-exit door and swung it open a fraction, ready to wedge the box of tissues in place. There was a loud ringing in her ears.

She'd set off an alarm!

Chapter Six

Le Fay didn't panic. She slipped out into the street and began walking ever so casually along the pavement, looking as if she didn't have a care in the world. She glanced up at the clock on a building opposite. Five minutes to three. The others should be there soon, but how was she going to get them inside now? What she needed was Plan B, and she didn't have a Plan B!

The hotel alarm stopped and The Dell's chief house detective, Twinkle-Toes Tweedy picked up the squashed tissue box wedging the fire-exit door open. He looked out into the street – left and right – making a mental note of the people he saw there. He then swung the door shut. Le Fay didn't see him, of course, because she was walking away from the scene of her 'crime'.

She walked around the block a few times, keeping an eye out for her brothers and sister.

Three-fifteen came and went, and there was still no sign of them. She had no way of knowing that the coach had been abandoned and that they were, at that moment, in the cab of a breakdown truck singing *I'll Tickle Thomas*, as they reached the outskirts of the city.

When the clock across the street read 3.30, Le Fay decided to go back up to her room to call the coach company. Jackie had given her the number, 'in case of emergency', when she'd bought the tickets.

Le Fay walked through the brass and glass revolving door into the fabulous foyer of The Dell. Everything gleamed. It all looked so clean and shiny to Le Fay. Her jaw had dropped in wonder when Malcolm had led her through it a few hours earlier, and it seemed just as magical now.

She made her way across a carpet so plush that even her light weight sank into the pile. She reached up and pressed a button to call the lift. A man in a checked suit appeared, as if out of nowhere, at her side.

'Hello, little lady,' he said quietly. 'And where might you be going?'

Le Fay pulled her door key out of the pocket at the front of her dress. 'To my room,' she said, nervously. She knew she looked out of place in such a swanky hotel.

'So you're a guest, are you?' said the man.

61

'Yes,' said Le Fay. 'I'm a finalist in the Tap 'n' Type competition here tomorrow.'

'That's great,' said the man. 'Congratulations.'

Le Fay looked up at the man properly. He had a kind, round face. 'Are you a guest too?'

He shook his head. 'No. I'm Charlie Tweedy,' he said. 'I'm the hotel's chief house detective.'

Le Fay went bright red.

'Don't I know you from somewhere?' said Tweedy. 'Your face seems very familiar.'

'I don't think so, Mr Tweedy,' said Le Fay.

At that moment, the lift door opened. Le Fay hurried inside. Twinkle-Toes stayed in the foyer. 'Nice meeting you, Miss . . .?'

'Le Fay.'

'Miss Le Fay,' he said. 'Good luck in the competition tomorrow.'

'Th-Thanks,' stuttered Le Fay as the lift doors closed. Tweedy stared into her eyes and she could imagine him reading all her inner thoughts. She gulped. She had to smuggle Jackie, Fergal and the twins not only into the hotel, but also past Mr Tweedy. Things were getting tougher by the minute.

Twinkle-Toes Tweedy's office wasn't really an office at all – which makes this sentence an oxymoron (which may sound like an idiot with breathing difficulties, but actually means something that contradicts itself, such as the statement: 'All light is dark.'), but I'm sure you know what I'm getting at. He thought of it more as a cubbyhole but, if the truth be told, what it really was was a large built-in hotel linen cupboard with the door taken off. You could see on the door frame where the hinges had once been. The spaces had been painted over, but even the screw-holes were still there. To the left of the door frame was a sign printed on to card which read:

CAPTAIN C. TWEEDY (RETD) CHIEF HOUSE DETECTIVE

in a typeface that Tweedy secretly thought was better suited to a menu in a swish Manhattan restaurant than announcing a man of his profession. The 'retd' in brackets meant that he was a retired captain, not a retired house detective. No, sir. He was still very much on the case when it came to odd goings-on in *his* hotel.

Under this official sign, provided by The Dell management, was an unofficial sign added in the detective's own, fine handwriting. It read:

MY DOOR IS ALWAYS OPEN

which those of you with more intelligence than a cake of soap – which, no doubt, includes *most* readers of this quality book – will realise was, at least partly, a joke . . . because his cupboard/cubbyhole/office had no door. Having said that (which is what I've just done), Twinkle-Toes Tweedy would have had an open-door policy even if he'd had a door. In other words, door or no door, his door (or no door) was always metaphorically open. Clear? Don't lie.

Let me put it another way: Captain Twinkle-Toes Tweedy (retd) didn't believe in shutting himself away and making himself self-important, unlike a number of ex-policemen who ended up in private security jobs. Twinkle-Toes thought that the best way to keep law and order in a big hotel like The Dell was to know all the latest gossip and rumour, and the best way to do that was to welcome anyone and everyone who felt like coming to his office for a nice chat and a cup of something hot.

When junior management came in for a chat, they'd describe it as 'touching base' or 'keeping him informed'. If one of the women from the laundry came in, she might say that it was for a 'good old chin-wag'. Golgotha (the man who looked after the boiler and central heating) called it 'a jaw' and the ladies from the waitress staff might have 'a good old natter'. Other expressions for talking to Twinkle-Toes included 'a chit-chat', 'sharing the craik' (pronounced 'crack') and, more honestly than most, 'having a good old gossip' or 'dishing the dirt'.

In order to make sure that people kept on coming back to him, the house detective had three important rules:

1. Never to reveal his sources.
2. Always to have a good supply of tea and coffee.
3. Always to have a good supply of the very best chocolate biscuits in the hotel.

Number one was so that people wouldn't be afraid to tell him things. If a bit of gossip led to him catching members of staff stealing, for example, he'd never let slip who might have pointed him in their direction.

Number two was straightforward enough, except that at the time that these events took place, as well as huge holes springing up out of nowhere, there was a terrible world coffee shortage, for some reason. Don't ask me why. It probably had something to do with a severe frost in the main coffee-growing countries killing off all the little coffee beans, but I'm only guessing. Although I'm married to someone called Doctor Coffey – it's true, I promise you (her name is spelled with an 'ey' instead of an 'ee') – that doesn't make her a coffee expert either. Anyway, getting hold of a catering pack of 1,000 teabags was no problem for old Twinkle-Toes, but having so much as a small jar of instant coffee to hand meant that the retired police detective had to call in a lot of old favours, twist a lot of arms and pull a few strings (to involve as many metaphors as possible). Whilst many of the guests were being served poor quality coffee mixed with chicory, down in Twinkle-Toes Tweedy's office you could actually get yourself a cup of the stuff that actually tasted like coffee!

The chocolate biscuits were the icing on the cake, if you see what I mean. They were to bait those who weren't hooked by the 'never-reveal-his-sources' or 'chance-of-a-decent-cuppa' rules.

Sitting in Tweedy's cubbyhole that afternoon,

sipping a cup of the detective's prized coffee, was Mrs Doon, head of housekeeping. It was her team of women whose job it was to make the beds and clean the rooms in The Dell. It was also their job to replace the boxes of tissues when they were empty.

On the desk between them sat the crumpled box of tissues that Le Fay McNally had used to wedge the fire door open, and triggered off the alarm in so doing.

'It's definitely from one of the rooms, is it not, Mrs Doon?' the detective was asking.

'Either that, or taken from the stock room or from one of my girls' cleaning carts, Mr T,' replied Mrs Doon. She always referred to Captain Tweedy as 'Mr T' and her team of chambermaids as 'her girls'. Some of them were girls, barely of school-leaving age. Some of them were not. Some of them had grandchildren or even great-grandchildren. To call them 'girls' was a bit like calling the pope 'slightly religious'. It was misleading, to say the least. The cleaning carts she also mentioned, by the way, were the carts 'her girls' left outside the rooms as they cleaned, containing replacement bars of soap, sachets of shampoo and shower gel and little boxes of neatly furled shower caps. (I'm not 100 per cent sure one can furl, or unfurl, a shower cap but, as one can furl and unfurl a flag, I thought why not give it a go.)

'Good point,' said Twinkle-Toes Tweedy. 'And your girls are unlikely to be able to tell if someone took a packet off their carts, aren't they?'

'I'm afraid so,' said Mrs Doon.

'Do many guests take the tissues with them when they leave?' asked Tweedy.

He knew the answer before he asked it. He'd worked there long enough. He knew that the average guest took all the toiletries in the bathroom; then there were those who stole the bath plug along with the odd towel or three as well; and then there were those who took all of that, plus the tissues, plus just about anything else that wasn't nailed down or that could be smuggled out. Some chancers even

68

lowered the television sets out of their windows to accomplices waiting below. Once Tweedy had caught a man trying to leave the hotel with an ironing board and a full-length mirror (which he'd unscrewed from the inside of the wardrobe door) inside a zip-up cover designed to contain a surfboard, carried out along with a whole host of other sporting gear from skis to lacrosse rackets! It turned out that the thief had been stealing ironing boards and full-length mirrors in all the hotels around town and no one had been able to work out how, so Tweedy was a local hero among hotel house detectives for a while.

'Yes, a number of them take the tissues, as you well know, Mr T,' said Mrs Doon. 'But the majority leave them be.'

'Well, what I'd like you to do is to instruct your girls to let you know which rooms on the east side of the building are without boxes of tissues tomorrow morning, please, Mrs Doon. I'd be extremely grateful.' He'd said 'east side' because the tissue box had been wedged in the door of one of the east-side fire exits. Of course, the door-wedger might have deliberately come all the way from the north, south or west side to be as far from their room as possible, but Tweedy needed to narrow the search somehow. And, anyway, he had a hunch.

'Of course, Mr T,' said The Dell's housekeeper. 'Anything you say . . . Any chance of another chocky bickie and another cup of coffee?'

Captain Twinkle-Toes Tweedy spooned out the coffee granules into a fresh cup as though they were gold dust. '*Of course*, Launa,' he grinned.

Le Fay wondered what to do next. She decided that all she *could* do was go back downstairs and hang around outside the hotel, trying to keep as inconspicuous as possible, until her family showed up. She closed her door, hurried across the landing to the lift and pressed the button, imagining the large house detective watching her every move. The man had been very polite and everything, but that was probably one of the tricks of the trade, to keep criminals off their guard so that they'd slip up and make a mistake. Not that she was a real criminal, of course, but she was planning to get five of them sleeping in a room meant for one!

There was a 'ping' and the lift doors opened. Le Fay's greatest fear was that she'd find Tweedy already inside, or the dreadful Graham Large. To her relief, there were a handful of total strangers. She smiled at them. One or two smiled back and the rest of them looked straight ahead (as people in lifts so often do) and she stepped inside.

The lift stopped on five more floors on the way down and, fortunately for Le Fay, no one familiar entered. Once in the foyer, she strode purposefully out of the entrance and took up position on the other side of the street.

She didn't have to wait long. Once Jackie and the others had been dropped off at the side of the hotel by that nice Mr Noble, Jackie had decided that they should walk briskly around the block until Le Fay put in an appearance . . . and, sure enough, here they were now.

Albie caught sight of Le Fay before she saw them. He nudged his twin, Joshua, in the ribs. 'There she is!' he said.

''Bout time too,' said Josh, who was feeling hungry.

They ran across to reach Le Fay, who, rather than stopping and hugging them, started walking off. 'Keep moving,' she instructed.

It was only when they were around the corner from the entrance and the possible prying eyes of the doorman, that Le Fay gave each of them a hug and a kiss.

'You made it!' she said.

71

'What's the hotel like?' asked Fergal excitedly. 'Does your room have a bath or a shower? Does it have feather pillows?'

'Is there a television?' asked Albie.

'Are there blankets or a duvet?' asked Joshua.

'Do they feed you?' asked Fergal.

'Give the girl a chance!' laughed Jackie, in her big-sister role.

'What kept you?' asked Le Fay.

'Holes!' the twins chorused as one.

'A great big one opened up in front of the coach,' Fergal explained. 'We got a lift from a man in a pick-up truck.'

'Save that story for later,' said Jackie. 'Have you found a way to get us inside?' she asked Le Fay.

'I had a brilliant plan,' said Le Fay, and she told them about the back stairs, the fire exit and setting off the alarm.

'Oh dear,' said Jackie. 'I'm beginning to think you'll never be able to smuggle us in there!'

Chapter Seven

In the end, after all that planning and worrying, getting her sister and brothers into the hotel and up to her room was as easy as pie. Why pie should be easy I've never been quite sure. I personally have trouble making pastry, so would rather say 'as easy as stew', but the saying is 'as easy as pie', so I feel safer sticking with that.

Le Fay, Jackie, Albie, Joshua and Fergal were all standing around the corner from the entrance to The Dell, trying to come up with a Plan B, when Malcolm Kent from Tap 'n' Type appeared, shopping bag in hand.

'Hello, Le Fay,' he said. 'How are you enjoying things so far?'

'Very much, thank you,' said Le Fay.

Malcolm put down his bag of shopping. 'This must be your family,' he said (which, with their wiry ginger-red hair, freckles and – with the exception of Jackie – buck teeth, was an easy assumption to make). He put out his hand and shook Jackie's. 'Aren't you going to introduce me?'

'She's my big sister, Jackie,' said Le Fay.

'How do you do?' said Malcolm.

'How do you do?' said Jackie.

Back then, that was the correct response to a how-do-you-do? Nowadays people respond with a 'fine, thanks; how about you?' and then the first person says 'fine', and it takes up far too much time.

'Here to support Le Fay at the competition? Lovely.'

'I'm Albie,' said Joshua.

'And I'm Josh,' said Albie.

'I rather suspect it's the other way around,' said Malcolm as he shook their hands, which was pretty impressive, since he'd never even met them before.

'How on Earth did you know that?' asked Le Fay, so impressed that she forgot her shyness.

'Well, if I was a young near-identical twin, I think I'd pretend to be the other one, just to confuse grown-ups,' said Malcolm. 'And last but not least?'

'I'm Fergal,' said Fergal. 'The brains of the family!' which, as time will show, was rather an ironic thing to say.

'A pleasure to meet you too,' said Malcolm. 'Are you staying locally?'

'At a B&B,' said Jackie hurriedly. The tip of her nose went pink, which the McNallys knew meant that she was telling a fib.

Malcolm picked up his shopping bag and turned to Le Fay. 'Why not show them your room before they check into their B&B?' he suggested. 'That way they can see you're all settled in and ready for tomorrow's competition.'

Fergal had no idea what a 'B&B' was and was still impressed by Jackie's quick thinking . . . and delighted that they'd found a way inside. Of course, the poor chap had no way of knowing that this would be the building he'd fall to his death from; but perhaps that was a good thing. Think how gloomy *that* piece of news would have made him.

It turned out that Malcolm had nipped out to buy some additional balloons and streamers to add the finishing touches to the room where the grand finals of the competition were to take place. He was showing Jackie the contents of his shopping bag as they sauntered through the entrance of The Dell and walked over to the row of lift doors. Being with Malcolm of Tap 'n' Type and Le Fay, who was booked in with a room, the others felt as though they had every right to be there, so didn't look in the least bit shifty. Shabby?

75

Yes. Shifty? No. Not that they had any intention of looking around their sister's room and then heading off to check into some non-existent bed-and-breakfast place.

Once Le Fay had proudly fished the golden key out of her pocket and unlocked the door, the others piled into her hotel room and went over every inch of it.

They all liked the en suite bathroom best. You turned on the taps and water came straight out – *hot* water at that, if that's what you wanted – and there was a shower *and* a bath . . . and it was all just for them. Well, just for Le Fay really, but the five of them would be using it (sooner rather than later, as it turned out).

In fact, the first thing Jackie insisted on was that they each had a bath or a shower, one after the other. Now, one or two of you may not be a big fan of washing, but the good thing is, if you *have* to wash – say you've fallen on a doggy doo or something – it's good to know that there's hot water if you need it. For the McNallys, a shower was when it wasn't raining very hard and a bath was a very rare event in an old tin tub, so they had a great time washing.

By the end of it, their skins had never looked so pink and they'd never felt – and smelled – so clean!

Le Fay told them about the chicken sandwich and the mug of hot chocolate you could get by picking up the phone and just asking.

'I could do that just before I go off to supper,' said Le Fay, checking her itinerary ('Dinner with our Generous Sponsors in the Sizzle Grill at eight o'clock').

'But they'll be rather suspicious if you ask for four more sandwiches and four more cups of hot chocolate,' said Fergal. 'We don't want to risk being found out.'

'Good point,' said Le Fay, thinking back to her brief encounter with Captain Charlie 'Twinkle-Toes' Tweedy, chief house detective.

'I don't think it's only chicken sandwiches you have to order,' said Jackie, who was that much older so, though never having been to a hotel before either, knew that much more about room service. 'If you ordered a large piece of fish with extra chips, that should easily feed the four of us, and they'll simply assume that you're really, really

77

hungry. Try asking for cod.'

'OK,' said Le Fay, doubtfully. She picked up the phone and dialled '1'. When the woman answered at the other end, Le Fay asked for a large piece of cod with extra chips.

'Breaded or battered?' asked the voice.

Le Fay had no idea that 'breaded' meant covered in breadcrumbs, so said, 'Battered please,' (which you might have guessed, if you remembered what I said on page 11).

'One large battered cod and chips with extra chips,' said the woman. 'It comes with a selection of sauces: vinegar, brown sauce, ketchup. Would you like anything to drink?'

Le Fay put her hand over the receiver. 'Drink?' she asked.

Jackie shook her head. 'We'll have water from the tap,' she whispered.

Le Fay spoke into the telephone. 'No thank you,' she said.

'It'll be with you in half an hour, dear,' said the woman from Room Service. 'Room 1428.'

Fergal, Joshua, Albie and Jackie hid in the bathroom when the knock on the door came and the food was delivered. The waiter'd barely gone when they piled back into the bedroom and inspected the food he'd left on the tray.

'It's a feast!' said Joshua excitedly, grabbing a

chip. Jackie slapped the back of his hand. 'That's one less chip for you. We share this out equally.'

The other three groaned, but they knew that fair was fair and that, if anyone had a little less than the others, it'd be Jackie herself. Her excuse was that she had less growing to do.

Le Fay looked on, proud that, whether she won or not, her getting this far in the competition had got them all a night in a hotel room away from their father, which, in turn, had got them a good meal and plenty of baths!

When Le Fay went downstairs for her supper, Jackie made the others sit on the bed and watch television with the sound down low, because they didn't want to arouse suspicion. (She'd made them wash their greasy fingers first, though.)

Fergal was so excited to get his hands on the remote control that he kept on wanting to change channels all the time. Jackie made them start off by watching a nature documentary on grizzly bears. Soon they were all watching it, open-mouthed. The picture was so clear it was almost as if they were there in the mountains with the bears.

'I wish we could stay in this hotel room for ever,' said Albie.

'Me too,' sighed Jackie.

*

The next morning was the morning of the Grand Final of the Tap 'n' Type competition. Although Le Fay had slept in the bed because, after all, it was her typing skill that had got them the room in the first place, she'd had a pretty sleepless night. She'd been lying awake thinking of nasty Graham Large with his spun-sugar hair, and the fear of losing to him of all people. Albie had slept on the sofa and Joshua had slept on the sofa cushions on the floor. Fergal had slept in the open bottom drawer of the chest of drawers (with extra pillows, found in the top of the closet, for padding). Jackie had slept under a blanket in the bath, when she wasn't on the prowl.

Le Fay had come back from the previous night's meal with a 'doggy bag'. Malcolm had spotted her slipping a bread roll into the pocket of her dress and asked one of the waiters to bring him a paper bag.

'If there's anything you can't finish now but

might want to eat later, pop it in here,' he had told the appreciative girl. 'Everyone does it!' he'd said. Malcolm, who started out a nice chap in this story was beginning to turn into a very nice one. If the truth be told, Le Fay hadn't spotted a single other doggy bag all evening!

By the time Le Fay had made it back up to her room, the bag had been fit to burst. Whilst she now went down to breakfast with Malcolm and the other contestants, she left Jackie to share out the contents of the doggy bag for a breakfast feast.

When Le Fay entered the Sun Deck Breakfast Restaurant, Peggy Snoot and Anna Malting were already seated at a round table covered with a cream-coloured linen tablecloth. Peggy was polite as always, and Anna was eager to talk about all the different fruits and cereals and how much her gerbils would have liked eating them for their breakfast. (Le Fay wondered if Smoky had caught any rats while they were away.)

Malcolm wandered over to the table with a fruit juice in his hand. He'd been getting a refill. 'Good morning, Le Fay,' he smiled. 'Sleep well?'

'The bed was very comfortable but I was awake thinking about the competition for a lot of the time,' confessed Le Fay.

'Me too,' said Anna, 'I was so excited.'

'And I'm so nervous,' said Peggy.

'So am I,' said Malcolm, 'and I'm not even taking part.'

The girls were laughing at this as the shadow of Graham Large's quiff appeared over the mini-pots of marmalade and jam in the centre of the table.

'Good morning,' he said. 'I was hoping for a separate table.'

'We need to sit together so that I can fill you all in on the day's events,' said Malcolm. 'Sorry.'

The boy sat in the seat between Le Fay and Malcolm. She could smell his scented, oiled skin and the various gels and sprays in his hair. It was a bit like walking past the perfume counter in a department store, with all the competing smells mingling into one very expensive one.

No wonder he's the last one down to breakfast, thought Le Fay. He must take hours preparing himself.

'How did you sleep?' Malcolm asked the boy.

'Terribly,' said Graham Large. 'There was a drip coming from my shower and the noise kept me awake . . .'

'Couldn't you have shut the bathroom door?' Peggy suggested. 'Surely that would have blocked out the noise?'

'But I would have known that it was still dripping,' said Graham, 'which would have been just as bad.'

'I'm sorry to hear that,' said Malcolm, though he later revealed that he wasn't sorry at all. Graham Large had a whole suite of rooms and if the drip-drip-drip had bothered his poor little sensitive soul that much, he could have slept on the pull-out bed in the sitting room, far far away from the bathroom.

'So what did you do?' asked Anna.

'I called the night porter and had him fix it.'

'Wow!' said Anna, clearly impressed. 'What time was that?'

'About three o'clock in the morning.'

'I'll bet he loved you,' Le Fay muttered under her breath. She and Graham had avoided eye contact since he'd sat down.

Graham pretended not to have heard her. 'It's what these people are here for, of course,' he said. 'To serve.' He snapped his podgy fingers together and cried out, '*Garçon*,' which Le Fay knew from her French lessons meant 'boy'.

A waiter in a red waistcoat appeared by their table. 'Sir?' he said, raising an eyebrow.

'Four on a raft and wreck 'em,' he said. 'White bread, and weak tea. China. And I mean weak.'

'Sir,' nodded the waiter. He seemed to understand what Graham Large had wanted, even though it'd sounded to Le Fay as if he'd been talking in code. (The 'four' referred to in 'four on a raft and wreck 'em' meant four eggs; the 'raft' was the toast on which they'd be served, which Graham had specified should be made from white bread. The 'wreck 'em' referred to the fact that the eggs should be scrambled.)

'Would anyone else like to order?' asked the waiter, turning to the others with a much more human expression.

'Ladies?' said Malcolm. 'You can have bacon, fried egg, poached egg, boiled egg, scrambled egg, sausage, beans, mushrooms, kippers, waffles . . . You name it, they've got it.' He turned to Le Fay. 'Of course, that's after you've helped yourself to fruit, fruit juices and cereals from the table over there.'

Le Fay felt as if she'd gone to Heaven. Little did

she realise that, less than twelve hours later, that's where everyone would be telling her Fergal had gone, to try to make her feel better after the SPLAT! incident. She settled for bacon, sausage, mushroom, beans and a fried egg. For those of you interested in food, Anna stuck with cereal and toast and Peggy had a plate of waffles and maple syrup. Malcolm had three kippers.

Le Fay had just cut into her sausage when Graham spoke. 'I know they'd be called stowaways if we were on board ship,' he said, 'but what do you call people who hide away in other people's hotel rooms without paying? Apart from "thieves", that is?' Le Fay stopped cutting and stared at her plate.

'What is this?' asked Malcolm. 'A crossword clue?'

'No, it is a matter of grave concern,' said Master Large.

'What do you mean?' asked Malcolm.

'I mean that I believe there to be people staying in this hotel who are here without the management's knowledge or permission,' said Graham.

Malcolm fixed the boy's eyes in a stare. 'I understood that perfectly,' he said, 'but what I don't understand is why that should be of grave concern to you. Unless Large Lunches has part ownership in this hotel?'

'No,' said Graham, a little put out, 'but don't you think it any honest citizen's duty to report a crime if he discovers one?'

'Absolutely,' agreed Malcolm, pulling a tiny fishbone from between his teeth. 'So where are these hotel-equivalent of stowaways? Hiding in the boiler room? Living behind the pot plants in the Palm Court Tea Room?'

Peggy giggled. Graham Large gave her the benefit of one of his nasty sneers. Le Fay kept on staring at her plate.

'I happened to get out of the lift on the wrong floor on my way down to breakfast,' said Large, turning to look directly at Le Fay now. 'I was walking past Room 1428, which, I would imagine from the closeness of the doors to each other was a single room' – he said the word 'single' as though it was something very nasty he'd just trodden in – 'when I heard a whole gaggle of whispering voices.'

'And what leads you to believe that these guests are – how shall I put it? – "uninvited"?' asked Malcolm. He knew full well that Le Fay's room number was 1428. Of course he did. He'd shown Le Fay to it only the day before. He also knew full well that Graham Large knew full well that it was Le Fay's room and, although Malcolm had no idea about the boy's visit to her room or the Large/Lard incident, he didn't like what Graham was up to (whatever the reason).

'Because I heard one of them say, "Keep the noise down, you don't want anyone to hear us."'

That would have been sensible Jackie, keeping order as always, thought Le Fay.

Malcolm put his knife and fork together on his plate and pushed it away from him. 'You're not quite the detective you think you are, Graham,' said Malcolm. 'The room you just mentioned is Le Fay's and, if you'd been up as early as she and I were, you'd have known that her family turned up first thing this morning ready to cheer her along at the competition. With all the hotel reception rooms so quiet this time of the morning, I suggested that they go up to Le Fay's room while we had breakfast. As for wanting to 'keep the noise down', the McNallys seem a very considerate family and wouldn't dream of interrupting the other guests . . . Think how much that dripping tap upset you!'

Le Fay couldn't believe what she was hearing. She wanted to throw her arms around Malcolm from Tap 'n' Type and give him a great big HUG! He must have realised that the whole 'B&B' business was made up and that the others had been there all night, but he was lying through his teeth for her.

Somewhat deflated, Graham Large suddenly looked a little smaller. Le Fay tucked into the remains of her breakfast with relish.

Chapter Eight

The Tap 'n' Type grand finals were introduced by the Chairman of Tap 'n' Type, Count Medoc Silverman. Count Medoc wore a pinstripe suit, but the stripes must have been drawn with a pretty thick pin because they were pretty thick stripes. He stood to the front of the stage in The Dell's Empress Conference Suite and explained to the audience how the competition would proceed.

'Above my head are four giant screens,' he said, though you'd have had to have your eyes shut or been blind to miss them. 'And each screen is connected to the keyboard of an individual finalist. That way we'll be able to see each and every letter appear as they type.'

There was a ripple of applause, mainly from Tap 'n' Type employees, who thought it was safer to clap at everything their chairman said, just in case he was offended if they didn't.

Each screen was labelled with a contestant's name. Top left read: G. LARGE; bottom left: P. SNOOT; top right: A. MALTING; and bottom right: L. MCNALLY.

There'd been some discussion between the organisers as to whether it should have been 'LF. MCNALLY', her first name being Le Fay, but it was decided that it was fairer if they were all given just one initial each.

Count Silverman went on to explain that it was a knock-out competition. At the end of each round of typing, the contestant with the lowest score would drop out of the competition. This meant that the final round would be a head-to-head between the two best typists . . . but there'd be only one winner.

On the word 'winner', the audience applauded the chairman once again. Now it was Malcolm's turn to speak. 'The first round is dictation,' he announced. 'So that no single contestant can have the slightest advantage of being familiar with the piece read out to them, or of having, accidentally or otherwise' – his eyes came to rest on Graham Large – 'seen it written down beforehand, our four grand finalists will be typing the words of our special guest, who will be making them up as he goes along.' Malcolm paused to catch his breath. 'So let's give a big Tap 'n' Type welcome to ventriloquist and beat poet Hieronymus Peach!'

Mr Peach – yes, *that* Mr Peach: the one with the great big moustache – bounded on to the stage with his valise in his hand. He saw the McNallys in the second row (behind the Large family and friends, who'd taken up the whole front row, on each side of the central aisle) and gave them a special wink.

'He didn't tell us he'd be here!' Fergal whispered loudly to Jackie.

'Shh!' said Jackie. 'He said we'd meet again.'

'Now the rules are simple,' said Malcolm. 'In this first round, Hieronymus Peach will make up three poems on subjects chosen by the audience. The contestants will type as he speaks.' He turned to the four contestants, seated at four separate desks, with four separate keyboards and screens. 'Are you ready, Tap 'n' Type grand finalists?'

'Ready!' they said together (as rehearsed beforehand). Graham Large added a sneer and a thumbs-up to his supporters.

'Good luck, each and every one of you. May the best typist win!'

There were cheers and claps, this time more from the finalists' families and friends than from the Tap 'n' Type employees. Malcolm wasn't the chairman, so they didn't need to suck up to him.

'Come on, my boy!' boomed a voice from the front row. No prizes for guessing who that must have been. The only boy in the competition was Graham Large, so that must have been his father, Mr David Large of Large Lunches.

Jackie looked over to him. He looked like an even fatter, more perfumed and coiffured version of the boy on the stage, whom Le Fay had told her so much about. ('Coiffured' means his hair had been made to look *really lovely*.)

'So let's choose a topic for the first poem. Any suggestions?' Malcolm asked the audience.

'Holes!' shouted Fergal.

'The Moon!' shouted Jackie.

'Prize roses!' shouted a smartly dressed woman in tweeds, who later turned out to be Peggy Snoot's mum.

'Doggies!' shouted a little boy, sitting on his own near the back.

'Doggies,' said Malcolm, with a little nod. He turned to Mr Peach, who was already rummaging

92

in his valise and pulling out a glove puppet in the shape of a black Scottie dog. 'Mr Peach, please make up your poem. Contestants, please type as he speaks . . .'

Suddenly, the dog appeared to be singing:

Don't let your doggy do
Doggy doos [full stop]
Don't let your doggy do
Doggy doos [full stop]
For if he does doggy doos [comma]
Then he'll end up
In the news [full stop]
So don't let your doggy do
Doggy doos [exclamation mark]

The Scottie dog glove puppet bowed, the audience cheered and everyone had their eyes fixed on the screens.

'Full marks to all contestants!' Malcolm announced, as Mr Peach put the puppet back in his valise.

'This isn't going to be as boring as I thought,' said Albie, who was really hoping that his sister would win and had been really looking forward to the coach journey and coming to the capital. It was just the typing part he hadn't been so thrilled about . . . and who could really blame him?

The next topic chosen by Malcolm from suggestions from the audience was 'nightmares'.

Mr Peach produced a glove puppet that looked like a gargoyle – a hideous head carved in stone. When the head began to speak, it somehow sounded old and evil and Fergal found it hard to believe that it was really the same Mr Peach who'd just made the Scottie dog appear to speak, and the snake appear to talk on the previous day.

At night when half the world is sleeping
[comma]
Into your dreams this thing comes creeping
[full stop]
Inside your head its thoughts invade
With flashes of fear from its slashing blade
[exclamation mark]
The nightmare seeps into your mind
And leaves no pretty thoughts behind
[full stop]
If you can't escape its deadly grasp
[comma]
This gasp of air – the gargoyle puppet appeared to make a desperate attempt to gulp down air – *could be your last* [full stop]

With that, the hideous head fell from the ventriloquist's hand and lay on the bare boards of the stage, still panting for breath. Those in the audience who'd spotted this leant forward with a gasp, then broke into loud cheers. This Hieronymus Peach was a crowd-pleaser.

In that poem, Anna Malting had put an apostrophe in 'its' and had left out the 'h' in 'behind' because she'd been typing too quickly. Peggy Snoot had spelled 'seeps' with an 'a'. With one poem to go in this first round, Graham Large and Le Fay McNally hadn't made a single mistake.

*

For those of you who enjoy the gruesome gory bits, thank you for your patience. You're probably far more interested in what happened to Fergal's lifeless body when the ambulance completed its journey than you are in the typing competition. Now, I could say, 'Tough luck,' but jumping forwards again has advantages for all you readers. If we can get a little more of the nasty stuff out of the way *now*, then we don't have to save it all up until the end.

Doing it this way, we've already had Fergal fall out of the window and we've already had him land on the pavement (or sidewalk, or whatever you want to call it) and we've already had him declared dead by the medical examiner and picked up by the ambulance. If we could just get his body to the morgue, then we could get back to some of the nicer, jolly stuff with him still alive.

This way, when you reach page 133, you won't

go away feeling really, really depressed but will have got used to the idea that poor little Fergal McNally is as squashed as a bug underfoot. So, to the morgue:

The ambulance pulled up at the back entrance of the Sacred Heart Hospital and backed straight up to the doors leading down to the morgue. Morris (the paramedic) jumped down and opened the rear door of his vehicle. He slid out the stretcher bearing Fergal in the black, zipped-up body bag and laid it on a gurney (which isn't an island near Jersey but a trolley on wheels).

It had started to rain and the pitter patter of raindrops on the body bag sounded to the paramedic like someone drumming their fingers on . . . on a body bag. He hoped it wasn't coming from the inside because there was no way that this DOA (Dead On Arrival) wasn't DOA (Dead On Arrival), not after the stain he'd left on the pavement.

He banged the gurney through a pair of swing doors into the dry. Now inside an old lift, he pulled the concertina doors closed, punched a button and the contraption lurched downward, taking him and Fergal McNally's lifeless body to the bowels of the hospital.

Morris wheeled the body along a dingy, ill-lit corridor (where badly lagged pipes lined the ceiling) into the pathology lab. The pathologist was nowhere to be seen, but sitting in the corner, reading a magazine, was a scruffy-looking man wearing a white coat. It was the assistant path lab assistant.

'Hi, Morris,' said the assistant path lab assistant, glancing up from an article on 'Caring for your Cacti'.

'Hi, Dennis,' said the ambulanceman.

'What have you got for us today?' asked Dennis. He put down his magazine and wandered over to the body bag.

'A young kid fell out of a hotel window,' said Morris. 'Terrible shame.'

'Terrible,' agreed Dennis, trying to look serious rather than bored. This was only a summer job, and he usually spent his summers selling ice creams over in Gerton Park. He had been hoping to sell ice creams again that year, but his cousin Barney had pipped him to the post, so he'd had to find something else to do, which is how he came to be working in the basement of the Sacred Heart.

'Where's the Doc?' asked Morris. 'The Doc' is what they all called the pathologist, who was in charge of the morgue. As well as telling everyone else what to do (which she was very good at, by the way), it was also her job to cut people open and work out exactly what they had died of by looking at the bits . . . I don't know about you, but I'm quite keen to change the subject.

With no one else around, Morris had to make do with Dennis, the assistant path lab assistant's signature. The reason why the ambulanceman was a little reluctant to get Dennis to sign was that a path lab assistant was someone a little more important than a monkey and just about as well respected as a hospital-trained cleaner. An *assistant* path lab assistant came somewhere below a monkey – if that monkey was circus-trained – in the respect department, but he did get paid more than a regular supply of bananas.

Dennis signed the ROD (Receipt Of Deceased) form and helped Morris lift the body-in-the-bag on to a stainless steel table. That done, the ambulanceman began wheeling the now empty stretcher on the gurney back down the corridor towards the rickety old lift, and Dennis got back to reading his article on cacti (which is more than one cactus).

What we could do, in the meantime, is get back to the point in the story where the first round of the typing competition was still under way, with Fergal in the audience, still very much alive.

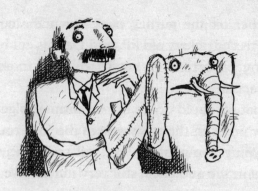

Chapter Nine

When Mr Peach had finished his fourth and final poem made up on the spot – this one was about pyramids, suggested by a grey-haired gentleman with a mop and bucket at the back – Malcolm bounded back into centre stage.

'Well, at the end of this first round, Graham Large and Le Fay McNally have yet to make a single mistake . . . Perfect scores, you two. Well done. Peggy Snoot has made two, and Anna Malting has made three . . . which means, I'm afraid, that we have to say farewell to Anna; but I must remind her that, in Tap 'n' Type's opinion, she's a winner to have reached the Grand Finals!'

He started to clap and the whole audience joined in as Anna stood up, lower lip trembling, and walked offstage. Passing Le Fay at her computer terminal, she whispered, 'I hope you win.' The two girls smiled at each other.

Anna's computer screen above the stage was switched off. Now there were three.

'In this second round,' Malcolm went on, 'Hieronymus Peach has ten sentences to say to you. Once each sentence has been spoken, you will type the words of the sentence in reverse order . . . We're not asking you to spell the words backwards, just to type the words in reverse order. For example, if he were to say, "The cat sat on the mat," you would type, "Mat the on sat cat the." Don't worry about capital letters, full stops and the like. Do worry about apostrophes. And stop typing the moment you hear the gong . . . Clear?'

'Clear!' said the three remaining contestants, who'd had it explained to them beforehand but, of course, had no idea what sentences the extraordinary Mr Peach might come up with!

'Ready, Mr Peach?'

'Ready,' said the moustached ventriloquist and beat poet. 'Sentence number one . . .' He put on the snake glove puppet the other McNallys had seen by the huge hole. 'Peter Piper picked a peck of pickled peppers.'

Le Fay frantically typed: 'peppers pickled of peck a picked piper peter,' which isn't as easy as it may sound – especially now Mr Peach already had another puppet on his hand, which appeared to be saying: 'Round and round the ragged rock

101

the ragged rascal ran.'

'ran rascal ragged the rock rugged the round and round,' Le Fay typed.

The sentences came thick and fast (which is a phrase I've been wanting to use for ages and it seems to fit really nicely here, without a join, so long as I don't call too much attention to it).

It was in the very last sentence that Le Fay made her first mistake. What Hieronymus Peach said was: 'Are you sure she sells sea shells on the sea shore any more?'

Le Fay typed: 'more any shore sea the on shells sea sells she shore you are.' The order of the words was fine, but – in all the confusion of having to do everything backwards – she'd spelled 'sure' as 'shore'. She realised this and was just about to change it when the gong for the end of the round was sounded.

Malcolm checked the screens and totted up the scores. 'Peggy Snoot didn't make a single mistake in this round (well done, Peggy), whereas both Le Fay McNally and Graham Large made one mistake each' – Le Fay sighed with relief. She was still in the game! – 'which makes the scores at the end of this round: Graham and Le Fay with one mistake each, Peggy with two, so I'm sorry, Peggy, we have to say "Congratulations and goodbye!" to you.'

There were claps as she began to walk across the stage; then everything suddenly plunged into darkness. The clapping stopped and there were murmurs of: 'What's happening?'

'Power cut!' shouted a voice.

The reason why it was so dark without the lights was that, although there was daylight outside, all the blinds in the room had been pulled down over the windows so that the stage could be lit with electric lighting to the best effect. (It'd taken a while to eliminate any glare from the four giant computer screens above the stage – all of which had now gone blank.)

There were sounds of scurrying around and then, a minute or two later, Malcolm opened one of the blinds and sunlight streamed through a window. 'Sorry about this, folks. We'll find out what's happening and –'

At that moment, the lights came back on, the computers booted up again and three screens flickered to life. Peggy's was switched off, now that she'd left the stage, which left Graham Large's screen top left, and Le Fay McNally's bottom right.

Malcolm pulled the blind back down and jumped back up on to the stage. Out of the corner of his eye, Fergal thought he caught a flash of something electric-blue lurking in the shadows by the edge of the stage, but thought nothing of it.

'Apologies for the added drama!' said Malcolm, who'd not only proved that he was a very nice man but also that he was very good at his job. 'Now we come to the final round of the Grand Final of the Tap 'n' Type competition. By the end of this round we will be left with one runner-up and one National Champion . . .'

This final round was straightforward enough. It relied on good spelling ability and speedy typing, without errors. Mr Peach slipped on a glove puppet of a crocodile wearing a mortar board (one of those flat, square caps with a tassel on it that teachers wear in old films and graduation students throw up in the air – a bit like a carpet tile) and began a quick fire of long words: 'immediately', 'coeducation', 'disinherited', 'unnecessarily' and so on. No sooner had he finished than the gong sounded.

In their second row seats, Jackie, Albie, Joshua and Fergal had their eyes glued on Le Fay's screen and what they saw horrified them. It was full of mistakes – littered with them. You name it, she spelled it incorrectly. It was a total disaster!

Had their sister finally lost her nerve? Had reaching the final round of the final been too much for her and she'd gone to pieces? She looked calm and confident enough sitting up there, but what was she feeling on the *inside*?

Graham Large was looking pretty pleased with himself as he sat at his keyboard, but he seemed to have every reason to. As far as Jackie could see, he'd only made two or three mistakes at most.

Malcolm walked back to the centre of the stage and thanked Hieronymus Peach for the final time as he popped the crocodile glove puppet into his valise and was cheered off the stage, waving to the audience. Malcolm then turned to the screens.

From where Le Fay was sitting, she could see the surprise on his face. He frowned again and looked at both screens carefully.

Feeling what he did about Le Fay and Graham Large, Malcolm didn't want to humiliate the young McNally girl in front of the audience by announcing the terrible number of mistakes she'd made in this, the final round. Instead, he went straight to the announcement.

'After local and regional heats, just four people made it to today's national Grand Final. Four people who can count themselves winners for just being up here on this stage today' – there were claps and cheers – 'but there can only be one runner-up and one champion. And the runner-up is . . . Le Fay McNally!'

The crowd cheered and Le Fay came to the front of the stage. She really thought she'd been in with a real chance of winning it. If only I hadn't made those few mistakes at the end, she thought. Whatever I think of Graham Lard as a person, he must be good at this, and deserves to win the competition.

Malcolm shook her warmly by the hand. 'Well done for being runner up, Le Fay,' he said. 'Let's have your family up here!'

Jackie, Joshua, Albie and Fergal didn't need asking twice. Le Fay might not have won, but they were all very proud of their sister. They all tried to hug her at once and Fergal, being the smallest, got pushed to the back and almost tripped over the spaghetti of wires, hidden behind a curtain, connecting all the computers, keyboards screens and lights.

Forever inquisitive, he realised how they 'switched off' one of the big screens above the stage when a contestant was eliminated. They simply pulled the particular cable jack plug from its socket. The two remaining screens – his sister Le Fay's and winner Graham Large's – were still plugged in: red jack plug into green socket and green jack plug into red.

Jackie was tugging him. Time to get off the stage with Le Fay holding the runner-up scroll.

When Graham Large went up to accept the winning prize from the chairman of Tap 'n' Type himself, Count Medoc Silverman, the whole front row of the audience leapt to their feet and clapped and cheered. Two photographers came forward, one from one of the Capital City's Leading

Evening Newspapers and another in an electric-blue suit.

Le Fay recognised him as the photographer working for the Large Lunches company magazine. Fergal recognised him as the electric-blue-coloured shape he'd seen lurking in the shadows after the power cut . . . lurking near where the wires were connecting the overhead screens to the computer. What had Fergal seen up onstage? A red jack plug in a green socket and a green jack plug in a red.

Then the blinding truth hit Fergal like a bolt of lightning (or like he would hit the pavement later on): the cables must be colour-coded. Green was supposed to go in green and red in red. The sockets had been switched in the so-called 'power cut', which meant that whatever Graham typed would appear on Le Fay's screen above the stage, and whatever she typed would appear on his!

All Graham Large would have had to do was type plenty of deliberate mistakes, which would appear on Le Fay's big screen as hers! He knew that she was good and would make very few mistakes, and that's what would appear on his screen. He was guaranteed to win, the cheat!

Fergal tugged at Jackie's arm and she leant towards him in her seat to hear what he had to say above the whoops and cheers of the Large family.

She had suspiciously good hearing for a mere human being. Her eyes widened in anger and amazement as she realised what her little brother was saying. But what should she do? She couldn't simply stand up and say: 'Cheat!' What if they were wrong? She couldn't be 100 per cent sure that the electric jack plugs and sockets were colour-coded.

Pushing her way past people in her row, with 'excuse me' after 'excuse me' as she banged against their knees, Jackie made it over to Mr Peach, who was standing in the side aisle. Fergal could see her explaining everything, with frantic hand gestures.

The next thing he knew, the ventriloquist had made his way up onstage and had disappeared behind the grinning Graham Large and his immediate family.

The room fell silent as Graham stepped forward and began his acceptance speech. 'The saying goes: "May the best man win,"' he sneered, 'and, as the only man, against three girls, you might think my winning a foregone conclusion–'

Just then there was a loud fizz and the two screens above them went blank, only to come to life again seconds later but with the badly spelled words on Large's screen and the ones with very few errors on Le Fay's.

There was a gasp, and muttering from the audience, and confusion on the stage, where they didn't know what was going on until, following the eyes of those below, they too turned to look up at the screens.

Malcolm Kent hurried back on to the stage. 'Ladies and gentlemen,' he said, grinning from ear to ear. 'I'm sorry to report that, owing to some confusion in the power cut, some misconnections were made, resulting in Master Graham Large's *twenty-six* typing and spelling errors' – he really emphasised the number – 'appearing on Miss McNally's screen by mistake. I therefore reverse the order of finalists and declare Le Fay McNally the rightful winner and Tap 'n' Type National Champion!'

He hadn't actually called Large a cheat, you'll notice – that's not good for business – but everyone knew what he meant. Everyone who wasn't a Large looked outraged and delighted both at once.

Before Le Fay knew what was happening, Jackie, Albie, Joshua, Anna Malting and her mum were carrying Le Fay shoulder high up the steps on to the stage.

Fergal's arms weren't long enough, but he (and Peggy Snoot) ran up with them. The disgraced Graham Large, meanwhile, was running offstage in the opposite direction, blubbing like a baby (but a very big one, old enough to know better).

Fergal felt a hand pat him on the shoulder. 'A nice piece of detective work, my boy,' said Mr Peach. 'Well done.'

Meanwhile, out in the foyer, a real detective was planning his next move. That was Twinkle-Toes Tweedy, of course, and he was about to haul Le Fay McNally off for questioning, in his linen closet of an office.

Chapter Ten

Captain Charlie 'Twinkle-Toes' Tweedy (retired), the chief house detective of The Dell hotel, was in a very good mood indeed. Housekeeper Mrs Launa Doon, had reported that – according to her 'girls' who had cleaned the rooms – only five rooms on the east side had been missing tissue boxes that morning. She gave him a list of the numbers.

It was a pretty safe bet, therefore (though admittedly not a 100-per-cent-watertight certainty), that one of the guests from one of these five rooms had used their box of tissues to wedge open the fire-escape door.

The detective took the list to the Reception desk and asked for details on the guests. Of the five rooms, three of the people had already checked out, which left two people to investigate on site. Of course, it was possible that the culprit had been one of the three who'd already left. It was also possible that it was one of the two remaining, so Tweedy would start with them. They were a Mr Norton Lisp in Room 1651 and a Miss Le Fay McNally in Room 1428. Next to Le Fay's name on her hotel registration card was written: 'minor'. This didn't mean that someone had wrongly recorded her profession as someone who dug for coal or tin or suchlike. *That* kind of miner is spelled with an 'e'. This kind of minor – with an 'o' – simply means that Le Fay was a child.

The card also said: 'In the care of Malcolm Kent, Tap 'n' Type competition.'

The cogs started whirring in Tweedy's brain. He'd met a little girl by the lifts who'd said that she was staying in the hotel and was in the typing competition. He'd also seen the back view of a girl – which could most definitely have been her – when he'd looked out of the fire exit wedged open with the tissues, alarm ringing. She'd been in the distance and walking ever so innocently, but it was the same girl. He was sure of it! He remembered having thought there was something familiar about the girl when she'd spoken those few words to him.

The detective was now convinced that Le Fay had been the one to wedge the door open. Call it a hunch. Call it a detective's intuition. Call it what you will. It wasn't a matter of having evidence or

113

undeniable proof. It was a gut feeling, after years on the job, that he'd found the guilty party.

But guilty of what? Wedging a door open. But why? To let someone sneak in the back way, of course. Tweedy made his way to Room 1428 and knocked on the door. There was no reply. He knocked again. Still no reply.

He pulled a large key out of his pocket. This was the master key. This key was what's called a skeleton key. It could open every locked door in The Dell. The chief house detective slipped it into the keyhole of Le Fay's room, turned it and walked inside.

The maid had been and made the bed, cleaned the bedroom and bathroom, changed the towels and replaced the missing box of tissues but, if there were still clues to be found, old Twinkle-Toes Tweedy would find them . . .

Some ten minutes later, the only strange thing he'd discovered was some strands of animal hair on the curtains at waist height. They were thick, like a dog's. Had the girl smuggled a huge pet into her room? Was that what all this had been about? But where was it now?

Tweedy picked up the phone and dialled '1'.

'Room Service,' said a cheery voice.

Tweedy explained who he was and asked what, if anything, had been ordered for the room since Le Fay McNally had checked in. He was told about the chicken sandwich and the hot chocolate and the large piece of fish with extra chips – all in the same day, when Tweedy knew jolly well that the competition included a finger buffet and supper.

Back downstairs, some fifteen minutes later, he talked with the waiters and waitresses who'd served dinner in the Sizzle Grill and soon learnt that Le Fay had taken a doggy bag of leftovers up to her room after the meal! There was no way she could have eaten all that food herself! A hungry dog, however, would have wolfed it down.

Tweedy was now sure that he'd almost solved the case – but for a few important details. Le Fay hadn't had the pet with her when he'd seen her back view in the street. She'd obviously planned to wedge open the fire escape and then come back with the dog, except that the alarm had gone off and the exit had been closed. How, then, had she finally managed to get the beast up to her room? That was the real puzzle. The hairs on the curtains and the amount of food ordered and eaten proved that she must have hidden and fed the creature . . . but where was it now?

These were the two questions that Twinkle-Toes wanted the answers to more than anything else, but they could be easily answered. Now he knew who the culprit was and what she was up to, he could simply confront her and get her to tell him.

Admittedly, smuggling a pet into one of The Dell's bedrooms wasn't the worst crime that had been committed in the hotel. It wasn't as if the girl was letting a whole bunch of people stay in her room without paying, or stealing anything . . . it was just that Charlie 'Twinkle-Toes' Tweedy didn't like anything to be going on in his hotel that shouldn't be going on. And now he was ready to confront the culprit . . .

*

With the National Championships of the Tap 'n' Type competition at an end, the doors to the Empress Conference Suite burst open and the National Champion – a certain Le Fay McNally – was whisked into the foyer on a sea of shoulders.

As the double swing doors swung open and the

people poured out, the chief house detective's eyes widened at the sight of them.

He recognised Malcolm Kent as one of the organisers and Mr Peach as the well-known beat poet and ventriloquist . . . and there was no mistaking Le Fay, though she looked a lot happier than when he'd spoken to her by the lifts. She was radiating happiness, beaming with pride and bursting with joy all at once. She was giving off so much heat that she'd have melted a snowman at ten paces. (Not that snowmen or women were allowed in The Dell unless, of course, they had a reservation.)

But it was the McNally family as a whole that struck Charlie Tweedy like a slap on the back: those red freckles, the sticky-out ears, the red wiry hair and the buck teeth . . . Surely they couldn't be? They *couldn't* be . . . but they looked so much like him, they *must* be! That's why little Le Fay had looked so familiar when he'd first laid eyes on her. They must be Rufus McNally's family. His children! McNally was a common enough name, but with those features? There was no doubt about it!

The chief house detective gasped and, for the first time in all his years at The Dell, he forgot his duty. He forgot that he should be questioning Le Fay about smuggling an animal up into her room, against hotel policy. Instead, he simply wanted to WHOOP with delight. So that's exactly what he did – and he broke out into a little dance on his tippy-tippy-toes. For a big man, he danced with great elegance, which was a strange sight indeed, made even stranger by the fact that he had the broadest grin he could fit on his face without planning permission. It was BIG.

Anyone who'd just walked into the foyer of The Dell off the street would have been in for a surprise. The Large family were leaving en masse (which is French for 'in one big lump', which is appropriate when you consider who we're talking about). Graham's dad, David Large of Large Lunches kept on slapping the back of his son's neck and calling him a cheat. Various other relatives were shuffling out, shamefaced with their eyes to the ground, whilst Mrs Large was bossing around some poor man carrying all their boy's luggage.

Le Fay, meanwhile, was still being carried shoulder-high around the foyer in a lap of honour, watched enthusiastically by everyone from Malcolm and Mr Peach to the Maltings and the Snoops.

And then there was Twinkle-Toes Tweedy doing his dance of pure, unadulterated happiness.

If this were a film, I might end it here, with the

118

camera pulling away from the action, up and out of the doors and away past the outside of The Dell. Because this isn't a film, the receptionist picked up a phone and called the duty manager.

'I need you in Reception,' he said. 'There're some weird things going on!'

Now I think I'd be failing in my duty as the narrator of these unlikely exploits if I didn't take the time or trouble to explain why Twinkle-Toes Tweedy was dancing with delight at having come face to face with Rufus McNally's five children: Jackie, Albie, Joshua, Le Fay and Fergal. Most of you will remember that he was a retired policeman, but some of you will also remember that, way, way back on page 27, I said that he was an ex-naval man. To put it another way, he'd once been in the navy. I also mentioned on page 5 that the McNally's dad – back in the days before he was bitter, sick and twisted – had, on three occasions, 'done heroic deeds to save others trapped as their vessels went down'. As a young sailor, long, long before he'd even joined the police department and become a detective, Able Seaman Charlie Tweedy had been one of those people Captain Rufus McNally had saved.

Tweedy had been trapped in the galley of a ship torpedoed by the Enemy with a capital 'E'. A ship's galley is its kitchen, and a huge stove had blocked Tweedy's only possible exit as the galley began to fill with water. Tweedy had known then that he was going to die. He was young and fighting to protect the freedom of his country, but he hadn't expected it to end like this: in a kitchen filling up with pounding seawater. Then Captain Rufus had appeared like some comic-book hero. This was Rufus McNally before he lost his leg. This was Rufus McNally the highly decorated ship's captain who never lost a man if he could help it. At great personal risk to himself, he'd made his way through the *Mary-Jane* and had already freed and rescued a number of other sailors before reaching Tweedy in the galley.

What's all the more brave was that this wasn't even Rufus McNally's vessel. He'd boarded the *Mary-Jane* when the ship had been hit and its captain hadn't answered his radio messages. A captain often went down with his own ship. Rufus McNally was risking going down in another man's.

Well, the very fact that Twinkle-Toes Tweedy was dancing in the foyer of The Dell hotel all those years later shows that the McNally's dad had somehow rescued Able Seaman Tweedy from the galley. He'd used every last ounce of his considerable strength and a crowbar to move that stove and get him out just in time.

There had never been time for proper 'thank yous'. Neither man had been badly injured and both had been back on active duty in a matter of days, but Tweedy had never forgotten the strange-looking Captain McNally with his wiry and unmanageable hair, freckles, and buck teeth.

When the war was done, he had gone out of his way to track down McNally to thank him personally. The Naval Office wouldn't give out his address, but had forwarded Tweedy's letters to Rufus who – now with one leg, and hate in his heart – had never even bothered to read them. He would have torn them up if his wife hadn't returned them unopened, out of politeness.

Although Tweedy had stopped actively trying to track down McNally (and, out of respect, he'd never abused his power as a policeman to find out from official records, not available to the public, where his saviour lived) he'd often wondered whether Rufus McNally had a family or what he was doing now . . . and, all these years later, Charlie 'Twinkle-Toes' Tweedy had absolutely no doubt that these were the man's children in front of him now.

Chapter Eleven

Back in Room 1428, the celebrations were still under way. Le Fay was a hero for having won the competition and Fergal was a hero for having exposed the cheat. In all the excitement, they'd forgotten about the prize itself, until Jackie caught sight of the golden envelope sticking out of the pocket in Le Fay's dress.

'Go on, Le Fay. Open it!' she said.

Le Fay opened it. Inside was a voucher for a very expensive, state-of-the-art, top-of-the-range computer with every conceivable attachment and gizmo: printer, scanner, camera – you name it, it had it.

'"Exchangeable at any electrical or computer store",' Le Fay read, her eyes widening in wonder. Then she looked a little sad. 'Of course, we must collect the computer and then sell it,' she said.

'Yeah!' said Albie excitedly. 'Think of all the

123

shopping we can get with that –'

'The repairs we can do to the apartment –' said Joshua.

'We could feed Smoky every day so she doesn't have to catch rats –' said Le Fay.

'We could live off the money from selling the computer for ages,' said Fergal.

'No,' said Jackie.

'No? What do you mean "no"?' demanded Albie.

'I mean that Le Fay won the computer so she gets to keep the computer,' said Jackie, quietly.

'We could always sell the computer and buy a cheaper one along with all the other stuff we need,' said Le Fay.

'No,' said Jackie. 'You won it. You deserve it and – who knows? – we might even find a way of you making money with this fabulous computer and your keyboard skills.'

Le Fay threw her arms around her big sister and gave her a hug. 'Thank you!' she cried.

Albie was about to protest, until Jackie gave him one of her no-nonsense stares over Le Fay's shoulder. He knew when he was beaten.

There was a knock at the door.

'Who is it?' asked Le Fay. She and the others half-expected it to be Malcolm Kent, who'd been so nice to them from the word go.

When the person the other side of the door announced himself to be 'Charlie Tweedy', it threw Le Fay into an unnecessary panic.

'It's the chief house detective!' she hissed.

If any of them had stopped to think rationally for one minute, it would have occurred to them that they could have pretended to have all gone up to the room at the end of the competition to celebrate. No one need know that they planned to spend one last night in it. But Le Fay had told them about her meeting with Captain Tweedy, and they'd all witnessed the very strange way he'd behaved in the foyer earlier . . . and Le Fay's irrational panic was contagious. Albie and Joshua ran straight for the bathroom at the same time and became briefly wedged together in the doorway. Jackie snatched up what evidence there was of their being in the room and was about to head into the bathroom too, when she saw Fergal leaning out of the window.

Le Fay later said that she thought Fergal might have been looking to see if there was an outer ledge that he could step out on to and hide.

Whatever his reason, Jackie turned and cried, 'Don't lean out of that window!'

But, as we all know from hindsight, it was too late. Fergal fell. Jackie dashed across the room and leant out, grabbing at thin air. She let out a pained cry of 'No!' stretching the 'o' to last a good fifteen seconds. What I neglected to mention before was that the cry turned into a howl and, by the time the remaining McNallys had thrown open the door, streaming past a startled Twinkle-Toes Tweedy – who'd heard the howl and had no idea what was going on – Jackie had turned into a jackal.

Why else do you think I said that there was more to Jackie's nickname 'Jackal' than her snapping and snarling, back on page 7?

Why else would she – a grown woman – have to 'jump up' to press the 'down' button at the lifts, on page 23? Who else do you think was the furry creature shown in the wonderful illustration on the same page? (Look between those running legs.) Who else could have left thick dog-like hairs on Le Fay's curtains? And what about Jackie's 'suspiciously good hearing for a mere human', I mention on page 109? Well, it's because she *was* no mere human, of course!

A shame none of the others had Jackie's amazing abilities, though that's not to say that they won't turn out to have some very distinct ones of their own. (Their late mother named them for specific reasons. The clues are there.) There are three books in this series and something has to happen in the other two! If Fergal had been able to turn into a golden eagle, or even a hedgehog with a parachute, things might have turned out very differently indeed!

And think how Captain Charlie 'Twinkle-Toes' Tweedy felt when he later pieced together what had happened (though, fortunately, he didn't realise that the 'dog' he'd seen dashing from the room and the big sister weeping by her dead brother were, in truth, one and the same).

He'd come to Room 1428 to share in the good news and delight at having come across them after all these years – the children of the man who'd saved his life as a young sailor – and in the process he'd indirectly led to one of them falling to his death . . . which wasn't the best way to say thank you.

Captain Tweedy was beside himself with mixed measures of grief, guilt and anguish. The only thing stopping him from falling to pieces was being strong for Jackie, Albie, Joshua and Le Fay. Someone else who was brilliant in that role was Malcolm Kent of Tap 'n' Type. I have to say that he's a person I'd be greatly honoured to call a friend.

Much of the rest you know. Fergal was taken to the morgue at the Sacred Heart Hospital, while Tweedy, Malcolm and the management of The Dell did what they could to comfort the McNallys.

'Should I ring your father?' said Malcolm, who hadn't found a contact number in Le Fay's competition file.

'We don't have a phone at home,' said Jackie. 'And I don't want anyone else going around telling him.'

In the end, they all went home that night. The Dell had a minibus they used for staff outings and special occasions. It had never been sent on such a sad mission before. Charlie Tweedy drove, Jackie gave directions and Malcolm sat with Joshua, Albie and Le Fay, the forgotten computer voucher crumpled in the golden envelope in her pocket.

Does some good come out of tragedy? In this case, I'm pleased to report, yes. The fall of Fergal certainly made a better man of Captain Rufus McNally. He cried at the news in a way that startled all his remaining children. They'd expected him to bottle up his grief like his anger, and to take it out on them and the bottles; but he sobbed floods of tears and – as they were to discover over the following weeks – those tears did much to wash away his bitterness, sickness and twistedness. He became much more the man he'd once been before collecting all those bottles. He became the kind of man Tweedy recognised as the person who'd saved him all those years before. Sure, he'd lost a leg and gained a big red nose, but this was the guy who'd risked his life so many times to save others. He even tore up the note from his doctor that said he was 'excused parenting'.

The two captains – one a retired sea captain and the other a retired police captain – became firm friends. Malcolm became a close friend of Jackie and the children. He became close enough to learn Jackie's secret that she could become a jackal, and the secrets of Albie, Joshua and Le Fay, as they themselves discovered them. They never forgot Fergal, of course, but not for the reasons you might think . . .

*

For some reason it was important for the pathologist to weigh Fergal's brain – perhaps to work out how much of it had slopped out of the boy's ears, nose, throat (and perhaps the odd eye socket or two). Unfortunately, the scales had broken when, during his lunch hour, Dennis, the assistant path lab assistant – whose usual summer job was selling ice cream, remember? – had tried to weigh his bull terrier in them, while the boss was out.

So what should Dennis do until they were fixed? He decided to pop Fergal's brain in one of the large jars he'd seen on the draining board by the huge stainless-steel sinks running along one wall of the morgue.

He picked up the brain with his gloved hands and glooped it into a jar. It reminded Dennis of an overcooked cauliflower. Now all he needed to do was to add some of that preserving liquid – what was it called? Formaldehyde, that was it – so that it'd stay in one piece until the scales were fixed and his boss could weigh it. Dennis was sure that his boss would be proud of his quick thinking and, as a result, wouldn't be quite so annoyed that Dennis had not only broken the special scales, but had got dog hairs everywhere in the first place!

The problem was that there wasn't a drop of formaldehyde to be found. Muttering under his breath, Dennis dashed out of the basement entrance of the hospital, up some stairs littered with ancient leaves from previous autumns, now dry and skeletal, and across the street. A few blocks down, he reached MA'S PICKLING STORE, along the bottom of the store sign of which was written: 'For All Your Pickling Needs'. He hurried inside and had little time to exchange pleasantries with 'Ma' who was, if the truth be told, Mrs Bloinstein, a friend of Dennis's Aunt Patty, and would no doubt report to her that her nephew, Dennis, had come to her store during his hospital working hours to buy a gallon of pickling vinegar.

Dennis dashed back down the street, across the road, down the steps and into the Sacred Heart Hospital's basement morgue, carrying the plastic gallon bottle of pickling vinegar as fast as his legs could carry him. He'd poured it into the jar containing Fergal's brain, and just fitted the tight-seal lid, when a man in a white coat appeared, wheeling a trolley stacked with store supplies.

'Hi, Dennis,' he said. 'No one else around?'

'No,' panted Dennis.

'Then you'll have to sign for this. A fresh supply of formaldehyde. OK?'

'OK,' said Dennis snatching the pen and signing.

The guy in the white coat wondered why Dennis was glaring at him as he piled the bottles of formaldehyde on to a wooden workbench. What had he done to upset him? He sniffed the air. 'Do I smell vinegar?' he asked.

'Don't be crazy,' said Dennis, handing him back the clipboard and pen. 'Who'd be mad enough to eat anything in here, what with all these bodies around?'

'True,' nodded the man. 'Hey, what happened to those scales?'

'Don't ask,' sighed Dennis.

That night, when the small, masked burglar broke into the morgue of the Sacred Heart Hospital he was very disappointed. He had hoped to find row upon row of jars of human brains to choose from. There were always row upon row of brains in

Frankenstein movies when the scientist's assistant Igor broke into the place, so why not here?

All the small, masked burglar could find was one. It was labelled:

**FERGAL MCNALLY,
JUVENILE.**

and had a slight whiff of pickling vinegar about it.

'It'll have to do,' muttered the small, masked burglar to himself (which is convenient for us). 'I only hope that the master is pleased.'

With that, he stuffed the jar containing Fergal's brain under his jumper, and hurried out into the night, heading for Fishbone Forest. The ground rumbled beneath him. 'Oh no! Not another hole,' he muttered . . .

Which was all very unlikely indeed, wasn't it?

THE END
of the first exploit

Epilogue

'*Philip!*'

What?

'*Is that really the end?*'

It says so, doesn't it?

'*But does it have to end here?*'

Every story has to end somewhere.

'*But here?*'

Here's as good as any place. Everything's rather neatly tied up, if the truth be told.

'*But what happened next?*'

Would you settle for: "And they all lived happily ever after."?

'*It's rather unlikely, isn't it? Especially if Fergal isn't living at all . . . And who's the small burglar, and who's his master?*'

Good point. I suggest you read 'Unlikely Exploits 2: Heir of Mystery.'

'*I didn't know you'd written a sequel.*'

That's because I haven't.

'*You haven't?*'

I haven't.

'*Then . . .?*'

Yet.

The Philip Ardagh Club

COLLECT some fantastic **Philip Ardagh** merchandise.

WHAT YOU HAVE TO DO:
You'll find numbered tokens to collect in all Philip Ardagh's fiction books published after 01/04/05. There are 2 tokens in each hardback and 1 token in each paperback. Cut them out and send them to us complete with the form below (or a photocopy of the form) and you'll get these great gifts:

> **2 tokens** = a Philip Ardagh poster
> **3 tokens** = a Philip Ardagh mousemat
> **4 tokens** = a Philip Ardagh pencil case and stationery set

Please send the form, together with your tokens or photocopies of them, to:

Philip Ardagh promotion, Faber and Faber Ltd, 3 Queen Square, London, WC1N 3AU.

Please ensure that each token has a different number.

1. This offer can not be used in conjunction with any other offer and is non transferable. 2. No cash alternative is offered. 3. If under 18 please get permission and help from a parent or guardian to enter. 4. Please allow at least 28 days delivery. 5. No responsibility can be taken for items lost in the post. 6. This offer will close on 31/04/07. 7. Offer open to readers in the UK and Ireland ONLY.

Name: ....

Address: ....

....

....

Town: ....

Postcode: ....

Age & Date of Birth: ....

Girl or boy: ....

Philip Ardagh Club
token number 3

For more infomation and competitions join the Philip Ardagh Club on-line.
Visit www.philipardagh.com